Happ' M ny.

Love,

Cheryl
"PUMA"

Behind
Closed Doors

Happy Birthday!

Behind
Closed Doors

———

An Erotic Novel

E. Lee Ritter ?!

Library of Congress Control Number:		2018904171
ISBN:	Hardcover	978-1-9845-2042-5
	Softcover	978-1-9845-2041-8
	eBook	978-1-9845-2040-1

Print information available on the last page.

Rev. date: 06/14/2018

To order additional copies of this book, contact:
Xlibris
1-888-795-4274
www.Xlibris.com
Orders@Xlibris.com
777741

Dedication

This book is dedicated to all the wonderful people whom I have learned from and shared my ideas with, as well as those who encouraged me to put pen to paper my zest for writing creative, erotic fiction. You know who you are, so "naming names" is superfluous. Four people, though, Keenan Rice, Elaine Chambers, Kay "Wheeler Dealer" Wheeler, and Nat Crump, are worth noting because they encouraged me, from idea to completion, to put my ideas to paper and complete this project. I am indebted to them for their open ears and ardent support. Further, I wish to thank countless individuals and couples who opened their hearts, minds, and mouths for sharing their most intimate experiences.

For years, I was apprehensive about writing erotic fiction for fear I would ostensibly be professionally banished. However, I have since recognized, along with being encouraged by a small cadre of peers, that not actualizing my dreams would be the penultimate form of banishment, akin to a fatal self-inflicted wound – the agony of not pursuing one's dreams.

Foreword

There comes a time in one's life when s/he is less concerned about what others think. When we are young, we generally prefer harmony amongst our peers. We embrace the idea of "fitting in" so as not to seem different, i.e., being labeled an outcast. As we mature, however, we become more aware of our own inevitable mortality. Thus, we are more likely to adopt the perspective that "life is short" and that we must begin to pursue our dreams, for our own good, versus doing so to please others. Complicating matters further are issues related to sexual mores because, arguably, we are even more static in our attitudes and pronouncements, at least publicly. But, what do we actually *do* behind closed doors? In public, we *talk* about the virtues of being a virgin until we are married. We *talk* about safe sex, whatever that means. In romantic relationships, we *talk* about monogamy. We *talk*, *ad nauseam*, about sex being an act reserved for procreation.

As you ponder the above questions about your own behavior, ask yourself, "What do *you* do behind closed doors?" How easy is it for you to judge others' sexual behavior now? If you are married, were you a virgin prior to the wedding? If you are not married, are you a virgin now? Have you always been monogamous? Have you only indulged in sex for the sole purpose of procreation? Have you always had "safe" sex? You need not respond to the above queries, for I suspect I already know most readers' responses.

I have no interest in making value judgments about others, for I am imperfect. My interest, then, is to stimulate dialogue, via this novel, about human sexual mores and behavior in an attempt to "free our minds." In other words, it should be obvious society's Puritanical perspective about sex leaves a lot to be desired. For example, some tenets fail to acknowledge that people actually, and often **do**, have sex prior to getting married. Others might point to religious texts to lend credence to their argument supporting monogamy. The irony, though, is how often some leaders and heads of organizations, with their virtuous, exalted admonitions, fall victim to the very actions they denounce.

Behind Closed Doors is largely a fictional characterization of one man's exploration of erotic life through the prism of what is called the *Lifestyle*, also known as *swinging* or *open relationships*. In one sense, though, it might be considered quasi-fiction because it focuses on a global community that actually **does** exist, and in very large numbers! Therefore, while there are some areas of embellishment, there are other areas that are ***very much authentic!*** The purpose of this account, then, is to stimulate dialogue and challenge the narrow boundaries of "traditional" sexual relationships. After all, boundaries are but sepulchers of the mind all too often defined and predicated by others.

Chapter 1

"What!" Glen blurted out. "Are you kidding me? You mean to tell me you're going to move back to Philly because you want to marry some chick you met last month in Chicago at a sex party? Not only that, but you're telling me you're okay with her having sex other men? Have you lost your mind, Theo? Where's the Hennessy, man, I need a drink!"

"Relax," I said. "As usual, you're misinterpreting what I said and how I said it. First, I'm **not** getting married to Stephanie. Second, I'm not moving back to Philadelphia **because** of Stephanie. Third, I didn't say she was screwing other men. I just said she's a swinger." "Oh," Glen sarcastically retorted, "excuse me, but I thought swinging **was** about sharing sex partners, so I guess this Stephanie chick is the only monogamous swinger on the planet."

"Hey man," I said, "don't chastise me with that holier than thou nonsense. Let's face it, Glen, you're no Saint, so spare me." By now, the vitriol in my tone heightened, and I initially felt guilty. I defended myself, embarrassed at being called to task. Still, I pressed, "Shall I refresh your memory? As I recall, it was **you** who had an affair with Vera, a married woman, by the way. Oh, I almost forgot… she was married to one of your co-workers! How 'bout the time you had to act like a Bellhop at the Hilton in Miami because Clarice's husband damn near caught 'ya'll screwing in their room during their vacation? Just fabulous! What about that gem of a woman, Caroline? I'm sure you remember her, don't you? Wasn't she the married angel who told her husband she miscarried because she knew the baby was yours? How convenient, huh? Now *that* is morality of the highest order, so perhaps I can learn a few things from *you* on the subject!"

Glen's back was turned towards me as he poured himself a drink. As I unleashed my verbal assault, he spun around, almost dropping his drink *and* my bottle of Hennessy. I thought to myself, "Oh shit! I may have gone too far this time." Before I could apologize, he gazed at me, eyes peering and brimming with rage. "Hey motherfucker," he shouted, "don't you preach to me! Yeah, I've made some mistakes in my life, and sometimes have let my dick think for me, but don't you judge me, man, don't you even judge me! You tell me about people knowingly being with others' spouses and *now* you want to play like you're Jimmy fucking Swaggert? Please, Theo, spare me the bullshit!"

Stalemate. I knew I was wrong for admonishing Glen, and he knew he was wrong for chastising me. The fact is, our behavior was far from the Puritanical upbringing our parents instilled in us while we were growing up in West Philadelphia. Glen's parents lived next door to my parents on 46th Street, not too far from the University of Pennsylvania, an Ivy League school where I later earned earn an MBA.

Our body language spoke volumes - pursed lips, heads held downward, rapidly blinking eyes; statues of bruised egos. We knew we went much too far, but I spoke first. "Hey man, I'm sorry. I really

2

am, Glen, and I didn't mean to come at you like that. I was wrong, brother, and I sincerely apologize." "Theo," he responded, "don't sweat it. I flew-off the handle, too, and I was way out of bounds. I apologize." We embraced and simultaneously echoed, "I love you, brother."

Tension exited my body as I poured a drink and invited Glen to my balcony that overlooked the Pacific Ocean. We sat, largely in silence, as sunbeams ricocheted off the ocean's waves. "Welcome to Los Angeles," I said, before we clanked our glasses, toasting his recent move out West.

Chapter 2

My legal name is Thelonious Ellington Williams, but everyone calls me Theo. When I was a child, I had difficulty saying Thelonious, and when people asked me my name, I would utter **Theolonus**, so the nickname Theo stuck with me. My parents were die-hard jazz fans, and my father, Earl Williams, was a popular jazz pianist who made a name for himself in Philadelphia during the 1960's. The story goes that he loved the music of jazz pianists Thelonious Monk and Duke Ellington so much that he wanted me, his only child, to be named in their honor. My father almost cut an album with jazz trumpeter Lee Morgan, but Lee got murdered outside *Slug's* in 1972, just one week before the recording date. My mother, Clora Williams, was fine with naming me after two jazz icons because she, too, was a jazz fan. She even had a short stint as a vocalist in a local trio, *The Chocolate Roses*, during the same era my father was gaining local prominence.

While I was born in 1963, I did not begin to *live* until 1996. This is the story of how my life changed in 1996, all with the click of a computer keyboard stroke that connected me to a website and community I *never* imagine existed. At the time, I was traveling regularly for an internationally renowned Cosmetics Company. My job took me all around the world, places I never imagined I would go, destinations I had only seen in travel magazines. In many regards, it was a dream job as a National Marketing Director with a generous expense account, upper-class accoutrements such as a condominium in Malibu, California with a view of the Pacific Ocean, a new Midnight Blue convertible Porsche Carrera, my dream car, and tailored suits.

While I thoroughly enjoyed the perks of my job and salary, which eventually grew to well over $250,000, it was tremendously stressful, and I worked long hours. But, the pact I made with my former business school roommate was etched in my brain, and I had no desire whatsoever to live off Social Security upon retirement. Fuck that! I would work hard and steadfast, keeping the end-goal in sight, which was to be financially sound in my latter years. No ratty-ass nursing home or government cheese for me, thank you very much. I wanted the best life had to offer, and I was determined to be rewarded for my hard work.

I had never been tech-savvy per se, so the internet was relatively new to me, at least in terms of a mechanism to meet women. In fact, meeting women was never awkward for me because I was always well-groomed, respectful, humorous, and fun to be around. I did not know it at the time, but my life was headed for a change that warm Tuesday in June of 1996 when I called my former business school roommate, Dennis Warfield.

After graduation, Dennis landed a job at the largest accounting firm in Chicago. Originally from Atlanta, Georgia, Dennis was the consummate Southern gentleman. He was always respectful and took great strides to help others. Even though he had a hefty salary as a forensic accountant, and also earned his MBA with me at one of the premier business schools on the east coast, his personal finances were often in shambles. He made excellent money, but often floundered it by partying or buying insanely expensive stereo equipment. In fact, I recall him bragging, "Hey man, I just brought a Clear Audio turntable for $3,000, a pair of Meridian Speakers for $8,000, and a McIntosh receiver for $4,000!" My response to his electronic braggadocio was always the same, "Yeah, but can that equipment screw your brains out and cook you breakfast?"

A mini-vacation from the demands of work, sales meetings, and flow charts was long overdue, so I called Dennis to let him know I had time for a much-needed weekend getaway and wanted to visit him in Chicago. "Hey man," he said, "come on out. It's about time you took a break from eating those avocado salads, selling lipstick and all that La-La-Land, tree-hugging bullshit!" We both laughed as I countered, "Yeah, and your ass will be calling me again next month when your mortgage is due and you're listening to John Coltrane on your elegant stereo system. 'Trane is the shit, but he can't pay your bills, can he?" We reflected on what we called our "'Trane Days" in college where we would scrounge-up funds to buy a twelve-pack of Rolling Rock, smoke a couple of joints, play Coltrane, Miles Davis, Ella Fitzgerald, and Duke Ellington, and eat pizza into the wee-hours, exchanging dreams of becoming wealthy one day. One day...

On Wednesday, I checked with my travel agent to confirm my flight from Los Angeles to O'Hare Airport in Chicago, leaving Friday morning and returning Monday mid-afternoon. I made sure my schedule was clear from Thursday evening until Monday evening because I knew a weekend with Dennis would require time to recover. I also anticipated having a hangover, so I wanted additional time to prepare for work on Tuesday.

I was upbeat about the trip because I had not seen Dennis since 1989 when we both celebrated earning our MBAs. When we graduated, we made a pact to become rich, travel the globe, and retire by the time we were fifty years old. Dennis moved to Chicago after graduation and my first job was with a large marketing firm in Dallas, Texas. I was the Assistant Vice-President of Marketing, primarily responsible for developing consumer marketing campaigns for the Beef Industry. Here I was, a city-boy from Philadelphia, Pennsylvania, MBA in-hand from a prestigious business school, and working on a beef campaign in bum-fuck Dallas!

There were three important lessons I learned about Dallas: 1) it was indeed a good ol' boy town, and if you made the right connections, your career could take leaps and bounds, 2) the Beef Industry was morbidly influential, and my income reflected how successful the firm made beef more popular than Cheerios, and 3) Texans lived, breathed, ate, and defecated high school football. Take a cursory drive through Plano, among other areas, and you will see high school football stadiums that rival Division I college stadiums! I used to call Texas the "Land of 3-B's," which stood for good ol' *B*oys, *B*eef, and (foot) *B*alls. I felt like an outsider because I was used to

7

the fast-pace, impersonal nature of the East Coast, but I made many contacts and learned the true value of networking.

I worked at the marketing firm for six years, and then began to get an itch to move to another city. I put feelers out to friends and former classmates that I was interested in moving to another city, perhaps somewhere on the West Coast. I visited Los Angeles several times, and enjoyed the consistent weather, but never imagined living there. After two months of networking, I received a phone message from my former undergraduate roommate, Steve Kirkland, who was an Executive Recruiter. "Hey man, if you're still looking for a gig in LA, I might have something for you to follow-up on. Give me a call when you can."

I called Steve and he told me about a National Marketing Director position at a company named Premier Cosmetics. My initial response was, "Man, I'm not developing cosmetics ad campaigns!" Steve countered by saying, "Okay, that's cool. I guess you don't need two-hundred grand." I exclaimed, "What? Did you say two-hundred grand, as in $200,000? Count me the hell in! I'll go door-to-door selling Avon for that much." Steve laughed before clarifying, "Cool down, Theo, the salary range is $190,000 to $200,000 with raises and bonuses over time. The maximum cap on the salary has the potential to grow to $300,000, and that's possible in few years if you really kick ass. Either way, that's a sweet salary for someone who's currently greasing palms of fat-ass Washington lobbyists that, of all things, tell the world that eating beef is cool." His comment, while humorous, stung because I was becoming disenchanted with my firm, and began to question the efficacy of my work. So, I felt compelled to hurl an obligatory "Fuck you, Steve! Have you seen beef sales over the past three years? Well, guess who's largely responsible for that!"

Chapter 3

On Friday, my plane landed at O'Hare Airport, surprisingly, on-time at 6:30p.m. Flying through O'Hare is like crawling through a maze blindfolded, and notorious for flight delays. I felt antsy despite my flight arriving on-time. Having experienced too many 11-hour work days, I was ready to party the moment the plane landed. I called Dennis on his cell phone, but got his voice mail. Frustrated, and fueled by jet-lag, I barked into the receiver, "Hey, dumb ass, I'm at the airport. Where the hell are you? I thought you were picking me up." I wasn't truly pissed-off because I knew Dennis, to put it diplomatically, was "punctually-challenged." He always had good intentions, but was truly exemplary of the adage, "You'll be late for your own funeral."

I made the trek to the baggage area and my mind wandered, reflecting on connecting with Dennis and re-creating our "'Trane Days." In business school, we always managed to carve-out time, and money, to hang-out at local jazz clubs even though school occupied most of our time. We were both avid music fans, and jazz was my favorite. Dennis always took time to remind me "Don't forget that the Godfather of Soul is from *my* home state, Georgia, not to mention Little Richard and Ray Charles." I would swiftly neutralize him by boasting, "Yeah, I know 'da Godfather, Ray, and Lil' Richard revolutionized music around the world, and God knows white cats stole their shit and became even more famous. But, I need to remind you that Lee Morgan, the Heath Brothers, *and* John Coltrane hail from *my* hometown, Philly! 'Trane was born in North Carolina, but he made his home in Philly. Need I keep going?"

I picked-up my bags from the carousel, exited the terminal, and called Dennis again. This time, he picked-up and screamed, "Where the hell are you? I've been driving around O'Hare for twenty minutes!" to which I replied, "Uh, I'm standing by the big ass sign that says ARRIVALS! You mean to tell me you've been so busy 'cooking numbers' at your accounting firm that you can't read anymore?" He blurted, "Oh, I see you. Is that you with that cheesy-ass Armeni blazer on?" to which I rejoined, "Uh, dickhead, it's called *Armani*, not Armeni." "Yeah, I know, but I also know you used to have a penchant for buying your threads at Marshall's, so I'll have to check the label." I hung up and saw him swerve, nearly running up the curb and coming to a screeching halt. I leaned over, stuck my head inside the car and said, "Damn, I see that forensic accounting is paying off, huh?" "Bullllllshit!" he responded, before exiting the car and walking towards me. "I paid for this S-Class in less than three years! Gimme' a hug, man."

We gave each other a hearty embrace, looked into the other's eyes, and almost simultaneously said, "I miss you, man." We were still in great shape, contrary to other classmates we had seen over the years. The years since graduation had done Dennis and I well financially, but most importantly, mentally and physically.

We drove along and began talking about one of the prettiest women in our graduating class, Cecelia Murphy. She used to be the Senior Vice-President of Finance for an automobile company in Detroit. However, she left the company, got married, and had four children. Our graduating class had not reached its ten-year anniversary, and word spread fast that Cecelia was still pretty, but after having four children, had a butt the size of a Christmas ham!

We also talked about another classmate, Timothy Greenfield, one of the most compassionate people in our class. He committed suicide. One afternoon, he came home early and found his wife, Mary, getting pounded doggy-style by their neighbor, Richard Halpern. She was still dressed in her blue Chanel pinstripe suit. Timothy had stood in a chair, wrapped a lizard-skin belt tightly around his neck and tied it to the chandelier in their bedroom. He left a note to Mary, written with red lipstick and in bold letters: ***Fuck you, too!*** Halpern, the consummate bachelor, relished in the fact that he was the youngest, wealthiest bachelor in Jupiter Island, Florida, one of the wealthiest cities in America. His bravado subsided and all but sent him to the psyche ward after Timothy's suicide.

Timothy and Mary were married only two years, and he loved her. In retrospect, though, most of us were curious as to how they even met. Timothy was not a troll, but he was very shy and timid around women. Conversely, Mary was gorgeous, educated, gregarious, and always flirtatious with men, even in Timothy's presence. She financed her undergraduate degree from Vassar College by modeling for a young women's fashion magazine. Word spread that Mary was cheating on Timothy within months after they married, but mere speculation and allegations did not bother him. He just took care of business, and over the short span of five years, had become *the* premier investment banker throughout southern Florida.

After Timothy's suicide, it was rumored the community of Jupiter Island was never the same, so much so that Mary packed-up and moved to the Hampton's in less than one month. Her move was the result of being shunned, effectively banished by her neighbors. She was unable to bear the strains of the scarlet brand she analogously wore: the wealthy MILF whose husband caught her cheating in the opulent, over-sized bed he purchased just three weeks prior!

Timothy was a hard worker in business school, and often helped others understand (and survive!) the maze of formulas during the semester of Dr. Jacobson's Forensic Accounting class. Dr. Jacobson was the academic reincarnation of Hitler. His demands and expectations were outrageously high. However, he earned a lot of respect because he prepared his graduate students to work in *any* accounting environment. When it came to accounting formulas, equations, and solving astronaut-like algorithms, Dr. Jacobson was *the* man.

Dennis zipped in and out of O'Hare traffic like Mario Andretti, and it's amazing he did not have an accident. Thirty minutes later, we were in downtown Chicago. The sun was setting as we listened to Thelonious Monk's tune, *Misterioso*. "Man, oh, man, you're bringing back memories of grad school with that cut," I said. Dennis replied, "Yeah, Monk never gets old. These young cats coming up today don't have a clue, and all that smooth jazz bullshit is killing *real* jazz!" He went on to lament, "The Chicago Summer Jazz Festival is going to hell! We used to have cats like Malichi Favors, El Khahil El-Zabar, Ernest Dawkins, and lots of other cats, but the organizers have been watering the festival down with these new wannabe jazzers. The music's depressing, so I don't even go anymore."

He went on to say, "Theo, I can't wait to show you my new turntable, it's amazing! People are all hyped-up about CDs, but I'll take vinyl any day! The sound of a high-fidelity album on my turntable is like making love to Halle Berry!" I was quick to chide, "Yeah, right, your taste is more like that of Grace Jones from the movie Boomerang!"

We laughed as Dennis approached a well-lit high-rise in the heart of downtown Chicago. I said to him, "Let's go to your place so I can drop my bags and take a shower before we go out." "Well, son," he said, "this *is* where I live. I don't make big money just to live on the South Side, although I do some volunteer tutoring over there with some hard-ass former gang-bangers. I've tutored some cats whose second home is Cook County Jail, brothers who would not hesitate to knock your teeth out." "Why do you do it?" I asked. "Because I never, ever forget that I easily could have gone that route. Yeah, I make crazy money now, but growing up in the projects in Atlanta was no picnic. I just try to help young brothers get on the right track. I'm not any better than them, I just do different shit." I responded, "The bottom line is, they steal from the Mom 'N Pop stores while your forensic accounting ass does corporate thievery – same ol' shit, different methods and bigger money." Brief silence. It was as if we were pondering our perceived privileged status as well-paid Black men, living in lofty abodes, and seemingly oblivious to economically destitute brothers on the South Side of Chicago.

The aura in the car became solemn as I said, "You know what, Dennis? Man, I make good money, work my ass off, pay my taxes, and try to do the right thing, but you know what? My very first weekend in Los Angeles, LAPD pulled me over as I was driving down Sunset Boulevard. Remember that old yellow Porsche Boxster I used to have? The racist bastards had the nerve to ask me what I was doing driving a Porsche. Ain't *that* some shit? I can't tell you how many times I've been pulled over by LAPD for that type of nonsense. I get even more wicked looks from them now because I have a new ride." Dennis replied, "Yeah, Theo, I know the feeling, and 'Chicago's Worst'… oops, I meant, 'Chicago's Finest' don't exactly welcome me to Mr. Roger's neighborhood either."

We pulled up to the entrance of the high-rise and an elderly Black doorman opened the passenger door and greeted me as I got out. He whisked around to open Dennis's door. "Good evening Mr. Warfield, shall I park it, or do you want me to leave it curbside?" Dennis shook the hand of the elderly man and put a crisp $20 bill in his crinkled hands. "No, Mr. James, please don't park it because we'll be back down shortly. Mr. James, this is my ol' roommate from college, Theo Williams. He's visiting from Los Angeles, and we'll be hanging out this weekend." Mr. James bellowed, "Welcome to Chicago, Mr. Williams! I hope you have a pleasant stay." I responded, "Please, Mr. James, call me Theo, and thanks for the warm welcome."

The lobby of Dennis's building, *The Ridgecrest*, was bright from scores of chandeliers. The smell of fresh roses waded through my nostrils, a serene environment completely antithetical to the musty American Airlines jet I recently deplaned. There was a gift shop to the left where an elderly Black woman peeked out. "Good evening, Mr. Warfield." Dennis turned, "Hello Mrs. James, how're you tonight? This is my friend Theo from Los Angeles, and he's visiting for the weekend." Mrs. James smiled and confided, "Mr. Williams, you're in good company with Mr. Warfield."

When Dennis and I boarded the elevator, I jokingly punched him on the shoulder and said, "Damn, man, you fuckin' Mrs. Jane Pitman?" We laughed, and then Dennis said, "Oh, you remember that movie? Nah, they're good people, been married 53 years and both have worked here for 30 of those years. Ain't *that* some shit? They've paid a lot of dues dealing with some of these wealthy spoiled-ass residents. I try to take care of them once-in-a-while." I countered, "Wow, 53 years? Man, that's some serious love!"

We reached the twelfth floor, veered right, and were soon inside Dennis's spacious bachelor pad. "Dennis," I queried, "promise me you're not doing some Michael Milkin-type illegal shit at that firm." "Well, Theo," he said, "another reason I tutor the gang-bangers is to keep myself grounded. Sometimes I see some questionable things at work, but as you know, my parents taught me well. There's nothing like growing up in the South and getting *real* home training. I like big-money, but I'm not going to throw away my future just to make an extra dollar. Fuck that!" He peered at me before saying, "On the other hand, look at Michael Milkin with that horrendous toupee'. He duped people out of insane amounts of money, got out of prison, did the lecture circuit, wrote about it, and now the dude is getting back on top. He got indicted on 90-something counts of racketeering and securities fraud. He was originally sentenced to ten years in prison, but the motherfucker actually *did* less than two! You let that shit happen to a Black man and he would still be *under* the jail. So, I'm not even thinking about doing anything crazy like that. Enough about the so-called justice system, come check out the stereo system."

I asked Dennis to put on some tunes while I took a shower. Coltrane's arrangement of *My Favorite Things* curled through the steam. When I got out of the shower, he was standing near his turntable, eyes closed, hands in the air, swaying back-and-forth as if he were conducting 'Trane's classic band. I teased, "What the hell are you trying to do, summon Julie Andrews from *The Sound of Music?*" I knew he was in a zone, just like I had seen him many times throughout college.

Dennis's love for jazz was secondary to his love for blues. He had a great appreciation for classic jazz, but his heart was with the music of "Blind Lemon" Jefferson, B.B. King, Elmore James, "Sonny Boy" Williams, and other classic blues cats. When we became roommates, we essentially swapped musical passions, Dennis enlightening me about classic blues and I teaching him about classic jazz.

I plopped down on the couch, beer in hand, towel wrapped around my torso as the dim lights took Dennis and I back to our 'Trane Days. It wasn't long before I, too, gesticulated to McCoy Tyner's mellifluous piano comps around Trane's saxophone. At the tune's conclusion, I jumped up, energized, and began to dress. Dennis, the consummate Southern gentleman, had taken time to iron my slacks and shirt while I was in the shower, so I said to him, "Man, you've always been so considerate of others. Thanks for ironing my clothes." "Well," he said, "you Northern dudes don't know how to iron, and I damn-sure ain't taking you out with *me* looking like Opey-fucking-Taylor!" I barked, "Well, that may be true, but you Southern cats would *still* be wearin' straw hats, rubber-band suspenders, and drinkin' moonshine were it not for us Philly cats schoolin' ya'll on how to do shit right."

Chapter 4

"Hey man," I asked, "how're your parents? I remember when they visited us our first year in business school and your mother brought all that food. For a moment, I thought she was going to pull a whole damn pig out the back of your father's SUV." We laughed, and then he responded, "They're doing okay, man, but I'm starting to get a little worried. Mom is doing well, but my dad's blood pressure is very high. I keep telling mom to keep tabs on his diet and cut back on the salt, pork, and stuff like that. They're old-school country folks, so between eating fried foods and leaving things in Jesus' hands, you really can't tell them anything." "I hear you, man," I said. "We'll have to call them before I go back to LA. Your parents, especially your mother, would kick my butt if she knew I came to visit you and didn't call them while I was here. You've got some good parents, Dennis, and they always treated me like their son whenever they saw me." "Yeah," he said, "they always ask about you, especially since your father passed away."

"Well," I said, "it's been about two years, and mom is hanging in there. She's still mobile, and able to get around, but I've been encouraging her to sell that big-ass house in West Philly. She says there're too many memories there, which I dig, but it's getting harder and harder to get up and down all those steps, although she won't admit it. She doesn't know it yet, but I've been pricing some condos at a senior community in Chestnut Hill. It's a pain in the butt trying to conduct real estate business in Philly while I'm all the way in LA. That's my mom, so, by hook-or-crook, I'm going to make it happen." As if he had just made an earth-shattering discovery, Dennis shouted, "Hey, I have a good friend, Stephanie, who's a realtor! She's the one who sold me this place. In fact, she'll be at the club tonight. Even though she's based out of Chicago, it won't hurt to ask her to do some digging around. She may just have some contacts in Philly."

Dennis and I were like blood brothers, looking out for the other's best interests all the time, and I was relieved he would contact Stephanie. Dennis had always been the type to focus in on a problem and persevere until it was resolved. He was driven, especially in business school, where he pushed me beyond my limits, helping me realize my potential. It's no wonder he became a very successful accountant.

There was an eerie silence before Dennis revealed, "Hey man, I'm really sorry I wasn't able to attend your father's funeral. You have no idea how much that messed with me." I consoled him, "Look, I understand. It wasn't a problem then and it certainly isn't now. Didn't you have to go to Hawaii for work?" He quickly responded, "No, the Cayman Islands. I tried like hell to get out of it, but our client's books were so fucked up. It took me an extra week to clean-up their mess. A client with *very* deep pockets always gets the attention, so my supervisor sent me. Frankly, I'm thinking about getting out of this business. It kind of fucks with me realizing I'm helping rich people essentially hide money just so they can make even more. Greedy bastards!"

I had never heard him express discontent with his job, so I dug further. "You're one of the best at your firm. Why would you leave? Aren't you close to becoming a partner? Besides, what the hell would you do?" His voice trailed off as he replied, "You'd never guess…"

I could sense he was still disappointed for not attending my father's funeral, so I consoled him. "Dennis, I *know* under ordinary circumstances you would've been there. Think about it. The fact that your parents were there spoke volumes about what they thought of me and my parents. Brother, you were damn-sure there whether you understand that or not. My Pops having a heart attack caught everybody off-guard, so it's not like you had time to plan a trip." We traded a robust hug as I quipped, "Okay, let's get out of here before you start crying like a lil' bitch!" "Yeah," he said, "besides, with all this hugging, I don't want to wrinkle your Bill Blas*t* jacket", emphasizing the *t*. "It's Blass, motherfucker, Blass!" I shot back. "Hmm, let me check the label…" he teased.

Dennis was dressed in a dark blue pin-stripe suit, soft red shirt, no tie, paisley pocket-square, and black Gucci loafers. Dapper. I was equally "showroom clean" wearing a charcoal colored blazer, grey slacks, white pin-point shirt, and black Bacco-Bucci loafers. We could pass for models, both of us standing just over 6'5", 225 pounds, muscular, and smooth chocolate brown, hairless faces.

21

Dennis looked me over as if I were finally worthy of being seen with him in public. "Okay, son, I see I taught you well. You're looking good." I laughed, and said, "Look, Southern boy, you are forgetting *I* was the one who 'schooled' your country ass in college. Before we were roomies, your ass was wearing bibs with a straw hanging out your mouth!"

Chapter 5

Mr. James saw Dennis and I exit the elevator and, like clock-work, had both doors to Dennis's Benz open for us before he bellowed, "Have fun this evening, gentleman, and don't do anything I wouldn't do." Dennis replied, "Don't worry, Mr. James, we'll be okay, but thanks for the words of wisdom." Once inside the car, Dennis popped in Miles Davis's iconic CD, *Kind of Blue*. Instead of playing the disc from beginning to end, he pushed the forward button and went straight to *All Blues*. As soon as the tune began, I reclined my seat and said, "Man, ***this*** is what jazz is all about. That is one of ***the*** baddest cuts ever made!" "You ain't lyin'" he said, "and it would be even better if you shut the hell up so we can hear it."

We were able to hear *All Blues, So What*, and *Blue In Green* by the time we pulled up to a classy-looking club in the Loop area called *The Spot*. As we strolled up to the red carpeted entrance, a bouncer called out to Dennis, "Hey, D-Dub, good to see you back" to which Dennis replied, "Hey Mark, good to see you. This is my buddy Theo from LA, and I'm taking him out to enjoy a ***real*** club experience." Mark Brewer, a rotund man of at least 6'9", 375 pounds, jovially barked, "Hammer don't hurt'em! Have a good time, fellas, and let me know if you need anything." Dennis slid Mark a $20 bill as onlookers gawked, "Who are they?" We walked into the club past a line of patrons at least twenty yards long.

A tall, sensuous hostess with sleek caramel-colored skin wearing a form-fitting red dress greeted Dennis with a hug and kiss. He introduced her as Gwen Robinson and she said, "Welcome to Chicago, Theo." I gave her a hug and peck on the cheek, saying "Thank you, Gwen. I'm having a great time already! If all the women here look like you, I may just have to move to Chicago." She smiled, a coy but decadent smile, and seemed receptive to my innuendo that I would be more than eager to explore her cervix until it cried for mercy!

Gwen led us to a private booth upstairs where another model-type woman greeted us. I whispered to him, "Okay, how much did you pay these chicks to act like they know you? You lucky bastard." He laughed and said, "Brother, it's not luck. It's my Southern charm." We barely had time to sit on the sofa before a waitress, Joann, walked up to us and said, "Hey Dennis! How's Chicago's most eligible bachelor doing? I see you brought a friend with you" as she demurely smiled at me. Dennis's good-natured side arose, and he responded, "Hey Joann, this is my buddy Theo from LA. Theo, this is Joann Neal. He's visiting for the weekend and I thought I'd show him why LA doesn't have anything on Chicago." Joann retorted, "You got that right, baby. What can I get for you gentleman?"

Either I was hallucinating or Joann was seriously checking me out in the brief moment since she entered our private booth. But, then again, considering how much money Dennis dropped in people's hands, it very well could have been plain ol' courtesy on their part. I quickly arose and gave Joann a hug and let her know *The Spot* seemed to be the place to be, especially since *she* was working there. She, too, took my advances in stride. When she brought our drinks back, she handed me her business card and said, "Well, I know you won't be in Chicago a long time, but I do get to LA on occasion. I model on the side. Perhaps we can keep in touch?" I tried like hell to be nonchalant because she was indeed gorgeous, so I sheepishly responded, "Oh, I would be honored to show you a good time… and then some." I smiled at her as she walked away and thought to myself, "Yeah, I'll keep 'in touch' with you alright…"

Dennis and I stayed at *The Spot* for a few hours, taking time to dance and talk with his friends who shared our booth. Frankly, I was impressed, but not surprised, with the caliber of people he associated with. There was Mike Adams, a pharmaceutical sales manager, a stunning anesthesiologist, Dr. Patricia Dunn, a well-dressed, nerdy Information Technology guy, "Skip" Thomas, a human resources manager named Sandra Lewis who lived in the same high-rise as Dennis, and Stephanie Culpepper, the realtor who sold Dennis his condo at *The Ridgecrest*.

We talked, joked, danced, drank, talked more, and danced even more. I was feeling very relaxed as I had two shots of top-shelf vodka, compliments of Stephanie. Dennis, the designated driver, encouraged me to enjoy myself, "Go 'head, have a good time, Theo, you need to cut-loose, so don't worry about me. I'm enjoying my Martinelli Sparkling Cider." Stephanie chided us by saying, "Oh, that's so sweet. The ol' college roomies are all mushy. I think another shot is due!

Let's have a toast for Theo!" Dennis followed, saying "Damn right, a toast to my main man, Theo, my brother from another mother!" He looked at Stephanie and said, "Stephanie, Theo's the consummate gentleman, but you better watch out, he's a tiger." I was embarrassed because he did a dreadful imitation of a tiger's growl, even gesturing his hand as if clawing the air. I took a mental note that Stephanie seemed intrigued by Dennis's comments as she uttered, "Oh, really?" while looking directly at me.

I felt taken aback by everyone's generosity. "Wow! All of you are much too kind." We clanked our glasses as everyone downed a shot of tequila, except Dennis, who maintained the grip on his cider-filled flute. As I was finishing my shot, Stephanie put her hand to my mouth and I noticed the inside of her thumb and pointer finger were coated with salt. "Would you lick this off for me, Theo? Please?" I meticulously curled my tongue against her well-manicured, fingers, licking the salt as slowly as I could. I, too, was intrigued! I became self-conscious of the bulge in my slacks, and was further surprised when Stephanie upped the ante by using her other hand to guide a slice of lime into my mouth. As she did this, we looked directly into each other's eyes, that *"Oh, I'm **definitely** fucking you!"* look.

After our shots, Stephanie, Sandra, and Patricia excused themselves to the ladies' room to "freshen up" as they called it. Dennis pulled me close to him and whispered in my ear, "Damn, Theo, Stephanie's acting like she wants to give you the pussy right here on the couch." I responded, "Yeah, she seems interested, and

I'm not going to lie, when she did that salt and lemon thing, my dick got so hard a cat couldn't scratch it!" We laughed out loud and gave each other a high-five, machismo gone awry.

I was having a great time with the group and felt as if I had known everyone for years, primarily because Dennis was the type of person that gravitated towards kindred spirits. Or, perhaps it was the inverse. His personality was so mellow and humble that people tended to enjoy his presence. While the ladies were absent, Dennis struck up a conversation with Skip. "Skip," he asked, "what's new in the computer world? Everybody knows you're on the cutting edge of technology, but I bet your pervert-ass is designing some robotic, latex fuck toy."

Skip swiftly countered, "Yeah, whatever, Mr. Accountant. You keep crunching numbers and let me handle the tech-stuff. By the way, did you get the link to *Global Connections* I sent you last week?" Dennis responded, "Yeah, but I didn't really have time to dig too deeply into it. I've had a lot of success with another site similar to *Global Connections*." Mike, the pharmaceutical representative chimed in, "Oh, shit, there they go again." He added, "Skip, don't tell me you're still meeting fat chicks from Peoria on the internet." There was a round of laughter before Skip shot back. "Okay, you Max Julian-wanna-be-motherfucker, you just worry about selling Viagra to old men with limp dicks while I line-up more pussy on *Global Connections* than you'll get in a year. I'm telling you, *Global Connections* is the shit!" He added, "You know I travel a lot, and I've hooked-up with women, fine women, in every damn city I've been to. No lie, the site's amazing."

The ladies returned from their near half-hour session of "freshening-up" and it was comical to see them acting like it took that long for three ladies to pee. The fellas all knew, or at least suspected, the real purpose of their excursion was to discuss me, the weekend visitor from LA. I mentally crossed my fingers, hoping like hell Stephanie was getting their opinion on whether it was lady-like to take me home and fuck my brains out or if she should make me wait. Secretly, of course, I imagined that was the tone of their discussion and she would choose the former option.

At about 1a.m., I began to run out of steam, and Dennis could sense my energy waning. As much as I wanted to be with Stephanie, or at least try to discover what lie beneath her meticulously cut dark blue sequined dress, I was physically and mentally exhausted. It had been a long day for me, and I was rapidly approaching nineteen hours, not to mention jetlag, the alcohol I voraciously consumed, and a relatively empty stomach. Dennis leaned over to me and said, "Bro, you look like you're running out of gas, it's your call. Do you want to jet or see if you can connect with Stephanie?" I responded, "As much as I want to go for it, I'm tired as hell, so let's head out." As if he were some high-level Consulate, Dennis stood up and bellowed, "Well, good folks, Theo has had a long day, and he's not used to real parties, so I think we'll bid ya'll adieu. The young lad needs some rest, and he'll need some energy for the rest of the weekend."

Stephanie was the first to stand up to say goodbye. She pulled me close to her as we hugged and whispered in my ear, "If you've some energy tomorrow, I'd love to *have* you for lunch… Oops, did I say that? I *meant* have lunch with you, tomorrow. I have an open house tomorrow, so maybe you can join me. Remember, I'm a realtor, and this is one 'open house' you *don't* want to pass up." I pulled her closer to me, discreetly kissed her on the small of her neck and whispered, "My dear, you can take that house off the market. Sold!" We both laughed, pulled back, and then she gave me a quick peck on my lips.

Dennis, always looking out for me, said matter-of-factly, "Hey, Stephanie, you have any real estate connections in Philly? Theo is looking for some property there." He elbowed me in the ribs and whispered, "Uh, son, you gon' jump on it or do you want me to tell you what to say as well?" Stephanie perked up even more, "I have some solid connections there. As a matter of fact, I've a real estate colleague who's been trying to recruit me to move there." She then took on an exaggerated, albeit humorous persona, "Uh, Theo, have *your* people call *my* people." We laughed and made the obligatory, trite exchange of air kisses, moving our heads right-to-left of the other's cheeks, but never actually putting our lips on the other's face. Dennis and I were about to leave when he announced, "Oh, before I forget, Mark the bouncer sent me a text message letting me know the cabbie that brought ya'll here should be back around 2:30a.m. Have fun."

Before we left, Stephanie said, "Seriously, Theo, I do have a friend in Philadelphia who owns a commercial real estate firm. It's one of the biggest firms in the area, so I'm pretty sure he can at least point you in the right direction if he can't help you himself. I'll give him a buzz first thing in the morning. Can that work for you?" "Of course it can, Stephanie. I greatly appreciate that," I said.

Chapter 6

During the drive back to Dennis's, the music of jazz pianist Horace Silver filled the car. Dennis knew that *Song For My Father* was one of my favorite tunes, especially when I was in a good mood. "Ahh, there you go again, man. That's the ideal tune, perfect timing. "Well," he said, "I figured now is a better time for Silver than, oh, say, one of my homey Little Richard's *Tooty Fruity* type of tunes. But, based upon your and Stephanie's connection, my man James Brown's, *It's A Man's World* might be more apropos. I think she's got your ass shook." I replied, "Maybe so, brother, maybe so. She's fine, smart, good sense of humor, and has a wonderful vibe. Have you 'hit' it before?" "Actually," he said, "I never tried. Stephanie and I always related to each other like hangin' out buddies, so we never treaded any romantic waters."

He went on to say "She's fun as hell to be around and we just didn't want to spoil things by mixing business with pleasure since she sold me my condo. There was just something about that space that she and I understood, certain lines we didn't want to cross. I guess you could call it mutual admiration and respect. Don't get me wrong, though. If things were different, I'd tap on that ass like Gregory Hines" to which we gave each other high-five, laughed hysterically, and finally allowed Horace Silver to work his piano magic.

Song For My Father concluded and a thought came to me. I pushed the forward button on the CD player to *Calcutta Cutie* and said to Dennis, "Hey man, we didn't finish our conversation." He asked, "What conversation?" and I reminded him. "Right before we left your pad to go out, you said something that stuck with me." His contorted face mirrored the semi-frustrated tone in his response. "Look, Colum*bro*, spit it out." "Well," I said, "you mentioned that you've been thinking about quitting your gig, but when I asked what you would do, you said, and I quote, 'You would never guess.' What the hell does *that* mean? Are you trying to become a Navy Seal or some shit?"

Dennis knew I wouldn't let him escape my query, but before entertaining the question, he said, "No, no, no! It's not like that at all. I'm not like one of those rappers that want to be an actor, and the damn actors want to be rappers. What kind of shit is that? Motherfuckers *need* to do what they're good at and stop treating other professions as novelties." Pensively, he continued. "Actually, Theo, I've been giving this a lot of long, hard thought. Remember I told you I volunteer with some former gang-bangers? Well, I've been doing that about three years and it's very fulfilling. I really dig working with the brothers because I see results. Imagine being with an ex-felon, a cat that did twelve years of a fifteen-year bid for aggravated manslaughter and car-jacking, who's now 30 and trying to turn his life around."

"This brother, Lamar Brewer, was straight-up hardcore when he came into the program. He was bitter as hell for the prison time he did because his future went down the tubes after he was busted for a joy-ride that went sour. The young brother was involved in a stupid joy-ride in a car he didn't realize was stolen. He's damn-near a math whiz, but got caught-up with the wrong crowd, and the joy ride was only part of it. He actually had a full academic scholarship to Grambling State University. In fact, he was offered a full football scholarship from Coach Eddie Robinson, but decided to walk-on because the academic scholarship was more secure in case he got injured. That's how forward-thinking this kid was."

I interjected, "Damn, that's really fucked up! You mean this young brother had a full-ride to go to Grambling and *that's* how it all went down?" "He was a senior in high school," Dennis said. "Just two months before graduation, he and some of his buddies were driving around in a car Lamar didn't know was stolen. The real owner of the car, along with some of his friends, caught up to Lamar's group and a fight broke out. Long story short, one of the fellas who came looking for Lamar's group was shot and killed. Even though Lamar was not the one that pulled the trigger, everyone in the car was charged because nobody wanted to admit who was guilty. So, all four of the fellas in the car did varying degrees of time for that nonsense." Stymied, all I could say was, "Damn! A young brother's life changed so drastically…"

Conversation between Dennis and I all but ceased after we talked about Lamar Brewer's demise as a youngster and his optimistic future as an adult. Instead of talking about horrific life experiences, we simply agreed, literally, to allow jazz saxophonist Pharoah Sanders' tune, *The Creator Has A Master Plan* to sift through our ears and deep into our souls. Perhaps it was Leon Thomas's yodeling, or it may have been Pharaoh's wailing saxophone, but we both drifted into another dimension.

Chapter 7

On the way back to Dennis's place, my stomach began to growl like I was Sasquatch. "Before we go back to your pad, let's get a bite to eat. I'm starving like crazy." "Cool." Dennis said. "What do you have a taste for? There's a late-night deli on the South Side that has some mean hoagies. Or, if you want, we can grab a full meal, just let me know." I responded, "You know what I'm craving? Don't laugh at me, but I *really* want some White Castles. We don't have any in Los Angeles, except the frozen version at grocery stores. Eating a microwave version of White Castles is not even close to the *real* thing."

"See, he said, I told you". All those health nuts in LA have you twisted. You *need* a good, juicy steak, fat-ass baked potato with mounds of sour cream, and a huge dinner roll. I bet you've become one of those grass-eating vegans, haven't you?" He didn't relent. "It's only a matter of time before you'll be wearing your signature Ralph Lauren Pol(*i*)o shirts, khaki pants, and Fairgame flip-flops." I barked, "You meant to say Polo and Ferragamo, bitch!" "I know, I know!" he said. "I'm just messing with you. "Seriously," I said, "I want some White Castles. I haven't had any since I visited my cousins in Louisville a few years back. Since I'm the visitor, buddy, you need to get moving." Dennis started impersonating Alfred - the dutiful butler of super-hero, Batman - in a horrendous English accent,

"Right away, sir, and shall we stop in the 'hood to pick-up a fifth of Mad Dog 20-20, too?"

We pulled into the White Castle drive-thru and my energy level increased. I hadn't wolfed down White Castles in years. I ordered four White Castles, an order of onion rings, and a large chocolate shake. Dennis ordered two White Castles, two fish sandwiches, French fries, and a large Coke. We resisted the urge to eat in the car, and opted to wait until we got back to his place. It was almost 1:45a.m. when Dennis maneuvered his Benz into the designated parking area for tenants. Mr. and Mrs. James were not in sight, either, and the serenity of *The Ridgecrest* was interrupted by faint sounds of rattling car keys, our loafers clacking against the lobby's marble floor, ice shaking in Dennis's soda cup, and rustling of our White Castle bags.

When we entered his condo, I made a beeline for the bathroom while Dennis dropped the bags on the kitchen table. I noticed he picked-up his universal remote control and clicked three buttons. In milliseconds, life came to his television and stereo equipment. He went into the second bedroom, which also served as office space, and turned his computer on. When I came out of the bathroom, Dennis had already begun reading his email before reluctantly taking his attention off messages to also go to the bathroom.

I said to him, "I had a great time with your friends tonight. They were all good people." "Yeah," he said, "they're all pretty cool, and we usually get along very well with no drama. I enjoy being around them, especially our diversity of thought and life experiences.

They're good people, and you would be welcomed to the fold if you ever move to Chi-town."

As usual, music was a part of everything we did, so Dennis said to me, "Okay, I've been picking all the good 'cuts' to play tonight, now it's your turn. The CDs are over there" as he pointed to the mahogany case, "and the albums are on the turnstile next to it. I have more albums in the other room. Remember, son, my stuff is in alphabetical order, so please don't screw-up my system." "You," I said, "are the most anal dude in the world! When you go to sleep, I'm gonna re-arrange all your CDs and albums and mix everything up." "You do that," he said, "and your ass *will* be hanging out with Stephanie the rest of the weekend!"

I sifted through his extensive vinyl collection and stopped abruptly when I saw a high-fidelity recording of Lee Morgan's *Search For The New Land*. "Oh man, this is one of my all-time favorites! My father and I used to listen to this when I was a kid. He used to sit me in front of the stereo and would play along with Herbie Hancock during the piano solo. He had this old Yamaha upright piano he used to play, especially on Sunday mornings. Man, my mom and dad were something else on Sunday mornings! I *still* remember them doing their rendition of Duke Ellington's *Black, Brown, and Beige* before we went to church over on Tioga Street. Mom did her best impression of Mahalia Jackson while dad sat coolly at the piano mimicking Duke."

"My mom confided in me once that my dad was devastated by Morgan's death. Dad was scheduled to have his first major recording

37

session on Morgan's album just two weeks after Morgan got murdered. That was going to be the highlight of his career, a move that surely would have put him on the international radar. So, he was shattered not only because he and Morgan were tight, but, perhaps, even more, because it meant his opportunity for worldwide exposure quickly vanished." A dream deferred.

I put the title track on, *Search For The New Land*, and we escaped along with Morgan and crew as they searched… and searched for a delightful fifteen minutes of the track. We devoured our White Castles before the tune ended. "Damn!" I said, "The food hit the spot, but the music took me to another place… back to Philadelphia growing up and, as a kid, being bathed in jazz." Dennis responded, "Oh, yeah, I feel you on that!" He sat in his chaise recliner while I lay on his sofa, as we now enjoyed another Morgan classic, *The Joker*.

Chapter 8

I was beginning to drift asleep and caught my head bobbing, so I decided to take a shower before going to bed. Dennis, eyes closed, sat fixated on Morgan's pyrotechnic trumpet lines. When I got out of the shower, I saw him at his desk in the other bedroom. He was tapping away at his computer keyboard. "Man, do you ever stop working?" I asked. He barely looked up, just enough to mumble, "I'm not working, I'm checking out *Global Connections*." I asked, "What's *Global Connections*? I heard you and Skip talking about that at the club, something about hooking up with fine women on the internet." "Yep, it is," he said. "It's a website for people in the *Lifestyle*, but you wouldn't know about that 'cuz you don't do anything but work and put Halle Berry in cosmetics ads." We laughed as I quipped, "Yeah, well, Halle's fine ass is part of the reason I drive a Porsche. When I signed her to our company, sales skyrocketed and I got a promotion." Playing the role of spoiler, he asked, "Yeah, you may drive a Porsche, but are you bonin' Halle?" Checkmated, I wryly panned, "No, but I'm not complaining."

I was lounging on a recliner when I kept hearing the sound of a bell coming from Dennis's computer. "Hey horn dog, I'm trying to relax, but that chime is a wee-bit disruptive." "My fault," he said. "I'm flirting with some women in a chat room on *Global Connections*. It seems I've intrigued the ladies, which should not be a surprise." "Yeah, well, they've not seen your face yet, so don't get too happy,"

39

I said. He motioned for me to come check out what he was doing. Admittedly, I was baffled that people in the chat room were so freely talking about their sexual interests. One lady in the chat room sent an instant message to Dennis saying, "I wish you were in New Mexico, I would invite you over now." I looked at him and said, "You must be bullshitting me! Are these chicks for real?" to which he replied, "You heard Skip earlier didn't' you? I know Skip well and I know he's telling the truth about connecting with women during his trips."

On one hand, I was embarrassed at the thought of connecting with women on the internet for dates, let alone sexual relationships. It all seemed so new, so open, and so… unbelievably decadent. "You should get an account, create a profile and see what happens. It's not like you have anything to lose, right?" Dumbfounded, I replied, "Yeah, you're right about that, but I don't want to connect with any crazy women who'll be stalking me." He tried to assuage my inhibitions by saying, "Well, according to Skip, this site is for serious people, meaning those who just want to fuck and, frankly, are **not** looking for relationships."

"Seriously," I exclaimed, "you've **got** to be bullshitting me!" He countered, "You heard Skip, didn't you? And, based upon responses from women I'm flirting with in this chat room, I've no reason to doubt either. In fact, I'm trying to set-up a dinner meeting with this babe tomorrow. She claims she's a dentist, divorced, tired of the dating scene, works a lot, and just looking for a safe, clean, reliable booty-call. I'm a Southern gentleman, so I can't neglect the lady's wishes, can I?"

I sat at the computer and flirted with the ladies and couples in the chat room. Incredulous, I shouted, "Hey, wait a minute! Are these couples actually inviting other men to join them so the wife can get some extra dick? I can understand why single women and men are here, but couples, too? You mean to tell me there're husbands on *Global Connections* who're looking for another man to bone their wives? Oh, hell no, that shit's crazy!" "It's called the *Lifestyle*," he said, "better known as *swinging*, and that's what's happening around the globe, Sherlock." He continued, "You have to understand it's **not** about falling in love. There's a *Lifestyle* saying that goes like this: 'Relax, it's just sex,' meaning people aren't trying to fall in love - they just love to fuck. Period." Bewildered, I flatly responded, "Damn!"

In college, I had my share of gang-bangs and small-scale orgies, but *Global Connections* was, indeed, a new frontier for me conceptually and morally. Conceptually, it was difficult for me to fathom the idea of having sex with another man's wife because that went against tenets I grew up respecting. However, *Lifestyle* tenets threw my perspective in-flux because the premise was the wife had her husband's permission! "Okay, I said to myself, I have to regroup and try to understand this." The more I **tried** to understand, the more confusing it became.

Morally, I was always taught "Thou shall not covet thy neighbor's wife." Again, that mantra was dispelled because it assumed the husband **did not know** his wife wanted, and was getting, a phallus that was not attached to her husband! What, then, if the husband knew? I just didn't comprehend the premise of the *Lifestyle*, in large part, because I knew I'd have grave reservations about giving **my** wife or girlfriend permission to fuck someone else! It did not register with me, so I remained confused. Everything I learned about sexual mores, particularly as they related to being involved with married women, went haywire.

The only thought I was able to recollect, albeit a movie, was the outright carnivorous debauchery of *Caligula*. I reflected on the time as undergraduates, my roommates and I went to an adult theater to see the movie. When the movie was over, we collectively bellowed, "Damn! That was some crazy shit. Those Romans were some wild motherfuckers!"

As I tapped away at the keyboard and flirted, I became more exhausted and told Dennis, "I think I'm gonna hit the sack. I've had enough flirting for one night… uh, morning." I went to bed where the Southern gentleman laid out some comfortable blankets and a goose-feathered pillow. He stayed at the computer a short while longer until, finally, I said to him, "Hey Mr. Horny, I'd like to get some sleep, but that damn chat room bell sound is interrupting my beauty sleep." "Okay, okay," he said, "Lord knows you need your beauty sleep with your Flava-Flav looking ass!" We laughed, but I got the last words in, "Well, yeah, I may look like Flava-Flav, but between the only two people here, *I* have Halle Berry's cell phone number!" I ***thought*** I had the last word, but he chirped, "Halle seems like the altruistic type, so maybe one day she'll give you some 'mercy pussy.'"

Chapter 9

When I woke up on Saturday morning, I did not realize how tired my body was. I slept well, like a rock for that matter, but my limbs strongly suggested I lay in bed a bit longer. Besides, I was on *my* time now, so there was no rush to get up. I did manage to take a bathroom pit-stop, and on the way back to the bedroom, I was drawn to the stereo. I sifted through the LPs and found a gem – a tune perfect for a Saturday morning sun: Billie Holiday's *Our Love Is Here To Stay*. I always loved the insightful lyrics, and Billie had a way of simultaneously making listeners' hearts smile and cry, sometimes in the same tune! Her lyrics waded through the living room. *"It's very clear... our love is here to stay. Not for a year, but forever and a day."* Wow! *Forever and a day...*

When Billie sang songs of love, one could not deny the fact that she touched on the deepest human emotions, whether love found or lost. I also felt a bit giddy about Stephanie. I was never the "fall in love overnight" type, but it was refreshing to be wanted by a woman who was unashamed of letting you know she wanted you, too.

At 11:00a.m., my cell phone buzzed. I looked at the screen, but did not recognize the number, except that it was a Chicago area code. Initially, I thought Dennis was in the other room calling me to see if I had awakened. However, when I answered, a sultry voice cooed, "So, Mr. Handsome, are we on for lunch today?" "Ahh, Stephanie," I said, "How are you this morning my dear?" She replied, "I'm fine, but

44

it won't be morning for too long. I thought I'd call, but not too early because I knew you were very tired when you left *The Spot*." She continued, "Are you fellas still lying around? If you are, you can just call me when you get a chance." I would have been foolish to refuse the obvious invitation, so I said, "Oh no, you didn't call too early. I'm just listening to Billie Holiday. I think Dennis is still asleep."

I have always been attracted to assertive women, so it was a turn-on when Stephanie said, "I've an open house today from 3p.m. onward and I'd love to have you join me for a bite to eat. I promise I'll behave, and who knows what may happen." There was something seductive and erotic about the way she said **promise** and **may** that I immediately got an erection. My mind raced as I responded, "Sounds good to me, and trust me, Stephanie, you can misbehave **all** you wish. Besides, if you're too bad, I'll have to cuff you." "Oh?" she exclaimed, "In that case, we won't have to use **my** cuffs." After that quip, my erection was in reveille mode! I thought about letting her know the physical impact of her words on my body, but was excited about the chase, so I refrained. Instead, I said, "I'll be ready at 2p.m."

Shortly after I hung up the phone, Dennis came out of his bedroom rubbing his eyes, and asked how well I slept. I told him I slept well, a combination of exhaustion from work and being in a different time zone. I asked, "What about you? I drifted off while you were flirting with women on the computer. Oh, and thanks for turning that damn chat room chime off." He laughed and said, "I stayed online another thirty minutes or so chatting with this lady in Rochester, New York.

I have to go there in a couple of weeks and we're going to meet for drinks. If there's some chemistry, we'll take it from there. She looks pretty good, at least in the pictures she sent me. She's originally from Belize and works for a Kodak subsidiary up there."

Dennis and I engaged in small-talk about the weather in Chicago in June, food, sports, and, of course, music. Finally, I asked him, "How long have you been checking out *Global Connections*?" "Not long," he said. "Skip recently turned me on to it, but I've been a member of another site, *Lifestyle Rendezvous*, for about two years." I knew Dennis enjoyed being around beautiful women, and had his share of many over the years, but I had absolutely **no** clue the depth of his involvement in these *Lifestyle* antics. I was, however, intrigued by the concept of *swinging*, but still had grave reservations about it all. I quizzed, "Are people **really** into having sex, essentially, with almost complete strangers they've met on the internet?" "Theo," he said, "you have no clue how popular this stuff is. It's truly a global phenomenon and, above all, a community." Still curious, I inquired, "What's the catch? Are all the chicks ugly-ass bus drivers or, to put it lightly, dogs?" "Hell no!" he screamed. "Trust me, Theo, I have met some of **the** finest women in the world and some really cool couples." He caught me off-guard when he said couples, so I said, "Wait one damn minute, you said couples! Do you mean to tell me you're out fucking wives and their husbands know it? What kind of shit is **that**?"

Dennis looked at me intently as he placed a CD in the tray, Traffic's *Low Spark of the High Heel Boys*. Traffic was one of the groups we used to listen to a lot when we were in business school together. He turned me on to them and I liked the way they combined jazz and rock elements, especially on *Low Spark of the High Heel Boys*. I think he put the track on to divert my attention from semi-chastising him about *swinging*, and it worked. "Do you remember how we used to play that tune on Saturday nights after we got home from the library and would drink beer and smoke weed?" He quickly noted, "Oh, hell yeah! That was one of our 'high' anthems." We both laughed and then I prodded further, "Don't tell me you're still smoking weed, too." Somewhere between being annoyed by my barrage of questions and silliness, he said, "No, man, I've not smoked since college. What about you?" "Same here," I said.

I to question him. "Now, let's get back to the issue. What's this about bonin' wives who have their husband's permission?" Finally, he spat it all out and told me, "Look, Theo, I hope you're not judging me. I work my ass off, long hours to be precise, and the *Lifestyle* just suits my needs at this point in my life. I'm not disrupting anyone's marriage or any nonsense like that. In fact, everybody's open and upfront. Ironically, there are no secrets, unlike people who sneak around and cheat behind their spouse's back. You remember the mantra of the *Lifestyle* I told you, the 'Relax, it's just sex' saying? Well, that's a reality. Believe it or not, respect and honesty are paramount, the very foundation of what it's all about."

I did not want to seem as if I were judging Dennis because I was truly trying to grasp and conceptualize the premise of *swinging*. We had been through so much during our friendship that I would never judge him, nor he judge me. And, we respected each other so much that there was a mutual understanding, an unwritten code, where we accepted the other "as is" without drama. There was a moment of silence accompanied by slight tension so I broke it by saying "You always wanted to be Goldie the Mack so I'm not surprised." We laughed, a somewhat nervous laughter, and I felt compelled to continue with "Hey man, you're my brother in every sense of the word, so I would *never* judge you. If you're enjoying what you're doing, then I'm happy for you. I mean that, Dennis." He sensed my sincerity and responded, "I know that, Theo. I would never worry about you judging me, and you know I have your back, too." With that, we gave each other a hug and then I headed to the shower.

As I walked away, I turned and told him that Stephanie was picking me up at 2p.m. "We're going to lunch and then she wants me to go to join her at an Open House or something like that. It sounded so cryptic, and I told her yes before thinking about whether or not you had anything planned. Is that cool with you?" "Sure, no problem at all," he said. "I pretty much thought that would happen when she asked you last night." Surprised, I asked, "How did you know she asked me?" "Well," he said, "because when she *thought* she was whispering in your ear, the DJ was between tunes. What was meant to be a whisper ended up being loud as hell and we all heard it. Besides, you better not worry about *me* at all, brother. You better worry about *Stephanie!*" He sneered as if I were being set-up for some surprise. "What the hell is **that** supposed to mean?" I barked. He just looked at me, smiled, and said, "Because she's a *swinger*, too. We initially wanted to connect on a sexual level, but like I said, we didn't want to mix business with pleasure. That works out because she trusts me to introduce her to good people, and she does the same for me." Again, as if on cue, he did his horrendous tiger growl impersonation, which was truly asinine.

Chapter 10

Dennis's doorbell rang at 2:00pm. I knew it was Stephanie, so I dashed towards the door, peered through the peephole, smiled to myself, and swung the door open. When her eyes met with mine, all I could say was, "Damn, Stephanie, you look wonderful!" She wore a black silk dress that was cut near the upper part of her shapely thighs, yet low enough to entice onlookers' imaginations. Her dress showed just enough cleavage to reveal a voluptuous set of 38-D breasts that silently begged me to caress them, at least that's what I fantasized! Her calf muscles were toned and firm, and her meticulously manicured red toenails were accented by six-inch patent leather pumps. And that butt... whew! She had a small waistline and a round derriere that I hoped to see from behind later that evening!

Accessories included a semi-glossy silver-colored silk purse the size and shape of a business envelope, black pearls around her neck, silver tennis bracelet on her right wrist and a silver Cartier watch on the left. To say this 5'7", 125 lbs. woman was a "bombshell" did her *no* justice. The color scheme of her dress, shoes, and accessories highlighted her bright caramel complexion and flowing, shiny black hair that trickled down her back, slightly over her left shoulder. At 32 years of age, she was built better and tighter than many women ten years her junior. *That butt...*

It was obvious I stood in the doorway admiring her longer than I was aware because she said, "Well hello, Theo. I was wondering if you were going to let me in today or wait until tomorrow." When Stephanie spoke, even during casual conversations, she had an air of confidence, sensuality, professionalism, and top-tier elegance. "Oh, yes, come on in." I took her left hand and brought her close to my body for a warm, thorough embrace. We hugged each other and as we pulled back, she planted her signature peck on my lips. The kiss was long enough to remind me that if I did not screw up, I would have the honor of viewing *that butt* from the rear, doggy-style. Yet, it was short enough to enchant me, making my mind race with possibilities. Tenderly, but certainly purposeful, she said, "Oops, I did not mean to get lipstick on your lips" as she used her pointer finger to wipe my lips. I swiftly retorted, "I don't think you did, but you can give it another try if you wish, just to make sure." Our tête-à-tête resulted in her saying, "There **might** be more where that came from later if you play your cards right." We broke our embrace and walked inside the foyer. I made sure to let her walk to the living room while I purposely took my time to close the door and enjoy the view from the back. *That butt...* I asked her if I could get her a drink before we left, but she declined and took a seat on the sofa.

"You look nice," she said, as I finally ventured into the living room. "Thank you". I wanted to look my best and, perhaps, make a good impression so you can sell a house today." I was dressed in tan-colored Armani slacks, matching double-breasted blazer, pink pin-point Oxford shirt, green pocket square, and dark brown Cole-Haan loafers. I was not much for accessories in terms of jewelry, and preferred the "less is more" approach, which is why my only accoutrement was a Tag Heuer dress watch.

I excused myself to Dennis's bedroom to let him know Stephanie was there. She sat attentively, soaking in the lyrics of the classic Johnny Hartman and John Coltrane collaboration. Admittedly, it was strategic on my part to have their arrangement *You Are Too Beautiful* playing when she arrived. I wanted her to remember the lyrics, *"You are too beautiful... and I am a fool for beauty."*

Dennis waltzed into the living room dressed in a grey suit, black dress shoes, white shirt, and black silk tie. Stephanie stood up and before giving him a hug, said, "Don't you look dapper. Are you joining us for lunch?" "No," he said, "I have a lunch appointment with a friend of mine "smiling. Stephanie countered with, "Well, I can tell it's not a beer and pizza date with the boys" as she hugged him and kissed him on the cheek. When Dennis pulled back from the hug, he said "You got *that* right!"

I walked into the living room and turned off the music. "Let's head on out, it's close to two-fifteen. How far away are the restaurant and Open House from here and each other?" Stephanie mentioned the restaurant and house were just five minutes apart, but the drive there was about twenty-five minutes. I looked at my watch and responded, "I doubt we'll have time for lunch if the Open House starts at three" and she replied, "You're right. I have some food already set-up at the house, so we can munch on each *oth*... I mean, the food, and have dinner afterward if that's okay with you." Her body language

52

suggested she wanted my feedback on the matter, so I replied, "I'm okay with that, and I can wait until you finish your work with prospective buyers. I kind of figured the schedule would be tight." Instinctively, I was curious about why Stephanie would set-up a lunch date a mere hour ahead of a business deal, but I let it go.

Chapter 11

While we were driving in Stephanie's bright red BMW 3-Series, I reached over and placed my hand on hers, which tightly gripped the stick-shift. The idea of a woman whisking through traffic, deftly shifting gears was a mental turn-on to me. I always perceived women who drove manual transmissions as feisty, the go getter types, which was appealing to me. In fact, it had nothing to do with sex. It was about perspective on life: you either wait for others or you seize opportunities. To me, a woman driving a manual transmission implicitly suggested a sense of enthusiasm and adventure.

Our eyes connected and I said "I appreciate you taking time out of your day to hang out with me and invite me for an afternoon of *Windy City* pleasure." "It's a pleasure, Theo. I've heard so, so many good things about you from Dennis, and I trust him a *lot*. He looks out for me. When he told me you were coming to visit, I was just as excited as he was. He thinks very highly of you, Theo, and respects you tremendously." She winked at me after she said that and, again, my mind began to race just thinking of the possibilities. So far, Stephanie possessed myriad qualities I preferred in romantic relationships: intelligence, savviness, attractiveness, wit, goal-oriented, assertiveness, compassion, and she was well-travelled. However, my mind kept envisioning… *That butt.*

We were about ten minutes into the drive when I abruptly screamed, "Oh shit!" Stephanie was startled and said, "What's wrong, Theo?" "Sorry about that," I said. "I just remembered that I forgot to call Dennis's mom. I can't be in Chicago visiting him without calling her. That wouldn't be right. Do you mind if I call her real quick?" Stephanie breathed a sigh of relief. "Damn, you scared me for a second. Whew! Sure, go ahead and call her."

I pulled out my cell phone and called the Warfield's, Ernest and Audrey. When Mrs. Warfield answered, I said, "Hi, Mama Warfield!" She always described me as her other son, and I was warmed by the love she and Mr. Warfield always showed me. Mr. and Mrs. Warfield were retired, she an elementary school teacher and he a social worker. My parents treated Dennis with the same amount of love and admiration his parents gave me. Mrs. Warfield beamed with energy, and in her deeply Southern drawl, asked, "Is this my uthuh' son in Los Angeles?"

I told her I was visiting Dennis in Chicago and wanted to make sure I called her and Mr. Warfield while I was there. Mrs. Warfield was one of the most compassionate people I had ever met, and she always took time to help others, particularly those in need. In her Georgia drawl, she asked, "How's ya' mom doin'? I've not spokin' to huh' in a few weeks, and the last tyme we spoke, Mr. Warfield and I were encouragin' huh' ta' move down heyuh. We've been tellin' huh' ta' sell that house an' come 'on down South." I was moved by the gesture. "Thanks, Mama Warfield. I appreciate you and Mr. Warfield looking out for my mom. That means a lot to both of us." In her motherly tone, Mrs. Warfield said, "Thas' the way it's 'spose ta' be, sugar, we need ta' look out fuh' one anotha'. Where's Dennis?"

I told her Dennis was at home and that I was now visiting with another friend of ours. I added, "I thought I would call you and Poppa Warfield before it got too late." She told me to hold on while she went to get her husband. When she gave him the phone, Mr. Warfield's thunderous voice echoed, "Theo! How ya' doin', son? Audrey told me you' visitin' Dennis. It's good to heyuh' yo' voice. How're things in Los Angeles? I hope you ain't mad that my Atlanta Braves are gonna be whoppin' yo' Dodgers to go to tha' Worl' Series," with a robust laugh. I shot back, "Well, Poppa Warfield, I guess things will balance out since my Lakers will go a lot further than... what's the name of Atlanta's basketball team? I can't remember if they have a team or not?" Mr. Warfield laughed, and was pleased with my quick- witted response. "Well, son, I 'spose ya' right. These here Hawks ain't doin' much-a-flyin' these days. Anyway, it's good ta heyuh ya' voice, son. How's ya' mom? Me and Audrey been tryin' to get huh' ta' move South." I told the Warfields I had been encouraging my mother to sell her house and move into a condominium, but my plea, thus far, had been unsuccessful.

"Well, Poppa Warfield, I just called to say hi real quick. Dennis and I will call you and Mama Warfield tomorrow. "Okay, son, he said "we'll be goin' to church in da' morning, so we'll be back 'round 2p.m. or so as long as none 'a these women gits' da' holy ghost, which means it'll be longuh' if they do. Call us ta'morrow, okey?" I chuckled and said, "I understand, sir. Tell Mama Warfield I said bye and will talk with ya'll tomorrow. I love you both!" Mr. Warfield's deep voice reverberated through the phone as he said, "We luv' ya', too, Theo, you-a-mighty fine young man. Talk ta' ya' ta'morrow." After I hung up, Stephanie looked over at me and said, "How're they doing? Dennis talks about them a lot and they seem like really nice people." "Oh, they are great folks indeed, continuing with. "They drove all the way to Philadelphia when my father passed away and were with my mother for an entire week before going back to Atlanta. They're like blood relatives."

Stephanie whizzed the BMW in and out of traffic, but she was not as much a risk-taking driver as Dennis. Her style was brisk, but calculated, and periodically she would look over at me, sensing I admired her driving ability. We finally pulled onto a winding road that led up a slight incline. Houses along the street were spacious, airy, and had well-manicured lawns. She pulled into the driveway of a two-story home that was decorated with various plants, roses, dandelions, and lilies. When she stopped, I hopped out of the car and whisked around to open her door. "My, what a gentleman" she said, to which I responded, "It's good home training, my dear, I'm no scrub." She led me to the door of the spacious house. I asked if we were going to pass on the restaurant before the Open House. She responded, "Uhhh, well, uhhh, it's better we come here." Hmm…

Once inside, the foyer, I soaked-in the view of the sunlight beaming into the living room. I could tell Stephanie was the type that enjoyed natural beauty; the type that appreciated the sun, mountains, plants, and life itself. All this was congruent with my own perspective, and

I was becoming more attracted to Stephanie the more I learned about her. As I took a seat on a soft, pastel-designed couch, she disappeared into the kitchen and returned with two glasses filled with champagne. I could also smell food, and I was still confused why we hadn't gone to the restaurant. Hmm...

"Wow! It seems this is going to be one hell of an Open House for people coming by." As soon as I said that, I realized I had not seen any "Open House" or "For Sale" signs on the lawn. Hmm, another "flag" that made me even more curious that something was going on. She went back to the kitchen, and the next thing I knew, the living room walls gently vibrated from the sounds of a piano. I knew it was not an actual piano being played, but was, instead, a Bob James recording, *Westchester Lady*. Apparently, the living room had hidden speakers in the walls, a nice touch, especially to an audiophile like myself. Even though this was an Open House, her attention to detail, i.e., the champagne and Bob James, was, again, precise and astute.

She returned to the living room carrying a tray of cheese and crackers. I asked her, "Do you need help setting up anything in preparation for the Open House visitors?" to which she responded, "No, I have everything in order, so all you need to do, Mr. Handsome, is just relax and enjoy yourself. I'm sure you'll help me in *many* ways today, so just relax. Take your jacket off and get comfortable, and I'll be right back."

I watched Stephanie ascend the spiral caste-iron staircase. She knew I was watching because she took each step methodically, suggestively moving her hips left-to-right, slowly, with each move upward. She was the *pungi* and I was the *cobra*.

Stephanie had been upstairs at least ten minutes, and I began to get a bit anxious. I knew she was not purposely being rude, leaving her guest alone, so my thoughts drifted as I asked myself, "What in the world is she doing?" Immediately after that query, I heard her call from upstairs, "Theo, please light a couple of candles. They're over the fireplace and the matches are next to them." "No problem," I said, and did as instructed. However, I could not help but wonder, "Who the hell wants to light candles during an Open House at three in the afternoon?"

After fifteen minutes, I heard Stephanie's heels echoing off the steps of the staircase. When I turned around, my eyes widened at their site: She was dressed in a silk Chinese kimono that was loosely wrapped, and millimeters below the intersection of the top of her legs, and she enticed me even further by revealing a generous amount of dick-hardening cleavage. This, as if not enough eye candy, was accented by red six-inch stilettos. Surprised, I mumbled, "Uhh... damn... what about the Open... damn... you look so damn... House. Uhh... What about the Open House?" Speechless, she continued to sashay towards me and placed a finger over her lips as if to say, "Shh..." No problem there. I knew when to shut the hell up and *this* was one of those times! By now, I was standing up... literally *and* figuratively!

When she reached me, she placed both her hands on the back of my neck and delicately pulled my head towards hers. Our lips met for a deep kiss. She rubbed the small of my back as we kissed, and pulled our bodies closer together. Rhythmically, her hips gyrated, first circularly then forward and backward. She knew exactly what I liked and did not hesitate to demonstrate how she, too, enjoyed the erotic union of our bodies. My brain whispered to itself, "Finally!"

It was obvious Stephanie felt my hardness because the intensity and tempo of her grinds became more pronounced and she began to breathe more deeply. I delicately ran my tongue up and down her neck, flicking it intermittently on her ear lobe. That clearly incited her as she now began to pull me, even while we were still embraced, to the couch where we plopped down, I on top of her. Our tongues danced about in each other's mouth, as she began to disrobe me, her left hand moving up and down my back while her right hand unbuttoned my shirt. Another futile, "Uhh, what about the Open House?" from me was countered by Stephanie darting her tongue inside my right ear and whispering, "Theo, *I* am the Open House!"

I immediately lifted my head, which was buried in the crevice between her neck and right ear, "What? I thought you said you were having an Open House and that you wanted me to help you out." She replied, "I said I '*have* an open house,' I did not say I was *showing* an Open House." My brain went into rewind mode, as I thought about what she said at *The Spot*. The words echoed in my ears (and now my loins!), "*I have an open house tomorrow, so maybe you can join me. Remember, I'm a realtor, and this is one 'open house' you **don't** want to pass up.*"

Damn! I couldn't help but smile. "You are a naughty woman, but in a damn good way. I had no clue your 'open house' was a matter of semantics, the difference between a capital O and H. Wicked, but I like it... very much! I might have to spank you for being naughty." She parted her legs and began wrapping them around my waist. "I can tell by that hard thing I'm rubbing against that you *do* like my naughty ways." Then, with a sinisterly expression, "I've been bad, maybe I deserve a good spanking. You think so? I promise I won't do it again. But..." I cut her off and said, "Oh, hell yeah, I'm definitely spankin' that butt! You *need* to be spanked, and I can tell you want it." Stephanie was the consummate tigress, and all she said was, "Theo, you turn me the hell on, bring it!"

We kissed, fondled each other, licked, nibbled and rubbed in the throes of passion until neither of us could take anymore. We both *had* to have it. "Let's go upstairs," I said, and she responded, "I thought you'd never ask. Let me turn the oven off while you take the candles upstairs. I'll bring the wine." I lifted her from the couch, and before she walked away, I was able to do something I wanted to do since I met her: rub her shapely, firm butt. Whew! She turned around and said, "Mmm, you're naughty, too, and I very much like that."

I carried the candles upstairs. Her bedroom was colored in earth tones that were delicate and serene. The bedroom was large, but decorated in such a way that resonated intimacy. I placed one candle on each of the two nightstands that outlined her bed. There were several decorative pillows on her king-sized bed, and while my carnal instincts urged me to cast them out of the way, I placed them on a nearby beige leather recliner. After ridding the bed of its pillows, I went to her stereo, scurried through her CD collection and came across several that demonstrated she had good taste in music, and were perfect for the occasion. I made sure to put the discs in their proper order: the first leading up to sex, the second during, and the third, after sex. I chose *Teddy Pendergrass Greatest Hits* as the first disc, Johnny Hartman and John Coltrane's collaboration as the second disc, and Earl Klugh and Bob James' *Two Of A Kind*. I programmed the CD player to start with Teddy's *Turn Off The Lights, Come Go With Me, and Love T.K.O.* For Hartman and Trane, playing the entire disc was fine, as well as that of Klugh and James. The music would embellish what I anticipated would be some serious sex, and I wanted to seduce the hell out of Stephanie. I thought to myself, *By the time Love T.K.O. comes on, I'm going to have her so hot she's going to beg me to delay my return to Los Angeles!* while the sheer bravado in me said, *I'm going to knock this pussy out!* Finally, I drew the curtains and, save for the candle lights, the room was relatively dark; just light enough to see the other's body, which is what I wanted.

Chapter 12

I heard her heels clanking against the stairs, so I immediately pushed PLAY on the CD. Teddy's mellifluous voice piped through the speakers, and as I turned around, Stephanie asked, "Mmm, nice choice. Are you trying to seduce me? I thought you were a jazz man?" I responded, "Me? No way. I'm not *trying* to seduce you. I *am* seducing you. Yes, I love jazz, but I'd be a fool to forget Teddy could talk the panties off a nun if he wanted!" We laughed while she handed me a glass of wine, "Well, I wouldn't fit either category because I'm certainly not a nun. And, I don't have..." With that, she untied her kimono and let it drop to the floor. I took our glasses and put them on a night stand and then walked back to her, embracing as we began to kiss.

She now proceeded to undo my belt. I slipped my loafers off, and as my pants dropped, she started fondling my erection through my boxers. "Mmm, and what do we have here?" she asked. "That, my dear, is what I've been waiting to give you since the moment our eyes met at *The Spot*." "Oh really? Well, had I known *that*, I would have slipped you away from everyone and taken you..." Her sentence trailed off and transformed into a moan when I began rubbing her butt while nibbling her breasts. "Mmm, you've got me speechless," she said, and then I picked her up and took her to the bed. I lay her down gently and pulled off my underwear. I stood at the side of the bed, dick standing at attention, while she caressed my thickness before fellating me. I leaned over and slid my fingers into her wetness. I moved my fingers in a circular motion on her clitoris and her hips started to writhe. We both were moaning before I finally lay on the bed with her.

I nibbled on her earlobe and whispered in her ear, "This is about *you*, baby. Your pleasure is *my* pleasure." With that, I moved down the bed, spread her legs further apart and admired her glistening vagina. "I can't wait to taste you" and she uttered, "I'm *all* yours, Theo, all yours," she muttered.

As I nibbled her inner thighs and caressed her erect nipples, I thought about my sexual encounters throughout my life. Women constantly described me as a "giver" in that I always *loved* doing things to/with them where fulfilling their sexual desires were my foci. Unfortunately, too many men are selfish, especially regarding oral sex. Regarding cunnilingus, I always thought, generally, there were three types of men.

One was the man who did it because the woman fellated him, so he reciprocated, but not because he *really* wanted to. The second type was the man who believed it was the quickest way to get her to fuck. He, too, did not do it because he really wanted to, but because it was a means to an end. The third type, which was the category I eagerly embraced, was the man who did it because he *loved* pleasing a woman. He *loved* hearing her moan and seeing her body squirm in pleasure. He relished the fact that he was doing something that turned her on, so he was unselfish. For him, the turn-on was mental for both partners, and it was unconditional giving and receiving. All these thoughts raced in my head before I placed Stephanie's legs on my shoulders and proceeded to nibble, lick and suck every part of her being.

She was passionate and vocal, both of which were *major* turn-ons to me. "Oh, Theo, right there... don't stop baby. Lick it. Mmm, yes! Suck my pussy, Theo... mmm. Damn, you have me so wet. Don't stop, baby, right there!" I wanted Stephanie to have as many mental orgasms as physical ones, so I purposely said things I suspected would turn her on, especially after hearing how forward she was. "Do you like my tongue sliding in and out of your pussy, Stephanie? That feels good, doesn't it? You like the way I tongue your pussy, don't you?" Her body was slithering to and fro with each query I made, and the more I queried, the wetter and more vocal she became. "Yes! Yes! Oh, Theo, damn! Don't stop, give it to me!" was all she could summon. She was just where I wanted her, so I abruptly said, "I'm going to stop eating your pussy. You don't want me to do it." I wanted to take her to the edge and bring her back, and then again. The mental cat and mouse game was driving her insane, and her response was, "No! Theo, please don't stop! Mmm, no, don't stop, you're making me cum! This is *your* pussy!" I countered, "Okay, baby, I'm not going to stop. I want to make that pussy wet, Stephanie, this is about making you feel good."

I licked and sucked Stephanie until she thrust her hips upward and screamed, "I'm cumming, Theo, I'm cumming... Oh God! I want you to fuck me, Theo, fuck me! Please, Theo, fuck me, I want you inside me, now!" Stephanie and I had essentially been oblivious to the music, but her orgasms seemed to conjure Teddy's spirit because right as she came a third time, I heard the lyrics, *"Looks like anotha' love T.K.O."* "You want this dick, baby, you want me to put it in you?" Her response was swift and concise, "Hell yes!"

I got off the bed, went to my pants, and pulled out a 3-pack box of *Magnum* condoms. I was reluctant to interrupt our sexual tryst by going back-and-forth throughout the afternoon to my pants, so I pulled all of them out, tearing off one and putting the others on the nightstand. She lay on the bed, legs spread wide, playing with herself. She rubbed vigorously, circling her hand around her clit, while moving her hips up and down. "That's it, Stephanie, play with your pussy. I like that. You've got my dick *so* hard. I'm going to give you some good dick. Play with it, baby." The more I tantalized her, the more she bucked her hips. Abruptly, she became the antagonist, and said, "You want this pussy don't you? You like watching me play with myself? See how wet you made me? I'll give you some if you stroke that big dick of yours." I complied, and began massaging myself. Stephanie began moving her hips, short, quick movements up and down as she inserted her finger inside herself. "Stroke it for me, baby. I *love* to watch a man jack-off!"

Stephanie glared at me as I stroked myself at the foot of the bed. The candles flicked in concert with my hand movement. "Mmm, that's it, Theo, do it. My pussy is *still* dripping wet and I think it's ready to be stretched out!" I saw her glistening fingers as she pushed in and out of herself. The mere sight of her actions and seeing how wet she was turned me the hell on, physically and mentally. Instinctively, we both understood the power of the *mind* during sex. Our union would not be like Aldous Huxley's *Brave New World*, where Alpha Plusses consummated as if they were emotionally bereft automatons. No, ours would be sweaty, scorching, and downright toe-curling - the "*I can't wait to have more*" type.

"I have something for you," she said, spreading her legs wide while motioning me with her pointer finger, "Come here, baby, I want you." I finished rolling the condom around my girth and crawled between her legs. We kissed and then I stopped and said, "Wait." Initially, she thought I was not going to continue, and I could sense her slight disappointment. However, my attention to detail took over. I said, "Oh, don't worry, you're getting this dick, but like I said, this is about *you*." I moved downward and continued all the way to her feet. Gently, I caressed her feet and massaged each. Then, I looked upward and asked, "Have you ever had your toes sucked?" "No, but that's a damn good idea, go for it." I flicked my tongue around her toes and then took her big toe into my mouth, sucking on it like a lollipop. I did this, delicately, while massaging her inner thighs. I moved one hand upward and spread her labia with my fingers, exploring until I reached that delicate button. She was extremely moist, and the bucking motion of her hips told me I was, indeed, achieving results.

I worked my mouth on her other foot, making sure to keep my hands busy massaging her legs. Once that duty was fulfilled, I crept upward like a cautious serpent, running my tongue up her inner thighs. I put the tip of my hardness at the entrance of her soul and slowly thrust upward. I wanted to tease her so I just put the head in. She craved me, and I her, but I was in no rush. This was not a sprint, it was a marathon. Any marathon runner worth a grain of salt understands the "3 P's", preparation, patience, and perseverance, are critical for success.

Slowly, I pushed in, and she let out a deep moan, "Ohhh, Theo, damn that feels good! Give me a little more" so I obliged and went deeper... and deeper until I was completely inside her. "Mmm, you feel so damn good!" Her inner muscles gripped me. "Those Kegel exercises *do* have benefits, you now. Do you like that, too?" I could only reply, "Oh, hell yeah! I'll have to send Dr. Kegel a thank-you note tomorrow by FedEx!" She laughed and quipped, "Admirable, but I'd rather you thank me." I thrust inside her deep and then withdrew, then back in again. I did this several times in quick motions and then slowed down to let her feel every inch of me.

She pulled me close to her and whispered in my ear, "What's *your* favorite position? Don't forget, Theo, this is about you, too." I answered, "Any position that turns you on" and after a sly grin, she said, "I want to do your favorite." I peered into her eyes and told her I wanted her on top. We both looked downward as she took me into her hands and guided me inside. "That's it, Stephanie, bounce on it. Put it all in there, deep, give me that pussy!"

For the next forty-five minutes, we tried a variety of positions: her on top, missionary, cowgirl, reverse-cowgirl, doggy-style, and finished off missionary. She wanted the latter because, in her words, "I want you to finish by pounding me deep!" There is nothing more sensuous than being with a woman who is vocal an unafraid to tell her partner how she craves to get fucked. In that regard, Stephanie was the consummate partner, and ever since our initial meeting at *The Spot*, our hormones and pheromones were in concert. But, my attraction to her, undoubtedly physical, was enhanced fivefold. She possessed that "it factor" I savored in women, meaning the complete package of brains, humor, sensuality, beauty, and carnal acumen.

Finally, we collapsed in each other's arms, bodies sweating with the scent of near-primal urges coming to fruition. It was not over yet, however. I told her to lay on her stomach and she replied, "My-oh-my, you are quite the Energizer Bunny, huh?" "No, my dear, it's time for a massage. You should know by now I'm not a selfish lover." She countered, "Ah, I like that, baby, you pay attention to detail." I found myself moving towards pensive mode. "You know what?" I asked. I don't want to get too philosophical, but I think we men sometimes miss the proverbial boat when it comes to sex. Sometimes, we just pounce on a woman, pump like a bunny for ten minutes, roll off, grab the remote control and turn on ESPN before falling asleep. I was very fortunate in that I had a girlfriend in undergrad who taught me how to be an attentive lover."

I continued, "We used to have crazy sex, but before we started, she would suck me and tell me to kiss her all over. Well, I surmised what she meant by kiss her all over, but I never ate the pussy. I was too naïve and caught up in the 'Black men don't eat pussy' thing, so I never did her. Well, one day I did it and she damn near hit the ceiling! After seeing how she responded, I vowed that day: To hell with stereotypes, I'm going to pay attention to what a woman desires. Those experiences transformed my perspective in myriad ways, but particularly as they related to women."

She laughed aloud and asked, "Oh, so you got caught-up in that trick-bag, huh? I've certainly had my share of Black men who would fuck me into oblivion, but when I asked them to suck my pussy, you would have thought I was threatening to cut their dicks off! So, Mr. Handsome, I'm glad you learned, because you *surely* know what you're doing. She laughed hysterically when I said, "You damn right!" and did my impersonation of the rocker Gene Simmons, sticking my tongue out as far as possible while making a slurping sound.

After I massaged her shoulders, legs, arms and back (not to mention sucking on her fingers one-by-one), we laid on our sides, facing each other. I stroked her face with my hand and then she asked, "So, how long have you been in the *Lifestyle*?" I was confused, initially, and asked, "The what?" She repeated, "The *Lifestyle*. You know, how long have you been *swinging*?" "Oh, I remember hearing

70

Dennis and Skip talk about that. Actually, I'm not in it and had never heard of it prior to coming to Chicago." Surprised, she asked, "Really? I just assumed you were involved because you and Dennis are so close. And, considering how much you made cum, I assumed you had years of experience." The humorous side of me came out, so I playfully boasted, "Well, I thought I was going to have to call 911 the way I put it on ya'. When Teddy was singing *Love T.K.O.*, I just knew I knocked the pussy out." I came back to earth and said, "Seriously, I was unfamiliar with the *Lifestyle* and had never tried anything like it. I felt something was up because Dennis kept making these comments about how I better watch out for you, but in a good way. It was as if the two of you conspired to have you 'jump my bones.'" I feigned betrayal by wrapping my arms around myself and said, "I feel violated" to which we burst into laughter with her stating, "Yeah, right!"

Stephanie confided, "That damn Dennis! He made it seem like you were in the *Lifestyle* when he told me about you and that you were coming out for a visit. Hell, I thought you were coming here to relax and go to some of the *swinger* parties. I'm going to kick his butt for not telling me the whole story." I felt very comfortable with Stephanie, so I did not mind chiding her with, "Look at Ms. Goody Two Shoes with her 'open house' tale. I ***thought*** we were going to have lunch and then I'd help you with showing the house to prospective buyers. I suspected something was up when I didn't see one damn 'For Sale' or 'Open House' sign out front. I knew there was a reason my radar went off." She inquired, "Your radar?" to which I responded, "Yep, my dick radar went off" as I slapped it against her leg. "You're so silly, but I like that. You know how to poke fun at yourself, and that tells me you're secure with yourself. That's admirable, Theo."

It was odd that the tone of our conversation, while light, was treading into serious-mode terrain. That was probably why we nervously joked and played with each other. Admittedly, while my relationship to and with Stephanie was brief and sexual, there was a lot I liked about her. As I lay next to her, my eyes conveyed that, but my conscience pierced my brain with a rhetorical "You know she's in the *Lifestyle*, but can *you* accept the idea of her fucking someone else and you knowing about it?" The question kept recurring as I desperately, but futilely, tried to shoo it away with "Shut the fuck up, I'll cross that bridge when I come to it." And I did, at least for a little while.

Chapter 13

"So, what's this stuff all about? How did you get involved in the *Lifestyle*?" I asked. "For me, it was all about trying to please my husband. I married right out of college and didn't really know who I was and, in retrospect, he didn't know who he really was, either. The bottom line is, we were too young to get married, but just didn't realize it at the time. Problems started about four years into the marriage when I noticed he wasn't paying much attention to me and our sex life deteriorated. When we first married, we used to fuck several times a week. I loved sex, and so did he, but when it began to fall off, it was like he mentally checked-out of the marriage."

Stephanie went on to tell me that her husband told her he was getting bored with their sex life and that he heard about *swinging* from a friend of his. Initially, her response was, "Oh, hell no! I'm **not** having sex with another man and you're damn-sure not having sex with another woman!" She told me they essentially were roommates after that, and that they barely spoke. So, it was a marriage of convenience. Or, as blues icon B.B. King sang, "It's cheaper to keep her." She further confided, "At one point, I was at my wit's end. My marriage was in shambles and I wanted to do anything to save it. My parents instilled in me the idea that marriage was a life-time commitment, and I brought-in to that, what I believe now as a bullshit philosophy. So, one evening I told my husband, "If you think it'll save our marriage, I'll give it a try, but if I'm not comfortable, end of story." He agreed, and the rest is history. "We went to a club and I watched for a while. There were a lot of men checking me out and my husband tried to get me to relax. Basically, he got me drunk and then started playing with my nipples while another man walked up and joined him. I was nervous as hell, but let it happen. Long story short, I just couldn't do it, and my husband was pissed off because all I did was give another guy a hand job. I watched my husband get a blowjob from another woman and I got jealous. Next thing I know, I told him, 'I can't do this. Let's get the fuck out of here... **now!**'"

I felt a sense of remorse for Stephanie as she recanted her experience, especially when she told me the marriage lasted one more year and then she couldn't take it anymore. She was dissatisfied sexually, but most important, distraught about her husband's lack of communication, attention to her, and her overall sense of loneliness. When the divorce was finalized, she decided to earn her realtor's license and pursue her dreams. She was successful as a real estate agent, but worked a lot to develop clientele, which meant her personal life was secondary. She told me, "Once I was firmly established professionally, I decided to spend more time on myself, but I didn't want a relationship. I didn't want to have anything remotely close to a long-term commitment. So, I did some investigating checking out different dating websites, but nothing worked out. It seemed all the men on dating websites talked about wanting friendship and all that, but, in reality, all they wanted was sex. I experienced one frustration after another and kept wondering why the men on the sites wouldn't be honest in their intentions. It was frustrating as hell."

Stephanie expressed her anguish with dating websites over the course of several months and then stumbled upon *Lifestyle Rendezvous*, a website for *swingers*. She decided to go to a "meet and greet" party at a club and met some nice people. She was not ready to "dive in" at the time, but remained intrigued. *Lifestyle Rendezvous* was an international site, but it also listed local contacts and events categorized by city, state, and country. Two weeks later, she decided to go to a *swinger* party after contacting the party's hostess. The hostess told her there was a strict rule that "No means no" and that any man (or woman, for that matter) who was disrespectful of anyone was requested to leave. The hostess assured Stephanie there would be a professional, but erotic atmosphere and that if she felt uncomfortable at any time, all she had to do was inform one of the bouncers.

She also told me that is where she met Dennis. "I was standing near the DJ booth, just having a drink and Dennis walked up to me. We struck up a conversation and he told me he was an accountant. I remember being surprised and saying to him, 'You're an accountant? I didn't know accountants did this kind of stuff. I'm sorry, but I just had a misconception that the only men who did this were horny losers who couldn't get laid anywhere else.'" She went on to say that Dennis confided, "You are gravely mistaken. People from all walks of life are in the *Lifestyle*. I personally know doctors, lawyers, businessmen and businesswomen who indulge. It's only about friendship and sex, so, let's face it, ***everybody*** likes sex, right?"

Stephanie continued, "Dennis was a gentleman. I won't lie to you. I wanted him to make a move because I was nervous as hell. But, he was professional, considerate and did not make me feel any pressure, especially after I told him I was new. He was like this mild-mannered Southern gentleman, so respectful. We continued to talk and I shared I was a realtor. He told me he was looking for a condo, so I went into business-mode. Two months later, I sold him his place at *The Ridgecrest*. Although I'm pretty sure he wanted to fuck me, and I him, we just kept the relationship on a business level." She continued, "We still hung out and developed a good friendship, but we never crossed the line. Eventually, though, I relied on him to introduce me to guys that would be respectful and not cause any drama in my life. Suffice it to say, Dennis helped get me more dick than I ever imagined, and he introduced me to some fantastic people along the way. Sometimes, we would even go to *swinger* parties as a couple. He would get his groove on and I would do the same, but he always kept an eye out for me to make sure I was okay."

While Stephanie articulated her experiences, I found my mind wandering again. Strangely, I felt a slight sense of jealously towards Dennis that was borderline anger. My mind raced, and I rhetorically asked, "How could he introduce this nice woman to fuck parties?" The irony, though, was that my displaced anger was directed towards

Dennis as if he had a sexual relationship with her; as if he were stealing *my* lady. But, he did not introduce her to sex parties because she was already there and attended on her own accord. Both my misconceptions subsided when I realized *I* was the one passing a value judgment that was not only misdirected, but inaccurate. I was simply jealous, so my brain teased, "Get over it, she's a grown ass woman and Dennis is a grown ass man. Dennis did not fuck Stephanie and she's damn-sure not *your* girlfriend, so why are you having these head trips?"

I felt renewed once I supplanted my self-pity and recognized I was emotionally out of bounds. Then, I told her, "Stephanie, I'm glad our paths crossed. You're a wonderful woman and I respect your perspective." She kissed me on the forehead and said, "Thank you, Theo. I'm glad our paths crossed, too, and I hope this is not the last I see of you" to which I responded, "I seriously, seriously doubt it. If you *ever* visit Los Angeles, you have a place to stay. I'll show you a great time and I'd surely commit another *Love T.K.O.* on you." She playfully tapped me on the shoulder and said, "You are a mess! I hope you're hungry because I cooked a delicious dinner for us. Not only do I know how to curl your toes, but I make a mean pot roast, too."

Chapter 14

I picked-up Stephanie's kimono and placed it on her curvaceous body. She said, "I have a robe you can wear, so don't worry about putting your clothes on. Besides, I have a feeling they won't be on too long anyway." We descended the spiral staircase, I in front holding her left hand along the way. There was something so sexy and open about seeing her naked body underneath the kimono. Perhaps my mind was focusing on the easy access I had to her. As I thought further, though, I began to realize I was having reservations about going back to Los Angeles on Monday morning. "Hell," I said to myself, "I deserve a real vacation, so I should take an extra day off." And, I began to question my emotions again, grilling myself with questions like "What the hell is wrong with me? Why am I beginning to feel an emotional attachment to this woman? It was *just* a hot fuck, so why am I feeling like I *really* like her?"

We reached the kitchen and I inquired, "How about some music for this wonderful afternoon?" and she said, "Good idea." I remembered earlier I heard the Bob James tune, but did not see a stereo, so I asked, "Where's your system? I heard music from the in-wall speakers, but I didn't see a stereo system." She told me it was inside the redwood bureau adjacent to the fireplace. "Nice touch," I said. "I like how it's hidden."

"What would you like to hear while we eat?" and she responded, "Hmm. Oh, I know what I'm in the mood for." I asked, "What would that be, sexy? You name it and consider it done." I could hear her run through a list of prospective CDs and then she shouted, "How about Earl Klugh's *Heartstring*? I love to listen to that when I'm relaxing on Saturdays, and I think it's such a romantic disc." "*Heartstring* it is," I said.

After placing *Heartstring* in the CD carousel, I went into the kitchen and saw Stephanie bending over to look inside the oven. My immediate reaction was, "Damn! I don't know whether I want to eat the pot roast or you." She stood up, turned around and said, "You sure know how to say the right things. You keep it up and you just may get some more of this" as she opened kimono, pointing towards her body. I approached her and put my arms around her waist, pulling her close to me. "That's one hell of a dessert," I said, and then began nibbling on her neck. She moaned and started rubbing both her hands up and down my back. We started grinding mildly before a timer buzzed. "Whoops," she said, "sounds like dinner is ready."

I remembered the "*3 P's*" so I knew it was not a good idea to attempt coaxing her to consummate on the table. Besides, there was no rush. One of the things I learned about women over the years was that it is usually not a good idea to be overly assertive when broaching the idea of having sex. My mantra has always been, "There's no need to rush anything. If it's meant to happen, it will." I always approached women from the perspective of thinking how I would like to be approached if I were a woman. I damn-sure would not like a man pawing all over me or being too consumed with getting my panties off. If I were a woman, a man who was attentive, compassionate, and a "giver" would appeal to me. So, I always paid attention to ladies' language just as much as words they spoke.

Stephanie took the roast from the oven and began slicing it, so I asked her where the dishes and utensils were. Initially, she seemed a bit taken aback that I did not just sit down and let her do all the work. I asked her why she looked surprised and she said "Wow! You're the first man I've ever cooked for that didn't sit on his butt and wait for me to do everything. I couldn't get my ex-husband to do anything related to kitchen work. He had this *Cro-Magnum* perspective about men's work and women's work. His jobs around the house consisted of cutting the grass, changing the oil in our cars, minor plumbing, painting, and things like that. My jobs were cooking, laundry, and decorating the house. I should have picked-up on some 'flags' early in our relationship, and that was but one. Don't get me started about the others." She went on to say, "I've always been turned on by men who cared less about so-called 'traditional' roles, whatever the hell that **really** meant. I like your vibe, Theo."

My back was turned as I reached inside the cabinet for dishes, so I did not see when she walked over to me, put her arms around my waist, and then patted me on the butt. I turned around and responded, "I like your vibe, too, Stephanie. I promise the next time we connect I'm going to cook you my world-famous grilled salmon in a white wine sauce." She exclaimed, "Wait one minute! You mean to tell me **you** can cook, too? Did I hear you say grilled salmon? You better stop lying, God don't like ugly." I laughed and said, "Well, yes, I can cook and I love it, but I don't carve out enough time to do it as often as I would like. And, yes, my salmon should be ranked among those of the top chefs of the world. But, I'm always working too much." I continued, "Seriously, I can cook and I actually enjoy it. Interestingly, I'm like you in that I always questioned 'traditional' roles and mores. When I was growing up, my mother taught me how to cook, do laundry, and iron clothes. To this day, I still find myself ironing my shirts even after they come from the cleaners. I just like a crisp, ironed shirt, and they just *feel* better. You know how the saying goes: 'When you look better, you feel better.'"

I went on to share that my mother used to tell me and my father, "There are no guarantees in life, so I want y'all to know how to do everything. I don't want y'all to be lost around the house when Jesus calls me back home." Fortunately, my father's perspective was similar to hers, so he taught her 'men things' like unclogging sink pipes, cutting the grass, paying bills, and painting. The irony, though, was that my father passed away before she did, and even though she mourned extensively, she was not lost without him.

My petulant inner voice returned: "There you go again! What's with all this emotional Freudian shit? You act like you've never had sex with a beautiful woman. Relax, it's just sex!" I quickly remembered that I had not been in a serious relationship in several years. In fact, close to ten years, if not more. So, here I was, bachelor extraordinaire, living the life, and beginning to feel attached to a woman I had known less than twenty-four hours, not to mention a *swinger*!

I threw mental punches at society's "masculine" mores that encouraged men to bed as many women as possible while avoiding emotional attachment. Equally, I jabbed at "feminine" mores that promulgated virginity for women until marriage, decrying that having sex for the sake of enjoyment was immoral. Why were men encouraged to get as much emotion-free sex as possible (before, during and, if applicable, after marriage!), while women were labeled as immoral, "loose" tramps if they desired intercourse prior to marriage? Why the dichotomy? Why the hypocrisy?

Apparently, I was thinking *too* loudly, as "Fuck all that nonsense!" inadvertently slipped out of my mouth. Stephanie turned to me and said, "Huh? What's the matter, Theo?" Ordinarily, and perhaps with any other woman, I would have responded, "Nothing. I was just singing the lyrics to this crazy song" or some other plausible line of bullshit. However, I felt compelled to be honest, telling her, "I'll tell you over dinner."

Stephanie snapped her oven towel on my butt and the popping sound coincided with a piercing sensation that darted the length of my body. She proceeded to retract the towel for another blow, but I dodged its path. Displeased with her miss, she instead settled on peering at me before saying wryly, "Okay, but if you even *dare* start rapping and scratch-mixing my albums, you *will* be walking back to *The Ridgecrest*!" I then gave her a light tap on her butt with my hand

and said, "No, sexy, it's not that at all, but if you want me to, I can show you some of my skills." I pranced around the kitchen, holding a wooden ladle to my mouth as if it were a microphone while grabbing my crotch with my other hand. Stephanie completely dismissed my entices, "Uh, look here, Mr. M.C., please get a bottle of Cabernet Sauvignon from the wine rack over there?"

Chapter 15

Dinner and dessert consisted of spinach pomegranate salad, pot roast, Cabernet Sauvignon, and bread pudding. We ate dessert in the kitchen, but moved to the living room to have more wine, relax on the couch, and listen to music. I placed our wine glasses on coasters while Stephanie went to her CD rack to play some more music. I heard her rustle through a few discs and it was not long before she pulled the curtains and sat by me on the couch. "Okay," she said, "close your eyes. You probably miss the ocean, so I'm going to bring it to you. Now, lay back… you better stop peeking!"

I laid back on the couch and closed my eyes while she sat on the floor parallel to me. She delicately massaged my legs and flicked her tongue, sporadically, on my inner thighs. It was fairly dark in the living room after she pulled the curtains, so my senses were particularly acute. My spine tingled after each flick, which transformed into nibbles. Slowly, the sensation from the lower region of my legs crept upwards until, alas, she took me inside her mouth.

My mind drifted, but I *thought* I heard faint sounds of the ocean. I said to myself, "Damn, she's got me so deep in the palm of her hands, literally and figuratively, that I'm hearing things!" However, I was not hallucinating, and soon recognized the tune she chose was Maze's popular tune, *Look At California*. The sound of ocean waves crashing against the shore served as the song's introduction before lead vocalist, Frankie Beverly, dove into a soul-stirring, *"Wooo…*

You know I heard somebody say, just the other day. How love... love ain't around..."

I recalled Stephanie's attention to detail, and her request to have me lay back on the couch was no exception. In some regards, I perceived her as my female counterpart. That is, I was always uncommonly attentive when I seduced a woman. From the moment of first contact until the conclusion of the evening (or morning!), I prided myself on setting the tone for romantic interludes: excellent food, well-chosen music, candles, bubble baths, and massages. This time, however, the roles were reversed and *I* was the one being seduced, and yet again! Through one prism, it was soothing to be pampered and made the center of attention. Through another came the reality that society's roles frowned upon women who were sexually liberated and vocal about their bedroom desires.

Stephanie fellated me as I absorbed Maze's soothing lyrics. When I became fully erect, she asked "Shall we indulge in Round 2 here or upstairs?" Frankly, I did not want to spoil the moment, nor the sensations, so I replied, "I'm in your hands this time, it's up to you." Apparently, she was just as interested as I was in maintaining our course, so we elected to stay put. "I want you to ride me reverse cowgirl," I said, and she complied by looking over her shoulder at me as she guided me into her moistness. "Watch it disappear," she said, and teased me by putting my erect bulb inside her, oh-so-slowly lowering her hips until I was fully inside.

She began to moan, "You like that, Theo? Does it feel good, baby?" All I could do was writhe and echo, "Yes, Stephanie, bounce on it. You like feeling me inside you and bouncing on that dick!" The more verbally explicit I was, the more she bounced and whimpered. And, the wetter she became. Similar to Round 1, we tried a variety of positions: doggy-style, cow-girl, reverse-cowgirl, and the coupe 'de gras, missionary.

It was going on 7p.m. and what I *thought* was going to be a real estate Open House turned out to be one of the most mentally and physically exhilarating days of my life. Frankly, Stephanie proved to be my sexual match, if not superior. I could not remember the last time a sexual partner exceeded not only my energy level, but creativity as well. What made her different from previous partners, too, was the fact that she knew (and perhaps, exploited?) how to mold, like warm clay, her body around my mind.

One of the most dreadful realizations we men experience is when a woman sexually wears us out to the extent we mentally yearn for a "rematch," sometimes even resorting to begging. I was well beyond that trite stage, and welcomed the experience, finally, of being with a woman who took her lustful desires to a higher plain than mine. If I were to become what was called "pussy whooped," then so be it.

Stephanie and I were exhausted and lay still on the couch. Finally, she asked, "So, what are you doing this evening?" I succinctly replied, "Sleeping!" and followed that up with "Seriously, I'm not sure. I'm guessing that Dennis will want to do something, so I'll have to check with him since tomorrow is my last night." She responded, "Well, if you want to stay in Chicago longer, you're more than welcome to stay here." My immediate response was, "Thanks, Stephanie, I appreciate that. I actually toyed with the idea of taking a couple of extra days off and staying, but I'm not sure yet." "I just thought I'd put it out there," she said, "just in case you want to stay longer." I assured her she would be the first to know if I changed my itinerary.

I went upstairs to retrieve my clothes, which were strewn all over her bedroom. I looked at the bed and saw how we virtually tore it apart during our throes of ecstasy. When I returned to the living room, Stephanie was sitting on the couch drinking a glass of wine. "You wore me out," I said. "I think I'll have a glass of wine, too." I went to the kitchen to pour myself a glass of wine and then my phone buzzed." It was Dennis. "Hey man," he bellowed. "I hope I didn't interrupt anything. Actually, since you answered, I suspect you're probably recovering from the fucking Stephanie laid on you. She's something else, isn't she?" I laughed and told Dennis I was going to put him on speaker mode. He yelled out, "Stephanie, I hope you didn't put a hurtin' on him. Will he be able to walk?" She and I laughed before she responded "I think he's okay, but he's walking like he just took a jab from Mike Tyson!" Trying to regain my sense of dignity, I said, "You must be kidding! *I'm* the one who put it on you, not the other way around!" Then Dennis dove in with, "Theo, save it, man. I've seen her in action, and I've seen her put down three guys in an evening, so stop bullshitting." Recognizing that I was in a no-win situation, I submitted, "Okay, okay! She put it on me *this* time, but I'll get her back."

I asked Dennis how his date went with his new-found friend from *Global Connections.* "It went very well. Man, she's fine as hell and fun to be around. I'm on my way back to my place now. I met her for lunch and then we went to her place. She's new to the *Lifestyle* and told me she wants to connect with me again, telling me she liked how I was a gentleman. Of course, she was correct in all regards." "Okay, Mr. Southern gentleman, don't pat yourself too hard on the back," I said. Dennis asked me what time I was going back to his place and I told him within the hour. "Okay," he said. "We can talk about what you want to do this evening when I see you."

After I got off the phone with Dennis, I told Stephanie I wanted to take a shower so we went upstairs and got into her walk-in shower. Since she had drained me over the last few hours, I was unable to achieve the same level of hardness I previously had. However, she proceeded to give me a hand job, apparently not satisfied until I was sexually incapacitated. It worked.

Stephanie pulled up to *The Ridgecrest* around 8:30p.m. Like clockwork, Mr. James rushed up to her side of the car and prepared to open her door, but she told him she wouldn't be getting out. Mr. James was coming to open my door, but I had already gotten out. I asked, "How you're doing this evening, Mr. James?" I walked around to Stephanie's side and proceeded to bend over to kiss her. Before I could, though, she had exited and, with open arms, embraced and kissed me. I could feel Mr. James' eyes peering at Stephanie's shapely body, which was accented by the tight shorts and low-cut blouse she wore.

After we let go of each other, she said, "If you gents want to hang out tonight, give me a call. If not, let's try to connect before you head back to Los Angeles. Oh, and don't forget about my proposition if you decide to stay longer." "That's a bet"! I said. "Thank you, Stephanie. I had a hell of a time. Yes, the meal was excellent and the sex was out of this world, but your personality was, and is, the cherry on top of the cake. I had a perfect day." She responded, "Theo, that's very sweet of you. I had a great time, too, and I hope that wasn't the last time." She kissed me on the cheek and then sped off.

As I entered the lobby, Mr. James sneered at me, winked, and said, "Well, Mr. Williams, how're *you* finding the wonderful *Windy City*? It looks like you're having a great time." "Mr. James," I said, "I'm enjoying my stay tremendously!" We both laughed and then he said, "Son, you and Mr. Warfield should enjoy life. I remember before I married, I used to have a ball dating. You both should do the same, and you'll know when you meet the right one. I've found the right one and we've been together 53 years. So, young man, enjoy it all!" I gave him a firm handshake, thanked him and then sauntered through the lobby, my legs wobbly from the thrashing Stephanie inflicted upon me.

Chapter 16

I rang Dennis's doorbell and when he opened the door, my ears connected to the sounds of Nina Simone's song, *This Year's Kisses*. He strolled over to the stereo, decreasing its volume before turning to me to ask, "How did it go?" I replied, "Man, she is amazing! I thought she was having an Open House, but she tricked the hell out of me. Her Open House actually meant she was free for the day, meaning her house was open. Long story short, she seduced the hell out of me, cooked a delicious meal, and then jerked me off in the shower before I left!" He laughed at the top of his lungs, bellowing, "Sounds just like Stephanie! Man, I've seen her at *Lifestyle* parties and when she's hot, she can go. I have personally seen her take on three guys at a party and wore them all out!" "You are lying your ass off!" I said. Without hesitating, Dennis barked, "I bullshit you not! With my own eyes, I've seen her fuck three guys until they couldn't get it up!" "Well," I sheepishly admitted, "she completely wore me out and I'm sure she would've gone on longer had I had the energy."

Dennis asked, "So, what do you want to get into tonight? I did not plan anything because I didn't know what time you were coming back. Besides, it's your trip so I want to make sure you enjoy yourself." "Hey man," I said, "I called your parents on the way to Stephanie's. I didn't want to call them too late because I didn't know what time I would finish hanging out with Stephanie. Your dad had me laughing talking trash about his Atlanta Braves, and your parents told me they have been trying to get my mom to move to Atlanta. Your parents are fantastic people, Dennis." Dennis told me he, too, took the liberty of calling his mother to let her know I was in town and that she told him "Theo jus' cawled' 'bout fifteen minutes ago."

Nina Simone was winding down the final lines of her song with, *"This year's crop of kisses are not for me, are not for me... 'cuz I'm still wearin' last year's... I'm still wearin' last year's... I'm still wearin' last year's... love!"* when Dennis asked me again what I wanted to do that evening. I told him I did not have anything in mind so he asked, "Do you want to go to a *Lifestyle* party tonight?" I was not sure if it was the directness of his question or the content, but he caught me off guard and the only response that came to mind was, "You mean a fuck party? Are you talking about the kind where people are laying around fucking and all that?" He knew I was not in the *Lifestyle*, and that I was very naïve about it, so with gentle sarcasm, he quipped, "Uh, yes, Sherlock, that's usually what happens at a *swinger's* party." "Man," I said, "I'm not sure if I am ready to do something like that. I won't lie, it sounds intriguing as hell, but I'm not sure if I could bone while a bunch of people are in the same room, especially watching me get it on." He responded, "Well, the cool thing is there is **never** any pressure. The fact is, if you don't want to play, you don't have to. Hell, you don't even have to take your clothes off. It's literally like a 'regular' party in that there will be music, movies, food, drinks, and even swimming. It's all up to you, so you do not have to *play* at all."

I was amused with my newly acquired *Lifestyle* vocabulary, and said to Dennis, "The language of this shit is hilarious. It all sounds so innocent - *Lifestyle, swinging, partying, playing.* Had you not told me, I never would have guessed you were actually referring to some *Bacchanalian* goings-on like fuck parties." "Well, what do you say, Grasshopper, you up for it or not," he queried. I thought about it and then responded, "What the hell, let's go for it. But remember, man, this is new to me so make sure you tell everyone that!"

Chapter 17

Admittedly, I was extremely nervous about the idea of going to a *Lifestyle* party. Hell, I barely understood all the terms, let alone what to expect! Dennis and I were dressed and ready to leave *The Ridgecrest* at 10:30pm. Just as we were about to leave, I heard Dennis say "Damn!" when his phone wrong. "Hold on a second," he said. "Let me see who this is." I heard him say, "Hey Stephanie! How're you doing? Yes. Yes. Actually, we're about to leave." When he got off the phone, he told me Stephanie was also going to the party, which was being hosted by a couple named Rick and Barbara Ballenger. I felt a lump in my throat when he said Stephanie was going to be there.

I was not familiar with many of Chicago's neighborhoods with the exception of the Loop area and the South Side. Dennis headed to an area called Burr Ridge, which I had never heard of. I asked about the party hosts and he told me, "Rick and Barbara are good people. They have been in the *Lifestyle* about fifteen years and throw ***the*** best parties I have ever been to. You will not believe the house they live in! It's huge, has several *play* rooms, pool, Jacuzzi, the works! They always have a good ratio, too." I asked, "A good ratio? Of…?" and he responded, "Of men to women. You never want to go to a *Lifestyle* party and it's a 'sausage fest' where there are tons of guys and only a few women. With Rick and Barbara, they usually have about ten couples, five or so single women and about five single guys. Sometimes, though, they will have a 'Greedy Girls' party and those are amazing!" "Uh, what type of party is that?" I asked. He told me those were parties where the ladies liked gangbangs and/or multiple men fucking them. Incredulously, I said, "You have **got** to be kidding me!" He looked at me intently and said, "I bullshit you not, Theo."

We were pulling into the driveway of Rick and Barbara's home, and for some reason, I was shocked because the house was so stately and reaped of a high-income community. I said "This does not look like a low-income area, obviously. What type of work do they do?" and he responded, "Rick owns a software company and Barbara is a high-end interior designer. They make major dollars and, surprisingly, Barbara's clients are some of Chicago's most noted professional athletes, some of whom even live in the area. By the way, Barbara is gorgeous, but do **not** let her size fool you! She's petite and all, but she can take some dick and she **loves** the brothers! Remind me to tell you about her '*BBC-themed*' parties." "Gee," I sarcastically muttered, "another acronym, I presume? I'm almost afraid to ask what it means."

"Do their neighbors know about their, dare I say, extra-curricular activities?" Dennis replied, "No, they keep that private although a couple of the *Windy City's* professional football players have been known to partake. Otherwise, they're pretty low-key, and their neighbors just think Rick and Barbara are throwing huge 'regular' parties. Man-oh-man, if the neighbors only knew! What you'll find in the *Lifestyle* is that people are very protective about maintaining discretion. It's a tightknit community." I then asked, "Dennis, how long have you been doing this? How did you get started?" "I'll share that with you later," he said. "Suffice it to say, it's been a great, fun-filled five years, and it keeps getting better!"

Dennis drove the car up the winding driveway, parked, and then asked me, "Are you ready? No pressure, Theo. If you're not feeling this, we can leave now. No harm, no foul, and if you feel uncomfortable at any time, let me know and we will leave immediately. Is that a deal?" "Of course," I said, "I'll let you know if I can't go through with it, trust me."

Before we exited the car, he said, "Here, take this. You might need it." He handed me a small blue pill that had Viagra 100mg written on it. I asked, "Is this what I *think* it is? I heard about this stuff and how it was recently released on the market. It's supposed to keep your dick hard for four hours. Is that true?" Dennis replied, "Yep, it's fairly new on the market. I have a prescription from my doctor. I actually don't need it in the strict sense because I can 'get it up,' but I take it when I go to parties. At parties, there may be anywhere from ten to twenty women who want to *play*, so I do what I can to uh... not let them down, so to speak." I said, "Hell, if this shit keeps your dick hard for four hours or so, I imagine that's enough. I'm not even sure I *want* a full hard on for four hours!"

I was apprehensive about taking the blue pill because I was not a fan of taking medication, let alone something like Viagra that was fairly new on the market. "Trust me," he said, "it'll be okay. I've used it before. Just take it in about fifteen minutes or so. By then, you will know if this scene is for you and whether or not you feel comfortable *playing.*"

Initially, I felt confident I was okay, but when I saw Stephanie's red BMW pull up right behind Dennis's Benz, I became skeptical. Again, questions arose and seared into my brain: *Can you handle watching another man fuck Stephanie? How are you going to feel if another man is fucking her brains out and you see that? What will you do if she's getting fucked by another man and she asks you to join-in?* I started to feel faint as beads of cold sweat accumulated on my forehead, then I finally answered the questions. "Fuck it! She's not my girlfriend, so why should I be jealous? Hell, I'll probably be too busy fucking other women anyway, and Stephanie better not bother me while I'm doing that! After all, I am not her boyfriend."

Stephanie exited her car and walked up to me and Dennis. Her first words were, "Hey there, you sexy guys! You both look wonderful. I think we're going to have a *lot* of fun tonight. How're ya'll doing?" I was the first to answer, and said, "Damn, Stephanie, you look good! I'm inclined to take you back to your open house." We all laughed, considering Stephanie seduced me earlier all with a mere manipulation of words, but I was *not* complaining. She purred, "Oh, really? Well, I suspect you gathered that I have a rather high energy level and I just can't say no to this" as she rubbed my crotch and winked at me.

The three of us walked to the entrance of the house and Dennis rang the doorbell. Within seconds, an attractive blond woman opened the door and said, "Well, hello Dennis and Stephanie! And who is this handsome gentleman you have with you?" "This is my buddy Theo. He's visiting from Los Angeles and I thought I would introduce him to some good people." She responded, "Well, hello, Theo. My name is Barbara, and welcome to Chicago. Since you're a friend of Dennis's, I'll do my best to make sure your visit is... uh... shall I say, memorable?"

She gave me a hug and as she did, purposely yet tactfully pulled me close enough so her pelvis rubbed against my leg. "It's a pleasure to meet you, Barbara. I've heard some very, very good things about you from Dennis." Barbara hugged Dennis and, to my surprise, gave Stephanie a kiss on the lips that was more than casual. The kiss damn-sure was not a "peck" so I found myself introspectively inquiring, "Damn! Does Stephanie go 'both ways?'"

Barbara was about 5'3", 115lbs, and easily a good 40DD! She looked to be in her mid 40's and had an elegant look about herself. She exuded class, but it was also very clear she was unabashed about expressing her carnal desires. When we walked into the foyer, a distinguished-looking gentleman approached us and said, "Welcome, Stephanie and Dennis!" He shook Dennis's hand and gave Stephanie a hug. Barbara introduced me by saying, "Rick, this is Theo. He's Dennis's friend from Los Angeles. I think I'll have to give him a special *'Windy City Welcome.'* Is that okay with you?" Rick said, "Theo, welcome to our home. I'll have to warn you in advance. Barbara is quite the hostess, once she's turned on, well, watch out!

Barbara my dear, it's all about *your* pleasure, and you should treat our new guest accordingly."

Immediately after Rick said that, he and Barbara embraced, kissed, and then she took me by the hand and said, "Thank you, honey!" She led me into the expansive living room. I shook Rick's hand right before Barbara whisked me away, and all the while I asked myself for clarity: *Did this guy **really** just give his wife the consent to fuck me, a complete stranger?*

Once I entered the living room, the uncertainty I previously had about being able to perform in a group setting waned because there were model-type women of virtually every ethnicity! In my preconceived notions about *swingers,* I imagined all the women would be morbidly obese, unattractive, and sexually undesirable. To my astonishment, I was very incorrect in my assumption!

Dennis walked up to Barbara and told her, "Barbara, Theo is new to the *Lifestyle* so may I ask that you 'break him in' gently?" "Don't worry, Dennis, I will make *sure* he has a good time and I will show him around... personally." She proceeded to walk me through their home, which easily could have been featured in *Better Homes and Gardens Magazine,* minus naked people walking around the place!

The living room was spacious, complete with a high, sky-light ceiling, two large couches, and several side chairs. There were four people sitting on the couch, apparently two couples who seemed to know each other. I noticed all four wore wedding bands, and my inner voice inquired, "I wonder who's fucking whom here." Initially, both women were sitting between the men, but as Barbara and I walked up to them, the men switched places and started caressing each other's woman. Barbara interjected and said, "Excuse us. This is Theo from Los Angeles. He's a dear friend of Dennis's and this is his first *Lifestyle* party. Be nice, ladies. I know he looks delicious, but you know 'house rules.' The hostess *always* cums first!" All the women smiled as their eyes undressed me.

Barbara introduced me to the couples. An African American couple, Wanda and Mitch Butler, welcomed me to Chicago. Mitch stood up to shake my hand and then Wanda stood up and gave me a hug. The other couple was a White couple named Warren and Dianne Grayson, and they were equally courteous. Warren stood up to shake my hand and Dianne rose to give me a hug. Both ladies wore short, scintillating dresses that revealed **lots** of cleavage and legs. As well, they both were very attractive and appeared to be in their early forties. Before Barbara and I left them on the couch, Mitch moved over to Dianne and started fondling her breasts while Warren and Wanda began their own erotic dance, touching and stroking the other's body.

Barbara took me to the kitchen, which was beautifully decorated with lots of stainless steel, high-end appliances, a granite island, and teak cabinets. There were all types of food and beverages in the kitchen as if the party had been catered on an expensive budget: shrimp, scallops, crabs, chicken breasts, oysters, salad, cakes, cookies, wine, vodka, gin, beer, soda, and chips. If anyone had the slightest of hunger pangs, they definitely were in the right place because this was not a "man party" consisting of beer and pizza. No, this was a class act. What I really found a bit out of place was that near a bowl filled with wrapped candy was a similar bowl filled with condoms of every brand!

We ventured to the backyard where there was a pool and Jacuzzi. Three couples and three ladies were in the oversized Jacuzzi as Barbara and I approached. Barbara introduced me by saying, "Everyone, this is Theo from Los Angeles. He's Dennis's friend and this is his first *Lifestyle* party as well. We're going to show him what it's all about, right ladies?" One of the ladies in the Jacuzzi, Lupe Cordova, was a stunning woman originally from Columbia, South America.

Lupe looked like she was in her late twenties, about 5'4", 115 pounds, stacked body, and long black hair. She retreated from the Jacuzzi, walked directly up to me and said, *"Hola Theo. Mi nombre es Lupe. Eres muy guapo y espero que tengo la oportunidad de jugar con usted. Espero que vuelvas a jugar conmigo!"* She was completely naked, and as she spoke, hugged me while putting her right hand around the back of my neck pulling my head downward. I was surprised that she kissed me, a complete stranger, on the lips. One of the ladies in the Jacuzzi who introduced herself as Nancy yelled, "Welcome, Theo. I think I see a bulge growing in your pants. Did you understand what she said or are you just trying to flatter us?" Laughter erupted from everyone, myself included. "Thanks for the welcome, Nancy, and, yes, I did understand what Lupe said. Trust me, I *will* return!" Seeing this beautiful, naked woman and hearing what she said to me reminded me that material things can always be replaced. So, I did not give a damn about her getting my suit wet!

Lupe tiptoed back into the Jacuzzi while Barbara introduced me to a few more people who were sitting alongside or floating inside the adjoining pool. Out of the corner of my eye, I saw a couple adjacent to the pool where a woman lay back in a lawn chair while a man buried his face between her outstretched legs. I also saw women in a "69" position on throngs of pillows on the grass while onlookers massaged each other's bodies, encouraging the ladies on.

I asked Barbara where the bathroom was and she motioned to a room adjacent to the kitchen. I walked into the bathroom, making sure to close the door behind me. I looked into the mirror and, as if I were speaking to someone else, asked, "Are you ready to do this?" I confirmed my interest, by replying, "Yes" as I slipped the Viagra pill into my mouth and then cupped my hand under the faucet to chase it with water. "Here goes," I said, as I took the plunge into the unchartered waters of sexually-enhanced prescription medication. I retreated from the bathroom and headed back to the kitchen where Barbara was speaking with a petite, attractive Filipina woman who introduced herself as Maria Rosario.

Barbara took my hand and led me towards steps that led upstairs. We were about to ascend the steps before Barbara asked, "So, Theo, what exactly did Lupe say? She seems to have made a very favorable introduction. She's a super-nice person, as is everyone else here, not to mention a bundle of sexual energy. I hope you get a chance to party with her. That is, if you've anything left after *I* finish with you." My response was, "Well, Barbara, *you* are the hostess and *you* have my undivided attention." She saw my erection standing out even further in my pants and said, "Oh, I can see I have your attention… in more ways than one." "Well," I said, "she told me she thought I was handsome and that she hoped to get a chance to play with me. She said she wanted me to come back and play with her." "Ah," Barbara said, "my Spanish is improving. I thought she said something like that."

Barbara led the way upstairs. I was always taught, "Ladies first," but it was also strategic on my part to make sure I was behind her walking up the steps. I wanted to see her voluptuous body from the rear, and it was blatantly obvious that under her sheer, thigh-high dress she was *au natural.* She, too, was keen on making sure to go first, and I saw her hike her dress up slightly as she ascended. About midway up, she looked back and asked, "What do you think?" I knew she felt my eyes glaring at the view underneath her dress, so I responded, "It depends on what you're taking about, whether the people I met, your home, or the wonderful view I have behind you." "Well," she said, "whichever comes to mind first." Unabashedly, I replied, "Barbara, you have a lovely body and your butt has me under a spell. I know you're doing that on purpose." I playfully smacked her on her backside just as we got to the top of the steps. To my surprise, she turned around and said, "I was wondering what took you so long to do that. I was beginning to worry you didn't like the view."

When we reached the top of the stairs, we embraced and started kissing. I ran my hands all over her body and then reached her hardened nipples, gently pinching them until she began to sigh, "Damn, that feels good." I felt her hands moving towards my zipper and she opened it, stroking my hardness with her right hand while using her left hand to unbuckle my belt. She then descended to her knees and started sucking me. I could hear faint voices coming from three of the bedrooms, and one voice I recognized was shouting, "That's it... deeper! Give it to me, Stan!" I recognized that voice as Stephanie's! My mind raced. It sounded like Stephanie was in the throes of sexual ecstasy.

At the time, I did not care because my mind and body were focused on Barbara, who was giving me a knee-buckling blowjob. My pants were around my ankles as I leaned my head backward to enjoy the sensations. Barbara looked up and said, "Theo, you have a lovely thick cock! I'm a bit tight, so I hope you'll be gentle before you stretch me out." "Don't worry, Barbara," I muttered, "I'll be gentle and won't give you more than you can handle. That dick is yours, baby." She finally stood up and said, "I like your perspective and think we're going to get along just fine."

I felt awkward as I stepped out of my pants, completely naked from waist down, but still wearing my suit coat, shirt, sox, and shoes. "Let's get you out of these clothes," Barbara said, so I stripped. She took my clothes and shoes to an adjoining bedroom. Dennis came out of one of the bedrooms wearing nothing but an erection and carrying a handful of condoms. He was about to go into another bedroom, but stopped to ask me, "So, what do you think? Barbara's fine as hell isn't she?" "That's an understatement," I said. "Man, this is some straight-up *Bacchanalian* shit! I thought you were exaggerating about these parties! I don't think we've been here more than a half hour and you and Stephanie appear to be fucking already!" Before walking into the bedroom, he turned, smiled, and said, "Have I ever lied to you, Theo? Did you take the Viagra?" "Yes," I said, "I can feel this stuff beginning to work, too!"

When Barbara returned, she was completely naked and proceeded to guide me to the doorway of each of the bedrooms. We peeked into each room, where several people engaged in various sexual acts on beds, floors, and even a couple that was fucking while standing up. I was so intrigued and, frankly, startled by what I saw that I did not recognize that Barbara was actually guiding me from room-to-room by my dick! Finally, she turned to me and said, "Let's go to my bedroom. It has a bigger bed and I think we're going to need more space. Rick and I do not let others play in our bedroom, so it's reserved for when he or I want to play with someone one-on-one." I mouthed, "No complaints from me" as she continued to stroke me with her guiding hand.

The room was lit by several candles, so I could see the large bed she led me to. Still standing, we kissed and groped each other near the foot of the bed. I guided Barbara to lay back on the edge of the bed with her legs spread wide. I got on my knees and started sucking her. Her body was already sweating, and her delicious canal emitted a sweet aroma. She tasted fabulous, as well-cropped pubic hair rubbed against my nose as I slid my tongue inside her. Barbara moaned as I heard her say, "Mmm, that's it, Theo, right there. Your tongue is amazing!" The more I licked, the wetter she became.

I had her under my control, so I took her to a higher level of pleasure by utilizing what I described as the "Butterfly technique." I whispered, "Are you ready for the 'Butterfly technique?'" "I don't know what it is," she said, "but whatever you're doing, don't stop!" I spread her legs as far apart as possible and held her ankles to make sure I would have total access. Then, I gently took her clitoris between my lips and swirled my tongue around it very slowly. My tongue moved clockwise, counter-clockwise, and then I flitted it against the tip. Finally, I darted my tongue in and out of her and felt her back arch while her hips bucked rapidly against my face. Her moans became screams and, still, she became even wetter as she experienced the first orgasm.

"Damn!" she said. "Where in the world did you learn that?" "That's only the beginning, Barbara. Suffice it to say, I am not a selfish lover," I said. "I can tell, Theo, and you are damn sure hitting the right spots. I can't wait to feel that big, thick cock of yours inside me." I wanted to get inside her mind, so I teased, "Are you sure you want it? Is this wet pussy ready to get fucked deep?" By this time, she was thrusting her hips upwards, and begged, "Oh, Theo, fuck me! I can't take it anymore."

I stood at the base of the bed and she moved to its center. She laid back, spread her legs and began masturbating as I grabbed a *Magnum* condom from a bowl on the nightstand. Barbara played with herself while I put the condom on. "I am such a slut for a man who uses *Magnums*. A hard cock is good, but a big, thick hard cock is so, so much better!" I responded, "Is that right? Well, you're about to get a thorough fucking."

I laid on top of Barbara while her hand gripped my phallus. "Take your time, this pussy isn't going anywhere. You're kind of big, so let me guide you in." I obliged and let her put the mushroom-shaped head inside. "I'll keep it like that, so you just move your hips upwards when you want more inside, okay? I'm not going to force it in. Just take your time, baby, it's about *your* pleasure." I kept my body still and waited patiently. She began thrusting her hips up and down, allowing me to give her more. She became extremely wet, and before I knew it, most of my dick was inside her. We got into a rhythm where her hips moved upward while I met each movement with a slight thrust downward. "Give it to me deep, Theo, I'm so ready." I eagerly pushed the entire length inside, balls deep, while I nibbled on her neck and massaged her breasts.

We fucked frantically for several minutes until I heard a sound coming from the door. Rick opened the bedroom door, peered in. "I see my hot wife is getting what she craves." Barbara responded, "Oh yes! You *know* how I am when I see a large cock, honey, and Theo is giving me what I need." Rick closed the door and sat in a chair across the room. "I *love* seeing my hot wife getting fucked! How is she, Theo?" I felt my erection waning because it was unsettling fucking another man's wife, let alone in *his* bed *while* he watched! I concentrated, trying to keep my mind from thinking about what was transpiring. This worked, and I felt my erection returning. Mentally, I tuned Rick out of the equation, but it was truly unchartered territory for me. This was strange, indeed! It helped that he was encouraging her and I by saying, "That's it, Theo, give that slut a good fucking, she needs it. You need that cock, don't you honey?" The more candid and raunchy Rick spoke, the faster she thrust her hips.

Rick watched me bang his wife for several minutes before saying, "This is making my cock hard, too. I think I better go downstairs and find Lupe." After Rick left, Barbara and I pleased each other another thirty minutes or so in varying ways. Exhausted, we collapsed and began caressing. She leaned over and whispered, "I've not had a fucking like that in quite some time. Are you *sure* you're new to the *Lifestyle*?" "Yes," I said, "this is my first time. I hope I made a favorable impression." She took my hand, guided it to her soaking pussy. "See how wet I am? I think you've made a *very* favorable impression, Sweetie. Let's go get a drink, I need to recoup. You did me very, very well!"

Before we got up from the bed, I turned to Barbara and asked, "Do you mind if I ask a personal question? If it's out of bounds, just say so. Please understand the context is me trying to understand the *Lifestyle*, so I am **not** being accusatory in **any** way." "Sure," she said. "Go for it." "Well," I said, "I won't lie. I felt strange at first when Rick walked in and started watching us. I'm sure you probably recognized I started to get soft for a moment. How did you and Rick get involved in this? I'm sorry if I sound too much like a 'newbie,' but I'm just curious. Again, if it's out of bounds, just let me know."

Barbara was candid, and it was as if we assumed the roles of teacher and student, I the latter. She then explained the tenets of the *Lifestyle*. "First of all, I know you're new to the *Lifestyle*," she said. "Your question is a good one, and well-taken. Rick approached me with the idea several years ago. We've been married almost twenty years, are very secure in our marriage, love each other dearly, and trust one another. We've pretty much done everything sexually that any couple could do from role-playing, watching pornographic movies together, to having sex in public places. Eventually, we started talking about our sexual fantasies and one night he told me he fantasized about me having sex with another man. I have always **loved** sex, but initially told him 'Fuck off!' At first, I was hurt and thought I was doing something wrong, but we talked about it further and he assured me he loved our sex life. I thought I was inadequate at first, and mentally shut down. Because of that, we didn't have sex for several weeks afterward. It was hard for me because I kept asking myself, 'What am I doing wrong that I can't please my man?'"

"He never pressured me again about it. Then, one night we were watching a porn movie. Specifically, there was a scene where two men were taking turns fucking a woman. Admittedly, I was turned on by the sight. We started fucking, and I asked him, 'So, you want me to be like that lady in the video taking on two hard cocks, huh?'" I asked how he responded and she replied, "When I asked him that, it was as if he went into a zone and fucked me like he had never done before. It was a tremendous turn-on for both of us."

I was still in amazement and tried masking my inexperience by saying, "Wow, that's hot as hell!" She went on to tell me they decided not to force the issue, instead, letting their foray into the *Lifestyle* happen organically. Rick was patient and worked at her pace, all the while taking time to do more research about the *Lifestyle*. He discovered in a *Windy City Swingers'* magazine that there was a community of *swingers* in Chicago, and they regularly hosted meet-and-greet events at upscale bars and restaurants. The meet-and-greet functions were primarily designed for "newbies" who were unsure about delving further, and there was never any pressure on people during events.

"I finally decided to attend a meet-and-greet function with the agreement that if at any time I felt uncomfortable, we would leave immediately. Rick was so excited when I told him I would attend. Hell, I could have told him 'I'll do it if you take a parachute off the Sears Tower' and he would have agreed!" I laughed and asked, "You're exaggerating, right?" "Well, slightly," she said. "At that point, he was so turned on by the idea he would have done anything I asked of him. In a strange kind of way, it was as if I had complete control over him from that point, a sort of power dynamic. You know, Theo, it's fascinating what a man with a hard dick will do in pursuit of pussy." I responded, "Tell me about it! I've had my share of late-night booty calls in the wee-hours getting up from sleep, knowing I had to work the next day. All in pursuit of the 'golden fleece,' so to speak."

She went on to tell me the *swingers'* meet-and-greet event went well, and she felt very comfortable with the people they met. They befriended another couple who was experienced, and Barbara confided, "The rest is history. I have no regrets, and have met some fantastic people from all walks of life. It allows me, with Rick's support and permission, to get all my sexual energy out of my system in a safe, comfortable environment. He has fun, too, so it's not all about my pleasure. I encourage you to explore it further, especially if you have a good time tonight." "Barbara," I said, "I've had a blast already, so make no mistake, I'm going to look further into the *Lifestyle.*"

We finally got out of bed and headed downstairs. As we were about to descend the steps, Stephanie was coming out of a bedroom with a thoroughly-fucked-look. Her hair, which was well-coiffed when we arrived, was now strewn about her head. She was accompanied by a gentleman whom she introduced as Stan. Stan was a mid-thirties White man, and he welcomed me to Chicago. He also said, "It's a pleasure to meet you, Theo, and I hope you have a great time. I would introduce you to my wife, Svetlana, but she's is in the bedroom with Dennis. Please make her acquaintance when you get a chance." I was struck by the contrast of formality and informality in Stan's tone. It was as if he was saying, *"It's a pleasure to meet you. Please be sure to introduce yourself to my wife and fuck her at your earliest convenience."* A voice echoed in my head again, "Damn, this is some wild shit!"

Stephanie walked up to Barbara and they started kissing. Stan was rather calm about seeing this and, frankly, unfazed. I, however, was shocked to see two women kissing passionately and rubbing each other's body. Barbara started sucking on Stephanie's nipples while Stan and I just stood back and watched. Then, Barbara got on her knees and started licking Stephanie!

My mind raced, wondering what I had gotten myself into, but I eventually relaxed when I saw Stan join in. He sucked Stephanie's nipples while Barbara started blowing him. My inhibitions waned, so I started rubbing Stephanie's legs and nipples. There we were, four people locked in an impromptu romp at the top of the steps. Stephanie got on her knees and joined Barbara in sucking me. They took turns sharing me before I ejaculated on Barbara's face while Stan obliged Stephanie with an ample amount of sperm on her face. I was torn between abhorrence and excitement as I saw Barbara and Stephanie, both with cream-coated faces, share another passionate kiss. The voice returned in my head, this time with more amazement, "What the fuck is *this*?"

Chapter 18

I went downstairs to the kitchen with Stephanie, Barbara, and Stan. I felt no embarrassment at being totally naked with them, as well as others, most of whom were *au natural*. Lupe, who was in the kitchen, saw Stephanie and they both were excited to see each other. Lupe walked over to Stephanie and kissed her. There was something erotic about seeing them kiss so delicately. Lupe noticed my staring, so she walked over to me and asked if I wanted to *play* with her. I said, *"Sí, Lupe, yo quiero jugar con usted, muchas gracias. Echa un vistazo a lo duro que soy, y que debería decirle lo mucho que quiero follarte."* She responded, "Your Spanish is very good, but I bet this is better," taking my fully-erect dick gently into her hand, stroking it. She knelt over and kissed its tip before taking my hand leading me upstairs.

Up to this point, I had not given much thought, perhaps purposely, to how I would react to seeing Stephanie with another man. I heard her when Stan was fucking her, so not seeing the act was bearable. I did, however, take solace in the fact I could emotionally handle her being with Lupe. I was not as confident and secure about seeing (and, hearing, for that matter) her with another man. The voice in my head appeared, and fired several unsympathetic questions at me. *Why are you being selfish? Why are you okay with Stephanie playing with Lupe, but not with a man? Are you afraid she might enjoy another man more than you? What gives **you** the right to feel* *jealous about Stephanie having fun? All you men are just alike. You can go out and get some extra pussy, but you cannot handle a woman going out to get some extra dick.* I thought about all these questions while maintaining eye contact with Lupe and finally said to myself, *You need to get over it. Have fun and stop being selfish.* I let my insecurity go and resigned myself to the fact that Stephanie was not my girlfriend. I had no right to tell her what to do, sexually or otherwise. Coming to grips with those facts opened a clearer dimension in my psyche because I finally let it all go. Stephanie and Lupe came over to me. I held them close to my pulsating body and whispered, "I want you both." Stephanie smiled and responded, "Oh, really? Can you handle ***both*** of us?" and I said, "Honestly, I doubt it, but I damn sure will do my best."

Before the three of us went upstairs, I went over to the island and filled my plate with shrimp, scallops, and potato chips. I was not interested in drinking alcohol because Dennis explained I needed to be cautious about combining alcohol with Viagra, especially since this was my first time taking the drug. So, I just decided on a can of *Canada Dry.* "Give me a minute to get some refreshments and then we can go upstairs." They agreed and ate as well. The three of us sat at the table before a tall blond woman wearing a silk sarong approached us. Lupe and Stephanie greeted her and exchanged embraces with her. Her name was Svetlana Krakov and she had a thick Eastern European accent, perhaps Russian or Ukrainian.

With her very strong accent and truncated English, she said, "You must be *Teo*, yes?" I replied, "It's a pleasure to meet you, Svetlana." She was an attractive woman, probably in her mid-thirties, tall, slender, dark blue piercing eyes, firm boobs, and a non-descript mole on her cheek. She continued, "I hear good things 'bout you, *Teo*, and Svetlana must find out herself." She kissed me on the cheek and winked. "Oh?" I said, "How did you hear about me?" and she replied, "Barbara tell Svetlana **everything**, especially about men who **really** take care of business." "I see, Svetlana. Well, I just hope I will live up to your expectations." "Based upon what I hear and see," as she looked downward, "you have already done so."

Just a week ago, I was confirming plans to visit Dennis. At no time did I ever fathom my trek would include having sex with some of the most beautiful, intelligent, decadently sensuous women from all over the globe! A drop-dead gorgeous, petite Columbian, a tall, sensuous Russian, a White American woman who had the sexual energy of women half her age, and an astoundingly attractive African American woman. This truly was one of those "Nobody is going to believe this shit!" experiences. Lupe, Stephanie, and I finished our food and then Stephanie asked if I were ready for some **real** fun. I was excited about the prospect of having sex with two women, but reality set-in, and I was worried I'd bitten off more than I could chew.

We entered a bedroom that was empty and laid on the bed. Initially, I was in the middle of both women before they started kissing and rubbing each other, effectively putting me out of the equation. I did not mind, though, because it was uncommonly erotic to see them *play* with each other. I moved to the outer edge and allowed them space to please each other. Lupe gently pushed Stephanie backward and Lupe moved downward and proceeded to spread Stephanie's legs to orally please her.

I watched for a few moments before I got behind Lupe to lick and suck her. There we were, a daisy chain, Stephanie being licked by Lupe while I feasted upon Lupe's nectar. They moved into a "69" position with Lupe on top while I sauntered over to the bowl of condoms on the nightstand to grab a *Magnum*. Lupe looked at me as I placed the condom on and said, this time in English, "Mmmm, *that's* what I've been waiting on!"

I angled myself behind Lupe to enter her "doggy-style," but before I could, Stephanie put me in her mouth and began sucking me while fondling my testicles. This excited Lupe, for she moaned, "Guía de él en mí, Stepanie!" People say sex is a universal language, but I found it a bit comical when Stephanie, slightly confused, uttered, "What the hell did she say?" so I had to translate. "She said, 'Guide him into him, Stephanie.'" Stephanie countered with, "Tell her I said, 'Of course I'll slide it in, but whatever you do, do not stop eating my pussy!'" I translated that to Lupe and she dove into Stephanie with a vengeance, simultaneously thrusting her hips back onto me. Stephanie lapped my balls as I eased into Lupe. We were in this position around fifteen minutes when Stephanie said, "Okay, it's my turn, I gotta have it!" I put on another condom and proceeded to slide into Stephanie doggy-style while Lupe feasted upon Stephanie. The Viagra was in full effect again, and I pounded Stephanie relentlessly.

I ejaculated yet a third time and, exhausted, fell to the side of Lupe and Stephanie. My body, overall, was depleted of energy, but my erection continued to peak. I said to myself, "I wish like hell I would have invented Viagra, this shit is amazing!" They continued with each other while I began to rub their bodies, providing ample verbal stimulation to encourage them on, "That's it, Lupe, eat that pussy. Mmm, Stephanie, I think Lupe's going to cum again. Don't stop... don't stop." My coaching had the desired effect because they now were flipping the other over continuously, attempting to prove who was in control. They, too, were verbal, "Suck my pussy! That's it, right there. Don't stop! You're going to make me cum!" They continued this for another fifteen minutes before, finally, Lupe mounted Stephanie's face, spread her legs and wailed, "You are making me cum so hard... I'm about to cum again! Stick your tongue in me deep!"

Lupe's back arched as Stephanie slapped her butt and inserted her index finger in Lupe's anus. I could not believe what I was seeing, but I was thoroughly turned on! I had never seen two women please each other, at least in person, but seeing them so attentive to each other's desires prompted me to stroke myself. Lupe peered at me playing with myself and began narrating, "Stephanie, Theo is stroking his big dick. Theo, I want you to cum on our faces!" "Oh yeah, cum on us, Theo!" was Stephanie's retort. Taken aback, I thought to myself, "Did

116

she just say what I **thought** she said? Did she tell me to cum on them both?" I started stroking vigorously and eventually screamed, "I'm about to cum!" When they heard this, they positioned themselves between my legs, mouths wide open like ravenous sparrows, and simultaneously moaned, "Give it to us!" Sperm jetted airborne, and landed perfectly on their entwined faces. They kissed each other as I rubbed myself, milking my balls of their contents. I looked down and saw them experiencing sexual nirvana, yet my mind raced, still in disbelief.

Our limp bodies lay in a pile as we proceeded to massage each other. The door opened and Barbara walked in with Dennis. "My-oh-my," Barbara said. "It looks like we missed a hot time!" I looked upward and said, "My dear, Barbara, that is a dire understatement. They just wore me the hell out."

I arose from the bed and stood in front of Barbara while Dennis stood behind her. We sandwiched her, rubbing our penises against her while teasing her nipples. She threw her head back and began moaning to our touches while Lupe and Stephanie continued massaging each other on the bed.

I quickly recognized my body was unable to summon any more energy, so I sheepishly stated, "I need to take another break. I'm completely exhausted and if I don't take a break, I may pass the hell out!" Barbara rubbed her leg against me as I walked past her, but said, "I hope you manage to garner some energy for Svetlana. I don't think she's going to let you go home until she *plays* with you. "Damn!" I said, "If ya'll keep *this* up, I won't be able to come back to Chicago for another five years!" They all laughed, but I was dead serious. I went downstairs to the kitchen to grab another plate of food before heading out to the backyard.

Chapter 19

When I walked into the kitchen, there were several people standing around talking, drinking wine, and eating shrimp cocktail. I introduced myself to those I had not met previously, and it appeared a few more single women arrived. The environment seemed so free and relaxed. There were some people who were completely naked while others remained fully clothed. I remembered Dennis telling me when we were en route to the party, "The environment is so chill. Everybody pretty much knows each other and, believe it or not, some people don't even come to *play*. They just come out for the fellowship. While a fair amount of the *Lifestyle* is about sex, it's actually more about trust, friendship, and being around like-minded people. It's just a cool community of folks." I found his comments to be fascinating, a historical throw-back to the '60's' "free love" movement.

Rick walked up to me. "How is everything going, Theo? Are you having a good time?" "Hi Rick. Yes, I'm having a blast! As you know, this is a first for me, but I have felt so welcomed by everyone I've met. This is truly amazing. Suffice it to say, I've been welcomed with open arms *and* legs!" He burst into laughter and responded, "We like to have a couple of parties per month, and we always welcome close friends of our regulars. Everyone thinks very highly of Dennis, so you, my friend, come highly regarded. Make yourself at home and let me know if you need anything. By the way, you made a wonderful impression on Barbara. Want to know what she said to me?" "Of course," I said.

"Well," she said, "and I quote, 'Theo is such a gentleman and he wore me out! It's too bad he's only here for the weekend. We need to go to Los Angeles instead of San Diego next summer!'" I looked at him in amazement and responded, "Wow! Just keep me posted, then. I have ample room and would love to show you both around the *City of Angeles* although I seriously doubt we would be anything remotely close to angelic." He laughed. "We'll see how things go, then. Thanks for the invitation. We take a vacation every other summer to a city we've never visited. Los Angeles and San Diego are two of those cities on the West Coast, so now it is **very** likely to be Los Angeles."

Just as Rick walked away, I felt a pair of warm, soft hands cover my eyes while the perpetrator blew into my ear, "I want you, *Teo.*" It did not take me long to recognize the thick Russian accent. It was Svetlana. I turned around and she grabbed my manhood, caressed it. "Mmm, this very nice, *Teo.* You have energy for me, yes?" "Don't worry, Svetlana, I **will** have some energy for you," I said. "Let me get something to eat and we'll *play.*" I never thought I would be in a situation of postponing the opportunity to have sex, but I was too exhausted. The Viagra was still working, but the rest of my body felt like pulp. She kissed me on the lips and rubbed her firm breasts against my chest before letting me know she would wait outside in the Jacuzzi whenever I was ready.

I was standing alone, soaking-in the sounds and views of carnal activities, when one of the African American men, Mitch, walked up to me and asked me what I thought about my first *Lifestyle* party. "To be honest, Mitch, this is mind-blowing. Dennis told me what to expect, but I guess I had no idea of the magnitude, how intense things would be. In another sense, it's difficult to imagine that people *do* this." Mitch said, "Yeah, I hear you. I remember my first *Lifestyle* party with Wanda. I pretty much felt the same way. It was about five years ago when she and I first got involved. The reality is, people definitely come here to *play*, and the ladies *will* fuck you mercilessly. But, what Wanda and I have found is the *Lifestyle* truly is a community of kindred spirits. We all work hard, and some of us even have children. We work diligently at maintaining discretion, ours as well as our *play* partners. Yes, it's about sex, but the deeper point is developing friendships. Frankly, sex is simply a bonus, but not the foci, per se. We never thought of it when we started, but there're also business relationships that develop out of the *swinging* community. We have a friend who is a dentist, another an architect, and yet another who sells Volvos! Suffice it to say, we have utilized the business acumen of all three!"

Intrinsically, I was struck by the recurring themes that everyone I met articulated: sex is a big part of the *Lifestyle*, obviously, but not necessarily the ***primary*** focus. Friendship, trust, and respect were terms I heard several people mention. My inner voice tapped me on the shoulder again, saying "Thou shall not covet thy neighbor's wife," but the voice was thematically muffled by the response, "It's **not** adultery if the wife's husband knows!"

Apparently, I was in deep thought wrestling with these issues and appeared to mentally drift because Mitch asked, "Are you okay?" A bit disoriented in thought, I said, "Oh. Yeah, I'm okay, I was just thinking. Mitch, may I ask you a question?" "Of course," he said. "What's **this** all about?" I do not want to spoil the vibe, but I have to admit this is new to me and I'm trying to understand the *Lifestyle*. "I understand what you mean," he said. "I used to spend an inordinate amount of time trying to understand it myself. Believe it or not, I am a philosophy professor! This is not quite the quest for the 'meaning of life', but I think *swinging* is a profoundly, fascinating endeavor."

Mitch went on to say "Modern man has often grappled with issues of life, procreation, marriage, monogamy, sexuality, morality, ethics, infidelity, and so forth. For me, a central question has been, 'What is it about man that he feels a desire to have multiple partners?' The irony, of course, is not every man and woman share this sentiment. What, then, about those who do indulge? Is a *Lifestyler* morally doomed because of his or her sexual activities? Are *Lifestylers* frowned upon by God? Or, for those who believe in God, do they believe they still have redemptive value in God's eyes?"

"From a Biblical perspective, one might consider the questions, 'Does a person who commits a murder a sinner?' Yes! 'Does a person who commits adultery a sinner?' Yes! 'What about in cases of war?' Do soldiers have redemptive value in God's eyes?' Therein lie the quandaries. That is, since a wife and husband give each other permission to *swing*, are they still considered adulterers? And, if they lead otherwise 'moral' lives, will they still be judged as sinners? These are intriguing questions to me as a philosopher. I certainly do not have all the answers, so I have simply learned to accept the *Lifestyle* as one facet of the totality of my existence." I understood what he was saying, yet my moral compass, admittedly, was not quite stable.

Mitch proceeded to share, "Yes, Wanda and I enjoy sex, but for us, it's more about the fellowship amongst our friends who have similar beliefs that having sex with someone else's spouse is not a wicked, damning thing. Wanda and I had some interesting discussions and debates when we were first considering becoming involved in the *Lifestyle*." Mitch laughed and noted, "She is an engineer, so you can just imagine the debates between an engineer and a philosopher about the merits of *swinging*." I laughed, too, and responded, "I can only imagine, my friend, I can only imagine!" I continued, "I greatly appreciate your incisive feedback, Mitch." "No problem, Theo. I hope my philosophical ranting made sense. If you have any other questions, do not hesitate to ask me. Before we leave, I will give you my phone number and email address. Dennis is a really good friend, so if you are a friend of his, you are definitely a friend of mine and Wanda's."

After speaking with Mitch, I could not help but think about the moral and ethical considerations involved in the *Lifestyle*. Once again, more questions than answers. I resigned myself to the fact I would ponder these issues later. For now, there was a beautiful Russian woman who wanted to have sex with me. So, I dismissed the philosophical underpinnings of *swinging* and decided to concentrate on the reason I came to the party. After all, this was a sex party, not a lecture on existentialism!

Chapter 20

I walked towards the backyard to find Svetlana and, as promised, she was in the Jacuzzi. She was accompanied by another Black man whom I did not meet previously. He introduced himself as Dave and then Svetlana chimed in, "Dave is his name, but everyone affectionately calls him Batman." I said, "Uh, okay. It's nice to meet you, Batman." Svetlana asked him to stand up in the Jacuzzi, and he complied. When he stood up, I knew why he held the moniker Batman! He was a slim man, probably in his late fifties, but extremely endowed, at least twelve inches! I have never been insecure or displeased about my size, but this gentleman made the other men at the party seem average, at best. Svetlana showed her appreciation by constantly stroking him while I eased into the Jacuzzi. He seemed to sense my apprehension about calling a grown man Batman, even though I clearly understood why, so he kindly said, "Please, call me Dave. Batman's more of a nickname the ladies call me."

"I hear this is your first *Lifestyle* party," he said. "Yeah, I'm new to the scene, but could not have asked for a better introduction into it. Everyone I've met has been cordial and understanding about my experience, or lack thereof. There has not been any pressure or anything, and the ladies have been most accommodating." "Oh yeah," he said. "the ladies who come to these parties are not bashful about their desires, but it is more than just a sexual romp. That is one reason I come. There is no drama, no false pretenses or anything.

I've even been here on several occasions where I did not even *play*. Everybody is so laid-back, the food is excellent, great music, and it's just a good group of people."

Svetlana started nibbling on his neck as he and I were in the midst of a conversation. It was obvious she was sexually revved-up, and not particularly interested in conversation. That became even more apparent when she asked me *"Teo*, your energy level is okay now, yes?" Her accent was so alluring that I thought better of correcting her mispronunciation of my name. "Svetlana is feeling a bit horny and there is only one thing that is going to cure me, right, Batman?" She continued "Well, actually, it is two things." I asked, "And what might those two things be?" to which she did not say a word. Instead, she grabbed on to my penis and Dave's simultaneously. "Well, Theo," Dave said, "you heard the lady, so I think we have to help her out."

I got out of the Jacuzzi first and then held Svetlana's hand to help her out. Dave got out afterward and then handed towels to me and Svetlana. We dried off and then the three of us walked through the kitchen and up the stairs. When we reached the top of the stairs, Svetlana motioned for me and Dave to follow her to the bathroom. The large bathroom had marble floors and a stately heir about it. Additionally, there was a walk-in shower that easily could have held five people in it. I noticed that, in addition to a shower, it had the capacity to be a steam room.

Svetlana turned the shower on while Dave and I followed. The cool water flowed down her ample breasts and summoned her nipples to attention. I got in front of her while Dave went behind. He and I massaged her body while she maintained an iron clad on our crotches. Her breathing became deeper and louder, and every time we touched her, she emitted slight moans while arching her back. I started soaping her body while Dave caressed and played with her nipples, which by now looked like tiny stones.

I bent over and began soaping her legs and feet, moving my hands upward very slowly. She parted her legs so I started massaging her labia. Her hips were now gyrating in a circular motion, and Dave started kissing her on the neck while his hands remained magnetized to her nipples. I used my left hand to rub her legs and then used my right index finger circularly, but counter-clockwise on her clitoris.

Svetlana's body was writhing and she began moaning loudly before finally commanding, "Let's go to the bedroom, now! I want **both** of these delicious cocks!" We got out of the shower and I proceeded to dry her off while she and Dave kissed. Even as I dried her body, my finger never retreated from her clitoris, but when I inserted my finger into her wetness, her body began to convulse.

We went to one of the unoccupied bedrooms and Svetlana jumped on the bed, spread her legs wide, and said, "Come here, gentleman, I have something for you both." Dave and I looked at each other and smiled before he said, "Welcome to the *Lifestyle*, Theo, I defer to you." "Thanks, Dave," I said, before proceeding to lie next to Svetlana.

Instinctively, she and I groped each other frantically as if we were college lovers separated after graduation, only to reconnect years

127

later. My lips found her nipples and she wrapped her legs around my waist. She thrust me on my back and then ventured downward to feast on my hardness. I saw Dave putting on a condom as he moved behind her. She was on her knees, butt pointing northward, so he spread her ankles. She let out a deep sigh as he entered her. Her body moved forward as he slid inside her, and his length caused her a brief, but pleasurable moment of anguish. "Go slow, Batman. You have to work that thing in me slowly."

Dave coached, "I'll just put the head in, Svetlana, so you just move your hips back when you think you're ready. We are in no rush, so take your time, baby." She moved her hips back slightly, but he was still too big for her. I began to soften in her mouth, briefly, because I could feel her teeth beginning to clinch. I pulled out of her mouth and just rubbed myself on her lips and face. "Slap my face with it, *Teo*." I complied and proceeded to slap my penis on her face and lips. I could tell she was excited because she began moving back on Dave's humongous erection with more voracity. Dave said to her, "You like that big dick stretching you out, don't you?" and she wailed, "Yes! Push it in some more!" I have never been too keen on getting a blowjob, especially when too many teeth were involved. So, I felt perfectly comfortable keeping it out of her mouth, particularly since she enjoyed it being rubbed and slapped against her face.

Dave's pace and intensity increased, and the more both did, the louder Svetlana groaned, accompanied by a barrage of grunts, gasps, and occasional rants of "Oh God! Slow down! Okay, right there!

Deeper!" Dave started thrusting in and out of her frenetically, and she took every inch. It was obvious she was turned on, but I could not refrain from jokingly saying "Man, you're going to get a felony charge the way you're killing that pussy!" He responded, "Brother, you don't know Svetlana. She **loves it deep and hard**. Just wait, you'll see." At that, Svetlana shouted, "You know how I like it. Get in there, Batman, and pound it!"

I moved my body to the side of her because her head was bumping against my balls and that was too uncomfortable. While Dave thrust in and out of her, I got out of the bed and retrieved a condom. He asked, "Are you ready? You need to try some of this good pussy." I was about to get behind Svetlana to do her doggy-style, but before I could, she looked at me and said, "I have **got** to have a *DP*!" I asked, "What's a *DP*?" She smiled and said, "Batman, tell *Teo* what it is" and he quickly said, "Double penetration." They knew I was a novice to the *Lifestyle*, so they didn't make me feel silly when I, like an excited and confused teenager, asked, "Do you mean one in your ass and one in your pussy?" Svetlana cooed, "Dah! Dah!" which was Russian for "yes."

I had seen that position in pornographic movies, but had no personal experience, and I couldn't mask the surprised expression on my face. In fact, I briefly stood there dumbfounded until Svetlana said, "So, would you like to try it?" "If that's what you want, I'm willing to give it a try." She instructed, "Batman, you lay on your back and I will get on top and straddle you. *Teo*, you have the honor of my 'back door,' if you don't mind. I do not think I am quite ready to let Batman go there." I thought to myself, "This is some truly wild shit!" Verbally, though, I answered, "Sure, why not?

Dave lay on his back while Svetlana mounted him. She eased down, and when he completely entered her, she belted, "Damn, you're huge, but I *love* it!" I retrieved some *Wet* lubrication from the nightstand and applied an ample amount on my condom. She and Dave got into a rhythm that began slowly, but quickly increased to the point she was virtually bouncing up and down on his firm slab. Svetlana used her finger to suggest it was time for me to get behind her. I inserted my pinkie finger into her anus to loosen it up. It was but a mere couple of minutes before she whimpered "Now, two fingers in." I did, followed by three!

When she was sufficiently loose, she said, "I'm ready, *Teo*. Go slow, though, please." She leaned all the way forward to the point her chest was pressed against Dave's. Dave moved both his legs together and mine were on the outer sides of his. Svetlana pushed her hips in the air and I placed the head inside. "I'll keep it there, so you just move back on it when you're ready." The head went in slowly and made a plopping sound. She pushed back further, inching more of me inside her tightness. Dave remained still while Svetlana groaned, "Okay, *Teo*, push. That's it, a little more. Wait! Okay, push..." I tried to comfort her by asking, "Are you okay? Take your time, I won't move." She dismissed my chivalry by abruptly saying, "Okay, that's it. Give it to me! Pound it, *Teo*, pound it!"

Dave and I got into a rhythm where whenever he pulled out of her, I pushed in. Like synchronized pistons, we jabbed her inner walls to the extent that the faster, deeper, and harder we thrust, the more she screamed for more! Svetlana was begging loudly, and when I looked to my right, I saw Stephanie, Dennis, Mitch, Barbara, Rick, and Wanda. Barbara got on her knees and began blowing Mitch while Rick bent Stephanie over the edge of the bed and entered her. Barbara took Mitch out of her mouth, briefly, to utter, "That's it, Svetlana, you naughty slut. Take those big cocks!" Dennis laid Wanda on the floor and buried his face between her legs.

Everyone was either grunting or moaning, and the sounds of sex excited me tremendously. I wondered if I was a closet voyeur because it seemed the more I watched the others, the harder I got and deeper I explored Svetlana. Then, out of nowhere, my primal sexual desires were overcome with the reality of watching Rick fucking the daylights out of Stephanie! At first, it was just visual, but swiftly became cerebral. "Oh, shit," I said to myself, "Stephanie is fucking another man!" My emotions bounced around like electrical ions, no destination, just pure chaos. *What the hell did I get myself into?*

The Viagra helped me maintain an iron-like erection, but watching Stephanie enjoy another man's dick almost led to my flaccidity. I felt myself getting soft, but Svetlana kept thrusting back on me, and she continued to moan ravenously, so I quickly recovered. I told myself, "Get over it, Theo! Remember, Stephanie is *not* your lady." When that reality set-in, I relaxed and focused on pleasing Svetlana and, ironically, began to get turned-on seeing and hearing Stephanie have a good time. "After all," I said to myself, "it does *not* look like Stephanie is worried about you, so you may as well have a good time. You were not complaining when Stephanie was with Lupe, so why the hypocrisy when she's with Rick? This is all about fun, so get over it."

I heard Dave grunt, "I'm going to cum, Svetlana!" She responded, "I want you to shoot that cum all over my tits!" I, too, was near orgasm, and yelled, "I'm about to cum, too!" to which Svetlana yelled, "Dah! Dah! I want both of you to unload all over me!" Almost simultaneously, Dave and I shouted, "Here it comes!" and, with that, I pulled out of Svetlana's tight hole and ripped my condom off. She hurled herself to the side of Dave, cupped her tits and squeezed them together, shouting "Give it to me, right here!" Dave lunged upward and got on his knees to the right of Svetlana while I did the same, but to her left. Within seconds, her nipples were covered with globs of semen as Dave and I jerked our dicks, milking them of every drop, splashing on her perky nipples. She rubbed our juices all over her chest, let out a long, "Ahh!" and then said, "You guys fucked the hell out of me!" As if she were maintaining some type of *swinger* etiquette, she said to Rick and Barbara, "I love you horny rascals. You always have the best parties where I let my inner slut out. That was the best *DP* I have *ever* had!"

Svetlana, Dave, and I laid on the bed while the others continued their sexual frenzy. One-by-one, there were an assortment of final affirmations such as "Oh God, I'm cumming!" "Yes, right there!" as well as "You fucked me thoroughly!" Virtually every muscle on my body ached, and I was sexually satiated, but the Viagra was still affecting me. I was not as firm because I had just ejaculated, but the tingling sensation reminded me that, if necessary, I had the capacity to spring right back into action. As much as I thought about having more sex, I decided I had enough and would spend the rest of the evening relaxing and getting to know the other *swingers*. Barbara came over to me and said, "Well, Theo, I hope you are enjoying your first *Lifestyle* party" to which I responded, "Barbara, I had no idea of what to expect, but, everyone showed me a great time." The demeanor of everyone in the room was lighthearted, so I jokingly asked of no one in particular, "Does this mean I am an official *swinger* now?" Everyone laughed and then Svetlana grabbed my dick and said, "Yes! You swing **this** in Svetlana whenever you want."

We all regrouped and then headed downstairs to the kitchen, Jacuzzi, and pool respectively. Dennis walked over to me as I was drinking a glass of water and said, "I noticed how you responded when you saw Rick fucking Stephanie." I said, "Yeah, for a minute, the insecurity bug bit me." "I figured that," he said. "I kind of sensed earlier today how your body language was elevated when you talked about the time you spent with her. Obviously, I could tell you had a good time with her this afternoon, yet I also sensed you viewed her more than just a sex partner." He asked, "Do you really 'dig' her?"

133

Dennis is my best friend, and he knows me inside-out, so it was futile being coy with him. "I like her vibe, Dennis. She's a nice lady, smart, goal-oriented, witty as hell, and fun to be around. Yes, the sex was torrential, but it was not all about that. Frankly, I had no clue it was going to happen, which probably made it even more special." He responded, "I hear you loud and clear, Theo, and I understand where you're coming from. I actually think you and Stephanie would make a great couple. However, you know she is a *swinger*, so that's something you have to be mindful of, if nothing else, for your own well-being. That's just a little food for thought, and you know, contextually, that I'm just looking out for you." I responded with "I appreciate that, Dennis, we definitely have to talk more about this before I go back to Los Angeles."

Dennis asked me if I was ready to leave so I told him "I had a great time, but have run out of steam, so I'm ready to leave, too. I want to take a shower first if that's okay with you." "No problem," he said. "I'm going to take one, too." I went upstairs to shower. The warm water comforted my depleted body, and before I began to lather myself, I stood there enjoying the sound and feel of the water. Suddenly, the lights went off and I heard the door close. The patter of feet echoed off the marble floor before I felt hands rubbing against my chest. It was Stephanie and she whispered in my ear, "I hope you had a good time, Theo." I clinched her body against mine and began kissing her neck, all the while running my hands across her breasts. I nibbled on her ear lobe and whispered back, "I had a great time,

Stephanie, and you made it all the more special. I could not have asked for a better experience, so I thank you for helping me create memories to last a lifetime." "That's sweet of you," she said, as our tongues explored the other's mouth.

Stephanie told me she was preparing to leave the party as well and asked if I wanted to spend the night at her home. I responded, "I think that's a great idea. I'll let Dennis know, and I'm sure he'll understand. Besides, knowing him, I would not be surprised if he takes one of the ladies here home with him." She laughed, "You are very astute, Mr. Handsome. Do not be surprised if he tells you he is taking Lupe back to his place. That usually happens when they see each other at parties. She is so much fun to be around and just an all-around free-spirited person. Sexually, when they get together, they simply cannot get enough. She continued, "Enough about all that. Are you up for one of my patented hand jobs?" I felt comfortable around Stephanie, even giddy, so I said, "Lather it up and slap it down." She planted her lips on mine and blurted "You are a nut!"

After the shower and Stephanie's knee-buckling hand job, I was so relaxed my entire body felt like mush. As she and I were in the bedroom putting our clothes on, Dennis was coming up the steps. He peeked into the room and said, "Knock, knock. Am I interrupting anything?" "No, not at all," I said. "Cool, I'm going to take a quick shower and then we'll head out. Lupe is going to follow us back to my place." My eyes connected with Stephanie's, and she had a devilish twinkle that conveyed a message that made words superfluous, that

"I told you so" look. Before Stephanie could gloat, I said to Dennis, "I'm going to spend the night at Stephanie's, so you and Lupe can make all the noise you wish. I suspect if I went back to your place that I would not get much sleep with Lupe there anyway, so it all balances out." "You got that right," he said, and added, "She actually asked me if I thought you would be up for double-teaming her at my place. I think I can handle things, though." I was giddy, so I chided, "I bet you can, Max Julian!"

Chapter 21

After Stephanie and I were dressed, we went downstairs where most of the party goers were in the kitchen. The party was winding down, so everyone was saying there customary goodbyes, all of which had the commensurate amount of kissing, groping, and even sucking. Barbara and Rick approached me and thanked me for coming. Barbara was kind enough to say "Theo, you are such a gentleman and, of course, a terrific sex partner. I certainly hope our paths cross again. Rick and I will be visiting California next summer. Our original plan was to visit San Diego, but I think I can convince him that we need to visit Los Angeles instead." We hugged, kissed, and she gave me her business card. "Call me anytime," she said. I felt welcomed by Rick and Barbara, and they both seemed to be genuinely good people. I told them, "Rick and Barbara, thank you both for your hospitality. This was *the* most fun I have had in too, too many years! Hell, I am surprised I can still walk after all that. You hot ladies wore me out. Most important, thanks for making my first *Lifestyle* party such a memorable one."

Svetlana walked up to me and thanked me, and candidly stated, "I enjoyed meeting you, *Teo*. You fucked Svetlana well. Stressful week, and I needed that!" One thing I learned about *Lifestylers* was that they were brutally honest and never minced for words, particularly the topic of sex. "Svetlana," I said, "if your travels ever bring you to Los Angeles, please let me know" as I handed her my business card.

She looked at the card and asked, "You work for Premier Cosmetics? Svetlana loves their products! No wonder I felt a special connection to you." I thanked her for her compliment, but knew intrinsically her perceived connection had more to do with my physical, sexual prowess than my cosmetics line. Nevertheless, I told her how much I enjoyed meeting her, and reminded her I, too, enjoyed the sex.

I walked over to Mitch and Wanda and thanked Mitch for his philosophical insight into the *swinging* community. We exchanged business cards and he told me, "My publisher is sending me on a book tour from mid-July to late August, right before my semester begins. My latest book just came out, so I will be doing the lecture circuit. I'll have some stops in California at UC-Irvine, UCLA, UC-Santa Barbara, Stanford, and UC-Berkeley. Let's keep in contact, and I hope we can connect when I am in the Los Angeles area. Wanda will be with me, so I know she will want to see Los Angeles and, of course, *party* a little bit."

"I would like that very much, Mitch," I responded. "By the way, what is your book about?" He told me his book was a philosophical critique and comparison of Dr. Martin Luther King, Jr., Marcus Garvey, Dr. W.E.B. DuBois, Booker T. Washington, and Elijah Muhammad. "In a proverbial nutshell," he said, "an examination of their work reveals they had more similarities than differences, but, in some cases, different approaches. I believe they all were correct in varying degrees, and all addressed philosophical issues about humanity, race, spirituality, social justice, ethics, and so forth.

Imagine if there were a way to combine everything they stood for, and put that recipe in a collective, concerted program. Whew! That would be powerful indeed." I countered, "Sounds pretty heavy, Mitch. I am fairly well-read, so I will be sure to come out and support you when your book promotion comes through Los Angeles."

Wanda approached. "It was a pleasure meeting you, Theo! It is too bad we did not get a chance to *party*, but you are definitely the type of guy we have in our circle of friends. We will have to make-up for that when Mitch and I visit Los Angeles in the next couple of months. Is that a deal?" I gave her a peck on the lips and said, "Oh, yes, Wanda. That *is* a deal, you can count on that!"

Before we said our final goodbyes to everyone, Lupe walked up to me and spoke in English. "I was hoping to *play* with you again later, but Dennis told me you were spending the night at Stephanie's. Hopefully, I will see you before you go back to Los Angeles, but if I do not, thanks for a great evening. I hope to see you again." "Lupe," I said, "you made a *very* favorable impression on me, and I hope to see you again, too. You are absolutely beautiful, and you have a wonderful personality. Oh, did I forget you are so damn sexy, too?" She smiled and kissed me on the cheek before walking towards the door.

Dennis came downstairs and told me, "I'll connect with you tomorrow. I don't have anything planned, so hang out as long as you wish with Stephanie. Just give me a buzz if you want to get into something." "Dennis," I said, "thanks for a hell of a time, man. All this would not have happened were it not for you. Everyone I met was just amazing, and it speaks volumes to the type of person you are. Thanks, man." We hugged each other and agreed to meet-up sometime on Sunday.

Chapter 22

Stephanie and I held hands as we walked towards her car. "I am so worn out," she said. "Do you mind driving, Theo?" "Of course not," I said, "just tell me which way to go and I will take care of the rest." I opened the passenger door and helped her get comfortable. Before I closed the door, I leaned over and kissed her on the forehead. As I walked around to the driver's side, I thought about how much I liked her beyond our mutual sexual attraction. I felt that she, too, had a connection to me. The way we looked at each other, smiled at each other, and touched each other suggested to me our admiration had the capacity to grow well beyond bedroom romps.

We drove off and she reclined her seat. After giving me directions to her place, she immediately dozed off. She looked so peaceful, and when I was able to drive without using the stick-shift, I placed my right hand on her left hand and caressed it. When she felt my presence, she awoke and reached over to kiss me on the cheek. I was encouraged yet surprised when she said, "I like you, Theo. You are a gentleman, fun to be around, and so compassionate. That goes a long way with me, so I want you to know I appreciate that." "Stephanie," I said, "I feel the same about you. I have to admit that, yes, I enjoy having sex with you, but it is different from other experiences I've had. I'm not sure if that makes sense, but I want you to know I like you, too. Even though I have only known you a couple of days, it seems like I've known you for much, much longer because you are so easy to get along with."

She went into humor mode by impersonating a Southern belle, cooing, "Well, I do deee-clare. If I didn't know any betta', I would think you were trying to get into my lil' panties." I laughed and said, "Well, Scarlett, you got *that* right!" She played along further by saying, "Well, my Southern gentleman, it would be mighty hard to get inside my lil' panties cuz', oops, I don't seem to have any on." She put her finger in her mouth, acting like she was an embarrassed damsel, but that persona subsided when she spread her legs, teasing, "See! Oh my goodness, I seemed to have misplaced my lil' panties. Where-oh-where could they be?" We both burst into laughter, and as I abruptly pulled the car to the curb, we kissed passionately. I leaned over to her seat and began kissing her neck, then her nipples, while my fingers explored her inner thighs, which were spread wide.

I was tempted to pull my pants down and position myself between her legs in the passenger seat. Instead, my rational side prevailed, so I was content with kissing and heavy petting, at least until we arrived at her place. After several minutes of intense fondling, I said, "We better save this until we get to your place" and she responded, "That is a good idea. I don't think the police in this area would appreciate pulling up on two people having public sex"

We finally arrived at her home and I helped her get out of the car. Then, I carried her to the front door and helped her stand to open the door. Once inside, we kissed and rubbed each other even more in the foyer. Our grip on each other remained as we took our clothes off while walking towards the spiral staircase. She was in front of me going up the stairs, and as we ascended, I massaged her round, firm butt. By the time we reached the top of the stairs, our clothes had been tossed to every part of the living room. We immediately went to the bedroom where she lit a candle and I pulled the comforter back. I crawled under the sheets and then she joined me.

"Stephanie," I said, "I want to show you how much you turn me on" so I proceeded to move downward and spread her legs. "I am going to touch, lick, and massage *every* part of your being, so just relax and be pampered." I started massaging her feet, making sure that every toe was attended to. I proceeded upward by kissing her ankles, calves, and inner thighs. As I nibbled, she instinctively arched her back, wrapping her legs around my shoulders to lure my head further between her legs. The pace of her hips increased, and the result was my face buried between the crevice of her legs. I used my fingers to spread her labia before I inserted my tongue. She was moist, so my finger glided in. I pleasured her with my tongue and finger while using my free hand to fondle her breasts. She moaned, "Damn, Theo! You are something else, baby!" I countered, "This is *all* about you, Stephanie. I want to please you, my dear. When you are pleased, I am pleased."

For the next hour, we continued at a frenetic pace, licking, sucking, and massaging. Eventually, I penetrated her. Afterward, we lay exhausted and fell asleep in each other's arms. I realized before I finally ventured into dreamland that Stephanie, to me, was not just a sex partner. I felt whatever would become of our relationship that we would be friends for many years. I also realized I was beginning to embrace feelings of vulnerability, perfectly content with sharing my feelings with her. And, I finally confronted the voice that previously resonated inside my mind, the one that pierced my brain with "Can you handle being in a relationship with a woman who is a *swinger*?" I considered the consequences as I looked at her sleeping peacefully and then confirmed, "I'm at least willing to give it a try."

Chapter 23

The soothing aroma of dandelions, roses, *Earl Gray English Tea*, mangoes, and oranges curled through my nostrils when I awoke. I was ravenous, and groggily peered at the tray table Stephanie placed adjacent to the bed. She greeted me with "Good morning, Mr. Handsome! Did you sleep well?" She pounced on the bed and we embraced. "I slept very well, thank you," I responded. "And you?" "Well," she said, "the last thing I remember was falling asleep on top of you. You curled my toes, you naughty man." I chuckled and said, "Give yourself some credit. You wore me out as well. My entire body is satiated, and I feel as if I ran a triathlon. But, that is ***not*** a complaint."

We kissed deeply, rolled to and fro in the bed, and then she said, "Let's eat first" to which I responded, "Oh, I have no problem eating ***you*** for breakfast!" She playfully tapped me on the head and countered, "Uh, I'm talking about the food, horny rascal." I said, "Oh yes, the food."

I placed the tray on the bed and we shared a tasty omelet. We alternated feeding each other slices of mangoes and oranges. After breakfast, we both sighed and lay back on the bed while staring through the skylight ceiling. She asked, "So, what are you and Dennis going to do since this is your last day in Chicago?" "I don't know," I said. "I will call him shortly to see what he wants to do. I suspect he and Lupe are either still asleep or fucking. Is there anything you want to do?" She responded, "I know you came to Chicago to see

Dennis, so I don't want to monopolize your time." "That's sweet of you," I said, and then I kissed her on the forehead.

I got out of the bed to retrieve my cell phone from my pants, but recognized my pants were somewhere on the living room floor. I went downstairs to get my phone and called Dennis. "Hey man, this is Theo. Are you and Lupe up yet?" His voice was groggy, but he managed to say, "Actually, she just left. We woke up early this morning and fucked like rabbits. Man, she has a ***lot*** of energy and just can't get enough dick." "You stud," I said. "So, what do you want to get into today?" Dennis told me he did not have anything planned and wanted me to let him know what my interests were. "I'm wide open," I said. "I don't feel the need to run around, so it's up to you." "Well," he said, "if you want, we can go see the Phillies and Cubs today. They are playing this afternoon at Wrigley Field at 3:00p.m. My company has box seats there, so we can check that out." I said, "That would be cool. I have not seen my Phillies play in a while, so I have been forced to adopt the Dodgers, albeit temporarily. Come playoff time, you know I have to go with my Phillies, though. Speaking of that, remind me to call your parents today."

We hung up and then I went back upstairs to hop into bed with Stephanie. She was reading the Sunday edition of the *Tribune*. I was surprised when I noticed she was reading the *Sports Section*. "Are you a sports fan?" and she replied, "Oh God yes! I love Chicago sports teams." I perked up and said, "Dennis and I are going to see the Cubs and Phillies play today. Would you like to join us?" I was struck by her sentiments of not wanting to be a "third wheel" when she told me "The two of you should spend some time together. You have not seen each other in a while so you should hang out and do some male bonding."

Truthfully, I actually wanted her to join us, but she was correct. I had not seen Dennis in several years, and even though we spoke regularly on the phone, we did need some time to reconnect. "Thanks, Stephanie," I said, "but if you want to go that's cool with us." "Nah," she said, "you boys need to be boys and do the baseball, hotdogs, and beer thing. I will be okay, so it's fine."

Stephanie and I laid in bed watching television for a while before I looked at the clock. "I'll hop in the shower around 11:00a.m. or so and then head over to Dennis's place. Is that cool with you?" "Yes," she said. "We can leave here by noon and that will give you time to get to Dennis's and then go to the game."

I leaned over Stephanie and picked-up the *Business Section* of the *Tribune*. It had been a few days since I examined the stock performance of my company, *Premier Cosmetics*. I was making very good money as an employee of the company, so two years ago I decided to buy stock as well. At the time I brought into *Premier*, its shares were hovering around $32.00 per share. Now, shares were going at $37.50 per share. By no means was I an investment whiz, but I knew I wanted my stock portfolio to be broad. Over the years, I purchased small shares of relatively secure companies, and made sure no particular industry dominated my holdings.

I started out with 200 shares of *Premier Cosmetics*. *Premier* had garnered the majority of cosmetics industry market share, about 54%. We were beginning to branch out and capitalize on our Marketing Research Department's forecast, which was the impending growth of people buying products via the internet. At the time, my work schedule was even more hectic because I spent more hours traveling overseas to broaden our global brand appeal.

One of my friends from business school, Keenan Rice, graduated at the same time as me and Dennis. Keenan went on to become a Futures Trader and lived in New York City. He worked at a large global investment firm and led a very comfortable lifestyle, so I always listened attentively to his investment guidance. We kept in contact over the years, and he always admonished me, "Keep your portfolio diverse. Never rely on one industry!" I had 30 shares of *IBM*, 20 shares of *Microsoft*, 25 shares of *Pfizer Pharmaceuticals*, 10 shares of *Browning-Ferris*, 15 shares of *Kraft*, and 10 shares of *Proctor & Gamble*. The performance of my portfolio was steady and I periodically received fairly decent dividend checks over the years.

When I first purchased shares of *Pfizer Pharmaceuticals* in the mid-1990's, they focused on consumer pharmaceuticals and various medical innovations. They became the breakthrough pharmaceutical company to finally harness, and receive FDA approval, for a drug, Viagra, that enhanced men's sexual performance. I found it humorously ironic, too, that my weekend excursion to Chicago would lend me the benefit of one of my holdings' products.

Stephanie looked over at me as I read the *Stocks* page of the *Tribune*. I playfully transformed myself into Dan Aykroyd's character in the movie *Trading Places*, Winthorp, and muttered, "Pork bellies! Hmmm. I have a hunch something very exciting is going to happen in the pork belly market this morning!" She grabbed the paper, swatted me with it and said, "You are so goofy." "What can I say?" I said, "I love those Eddie Murphy movies like *Trading Places* and *Coming To America*. I know just about every line of both those movies, and the barbershop scenes in *Coming To America* are classic! I could watch a whole movie of those barbershop scenes. Call me goofy if you will, but I prefer to call myself a novice thespian." "Okay. Well, you better get your thespian butt in the shower." I said, "See, you don't appreciate raw talent when you see it. When I 'blow up' in Hollywood, you'll be asking for my autograph. Don't forget, I *do* have Halle Berry's cell phone number!"

Stephanie and I showered, but this time we concentrated on actually cleaning our bodies rather than ravishing each other. Our previous forays into the shower always resulted in orgasms for both of us. This time, though, we simply enjoyed soaping each other up and feeling the hot water roll off our bodies.

We dressed and then headed over to Dennis's place. Stephanie took the scenic route, which included driving along the bank of Lake Michigan. The sun was shining brightly and it was an ideal day for baseball. I asked her, "Are you sure you don't want to go to the game with us?" "Yes," she said, "I'm sure. It would be nice, but you and

Dennis have not really spent much time together. On Friday, you went to *The Spot*. Yesterday, you hung out with me and then went to the party. You leave tomorrow, so today is the only real opportunity for you to be together." "You're right," I said. "The weekend has flown by and I will be leaving tomorrow. Now that I think about it, I have not seen him much."

We pulled up to *The Ridgecrest* a few minutes after noon. I was hoping to see Mr. James when we got to *The Ridgecrest*, but there was another doorman who approached the car. "Good afternoon, sir," he said. I responded, "Hello there. Is Mr. James off today?" The doorman said, "Yes. He only works Tuesday through Saturday. I can leave him a message if you wish, sir." "No thanks," I said. "I'm visiting Dennis Warfield."

I proceeded around the car to say goodbye to Stephanie. She got out of the car and we stood before the other, admiring ourselves without saying a word. She moved forward and hugged me and then we pulled back and looked directly into each other's eyes. Neither of us still had said a word, but our body language spoke: *I do not want to leave you.*

Finally, I said, "Stephanie, I really, really enjoyed meeting you. My weekend would not have been half the fun were it not been for you. I knew from the moment I saw you at *The Spot* that we would get along well. You invited me into your home, treated me like a king, and helped me appreciate some things in life I never thought about, or had long since forgotten. Thank you, Stephanie." She hugged me and countered, "Thank you, too, Theo. I felt that connection as well when I met you at *The Spot*. Dennis told me so much about you that I probably looked forward to seeing you more than he. Everything he told me about you was accurate, and then some. I ***really*** hope this is not the last time I see you, is it?"

We kissed and then I told her, "I assure you, Stephanie, our paths ***will*** cross again." She got into her car and I bent over to kiss her on the forehead after closing the door. Before she drove off, she said, "Oh, before I forget, I wanted to let you know I played 'telephone tag' with my realtor friend, Scott, in Philadelphia. I will keep you posted, but I did leave him a message regarding you looking for property there." I smiled and told her, "You are so thorough, and I like that. We'll talk later, my sexy friend." Before she revved off, she blew me a kiss and shouted, "I look forward to it... Winthorp!"

Chapter 24

When I reached Dennis's condo, music was curling from beneath the door. I rang the doorbell twice and there was no response. I was about to push the bell a third time when he opened the door, a towel wrapped around his waist and shaving cream on his face. I said, "You are always blasting that damn music. Your hearing is going to go bad before you reach fifty if you are not careful." He responded sarcastically with, "Yes, dear" as he walked towards the bathroom.

I went over to the stereo and turned the tuner down several decibels even though he was playing one of my all-time favorite tunes, *Summer Madness*, by Kool and the Gang. I walked in during the synthesizer solo, relished it briefly, and then went to the bathroom where Dennis was shaving. "How did things go with Lupe?" I asked. "Man, she is something else!" he said. "I don't think we went to sleep until damn near 5:00a.m.! Hell, at one point I wanted to call you and Stephanie over to take some pressure off me." We laughed and then he asked me about my evening with Stephanie. "It went very well," I said. "She is a hell of a lot of fun and a blast to be around."

I further confided, "I really 'dig' her, Dennis. It's been a while since I had a serious relationship, but if I were to venture into that direction, I would definitely consider her. Don't get me wrong, I know I just met her, but all things considered, she seems to be the 'total package.'" Dennis put his razor down and peered at me before asking, "Are you saying you think you might love her?" "I am ***not*** saying that!" I said. "What I am saying is she is the first lady in several years that has stimulated me on *all* levels. She is intelligent, funny, beautiful, independent, and even likes sports. What more can a brother ask for?"

"I hear you, Theo. I understand what you are saying. Believe me, there were times in the past when I wanted to approach her, too, and the feelings were probably mutual. We just never 'went there' and kept it business-like. We both have been in the *Lifestyle* a number of years, and we certainly have had ample opportunities. However, we pretty much became more akin to brother and sister type of friends and never broached anything sexual. I am glad because it seems that when you have sex with someone, who's a friend, the sex messes up the friendship and changes the dynamics. "God knows I have been there," I said.

"Theo," he said, "my suggestion is that you go with your gut feeling. If you really 'dig her' just tell her. We are not getting any older, man. I do not know about you, but I will likely get married one day. Yeah, I enjoy the *Lifestyle*, but there is no reason I cannot get married. And, it is likely that I will marry a woman who is in the *Lifestyle*. It's not mandatory, one way or the other, but I am at the stage in my life where if that happens, I will embrace it."

I could feel the ping in my stomach when he mentioned marrying a woman in the *Lifestyle*. "That," I said, "is what kind of concerns me at this point. I had to check my emotions last night when I saw Rick fucking Stephanie. At first, I felt jealous, borderline anger for that matter. But then reality hit me. I was like, 'How can I be mad and jealous when I am sitting here doing a DP on Svetlana?' Reality hit me even harder when I realized I was jealous of Rick fucking a mere associate of mine, yet I had already fucked his wife! I was trippin' for a minute."

I continued, "Fortunately, it did not take me long to regroup, but I have to admit I felt that way initially. I'm still wrestling with all this *swinger* stuff, so I have to give this some serious thought. It would not be my place to tell Stephanie that she would have to quit the *Lifestyle* if she and I got involved in a relationship. I'm just confused, man."

"The bottom line is, I have to take time to make sense of all this. It contradicts **everything** I have ever learned about monogamous relationships. And, it damn sure is antithetical to the way my parents raised me! I guess you could say I have some soul searching to do."

Dennis sensed I was struggling with these issues and, as usual, soothed me with his brotherly advice. "Hey man, I am here for you. If I can be of any guidance and support, do not hesitate to let me know. You are a brother to me, and I will always look out for your best interests. Do what is best for your mind, body, and soul. Whatever you decide, you have my steadfast support!" I said to him, "I know I do, brother, and I thank you for that."

Just as we finished that discussion, Weather Report's tune, *Procession*, filled the air. I shouted, "Man, I have not heard that cut in ages! That's one of my favorite tunes by Weather Report. I saw The Joe Zawinul Syndicate at the Hollywood Bowl last year and he was amazing." "Oh yeah," Dennis said. "Weather Report had some of the best jams during the *Fusion* era. By the way, what time is it? We better get going soon." I looked at my watch and told him it was 12:45.

Dennis told me we needed to leave around 1:30 so I went to the bedroom and grabbed a pair of jeans, sneakers, and my favorite t-shirt of Dizzy Gillespie, from my luggage. The classic t-shirt of Dizzy blowing a huge wad of bubblegum always elicited conversation among other Dizzy admirers. So, I thought I would dress Dizzy-cool for the ballgame. I ironed my clothes and Dennis called Wrigley Field to confirm that two of his firm's box seats would be used for today's game. He hung up the phone and told me it would be best to ride the El to Wrigley Field, especially since we'd be drinking alcohol.

A large crowd was already gathering when we arrived a block from Wrigley Field. "Man," I said, "Chicago fans love their baseball." My cynicism of the franchise's success contributed to an additional, "It's a shame they will not win the whole thing this year." Dennis laughed and said, "Ain't that a bitch! Actually, what team are you rooting for **this** year? Is it the Dodgers? Phillies? Yankees? Oops, I need to check the standings to see which team is your **current** favorite! You have more favorite teams than the league itself." I could not resist laughing as well because he had me cornered. "Come on, man, you know I bleed red and white. I grew up watching the Phillies, so I am not about to stop now."

"Yeah, I root for the Dodgers because I live in Los Angeles, but my heart is in Philadelphia. Your father gave me shit about the

155

Dodgers when I spoke with him yesterday and, of course, thinks 'his' Braves are going all the way. When I look at all the teams who have the ability, though, I would bet on the Yankees, but I have my fingers crossed for the Phillies." Dennis's response was, "Well, the way things are looking right now, we might see the Cubs and Braves battling it out for the National League pennant. But, you know how baseball is. A team can rattle off a string of wins or losses in a matter of days."

Dennis and I stopped at a bar near the stadium since it was only 2:00p.m. It was my suggestion to stop. I said, "I want to get a feel for Cubs fans, so let's grab a beer before we go inside the stadium." "That's cool with me," he said. We walked into a crowded bar filled with Cubs fans and ordered two Heinekens. There was a small contingent of fans dressed in Phillies jerseys and they were catching hell from Cubs fans. Everyone was civil, though. It was just mild banter about whose team was the best.

When I lived in Philadelphia, I saw my share of Philadelphia Eagles football fans who were some of the rowdiest, potentially dangerous sports fans on earth! On one occasion, I saw Eagles fans throwing hot dogs, mustard and beer at Dallas Cowboy fans in the stadium. Assaults on Cowboys fans were not only commonplace, they were expected. I remember asking myself, "Why do people take this shit so seriously? They are not on the Eagles' payroll and most of them do not know any of the players personally." I enjoyed professional sports, but I kept it all in perspective and referred to players and teams as "they" instead of "we."

We were able to find seats in the corner of the bar where it was not as boisterous. "So," Dennis asked, "what time is your flight tomorrow?" "I leave O'Hare at 11:00a.m. and have a layover in Denver." Dennis asked, "How long is your layover? If you are going to be there a while, we can check *Global Connections* and *Lifestyle Rendezvous* to see if we can get you laid in the *Mile High City*."

I screamed, "You ***must*** be kidding! Are you telling me it is ***that*** easy to hook-up with folks in the *Lifestyle*?" He looked at me intently and affirmed without hesitation, "Yes, Theo, very much so." "Damn," I said, "*swinging* is no joke, huh?" He went on to say, "Like I said before, it is truly a community of like-minded people. And, yes, believe it or not, if you are going to be in Denver for an hour or more, it is ***very*** possible that you could get connected with some *swingers*. Granted, it is short notice, so there are no guarantees, but it is certainly possible. Obviously, it would be contingent upon people's schedules, but the point remains. I am not bullshitting you one bit."

"Further," he continued, "in short notice situations like yours, it could be just an opportunity to meet someone or a couple with the intent of *playing* in the future. Essentially, it could be a 'meet and greet' situation. Like everyone else, *swingers* travel, so they are often looking for fun, clean, and safe people to *play* with in various cities." Still somewhat astonished, I countered, "That is ideal for someone like me who travels nationally and globally. I grapple with the concept, but I have to admit, it is ***very*** intriguing." "Hey man," he said, "stop trying to analyze and dissect it! Instead, just accept it as a part of people's lives. People do it for various reasons. You will be banging your head against the wall trying to understand every situation, trust me on that." I took the last sip of my beer. "I hear you, Dennis, and I will keep everything you said in mind." He gulped the remainder of his beer down and told me it was about that time to head over to the stadium.

Dennis and I were walking out of the bar when I felt a tap on my shoulder. I turned to my right and a college-age White guy said, "Dude! That's a cool shirt. I had *the* coolest professor for a jazz history class in college, and we learned a lot about Dizzy Gillespie. Dizzy rocks, man!" I knew I would not have time to talk with him about Dizzy, so we just exchanged a high five as I concluded, "Oh, hell yeah! Dizzy is *still* one of the baddest musicians to have ever walked the earth!"

Chapter 25

The Cubs smashed the Phillies 9-2. Dennis, of course, took the opportunity to badger me about the game. "I knew we would beat the Phillies!" I said, "We? Who the fuck is we? You mean *they* don't you? I did not know you were on the Cubs' payroll." Proudly, he responded, "Actually, Sherlock, the Cubs' organization is one of my firm's clients. So, technically, I am on the Cubs' payroll, smartass, but I do feel your pain." We both laughed at his comment because he was aware of my disdain for misguided sports fans.

The trip back to *The Ridgecrest* on the *El* was lively because several intoxicated Cubs fans continued celebrating after the victory. I did appreciate Chicago fans' support of the Cubs because their favorite team had come close so many times, yet disappointment always prevailed.

When we got back to Dennis's place, he plopped on the couch while I rustled through his albums. I decided on the live version of *Mr. Magic* by Grover Washington, Jr. This was one of Grover's signature tunes, and I liked it very much. But, I also wanted to play the music of a Philadelphia musician to help me forget about the game. "Ah," Dennis queried, "are you fucking with me by playing that cut? You know I know Grover is from Philadelphia, so I guess that is helping you ease the pain of the ass-whooping the Phillies received from *my* Cubs." I remained silent until I sat on the chaise lounge adjacent to the balcony's sliding door. I feigned ignorance by saying, "He sure is from Philadelphia. I forgot all about that. It never crossed my mind, but it sure is a coincidence." His response was, "You liar!"

Dennis asked me what I wanted to do in the evening, but I really felt content with just relaxing and watching television, which is what I told him. He wanted to make sure I enjoyed my trip to Chicago, so he asked, "Are you sure? We don't have to stay in. I am going to work tomorrow, but I do not want you to feel like we have to chill-out just because of me. We can go out for dinner and I can treat you to a good Chicago steak dinner if you want. Or, I can see if there is any good, live jazz going on tonight. It's up to you, Theo." "Seriously," I said, "I'm okay with just chilling here. Maybe we can have pizza delivered and watch a movie."

Dennis knew me inside and out, so when I mentioned watching a movie, he switched to sarcastic mode. "Oh shit, I bet you are going to make me watch *Coming To America* or, let me guess, *Trading Places*. Hell, you might even be adventurous and choose *Beverly Hills Cop*! Do you ever consider branching out and watching different movies? You *do* know there are a ton of other movies out there, right?" I said, "I know what we better do. It's coming up on 7:30p.m., so whatever we do, we better call your parents.

We talked to Dennis's mother first. She was happy to hear from me again and was especially pleased I decided to visit Dennis. As usual, she asked me if I were getting married anytime soon, and I told her what I always told her, "I need to find me a good country woman, Mrs. Warfield. I have not found one in Los Angeles, yet, but I am

160

looking." She encouraged me to take my time to find the "right one," and I was surprised when she warned, "That's right, Theo. You need a good Southern girl, not one of those 'fast' Valley girls from Los Angeles." I put my hand over the receiver and laughed before asking Dennis, "Hey man, what the hell does your mother know about Valley girls?" He said, "Since she retired, she watches all that bullshit on television and seems to believe everything she sees on the tube. I don't know what has gotten into her, but it drives my father nuts."

I handed the receiver to Dennis and he spoke to his mother for a few minutes before she gave the phone to his father. I was certain his father started talking about the baseball game because I heard Dennis say, "The Braves lucked out today, but it's not over yet. *My* Cubs will be in the playoffs, so don't get too happy too fast, Pop." Dennis handed me the phone and I spoke to Mr. Warfield about the Braves, his favorite topic. He went on to tell me how proud of me he was and how he and his wife would continue to speak with my mother about moving to Atlanta. "Well, Poppa Warfield, I am actually thinking about moving to Philadelphia, and it might be sooner than later. I will keep you and Mama Warfield informed, but that's the way it looks right now. A friend of mine is doing some research on property in Philadelphia, so if I find the right place, I'm moving back out there." He offered encouragement and then we said our goodbyes before hanging up.

When I hung up the phone, I said to Dennis, "Your parents are good people. You are blessed to have them both in your life. Treasure that, Dennis." He responded, "I do not take that for granted, Theo, and I keep in contact with them regularly. I get down there a few times a year and I also bring them up here at least twice a year. I owe them everything."

Chapter 26

My cell phone rang, but it was not in my pocket. "Where the hell is the ringing coming from?" I asked myself. The closer I moved my ears to the floor, the louder the ring was. Apparently, my phone had fallen out of my pocket and made its way under the lounger. On the fourth ring, I was able to reach it. Groggily, I said, "Hello?" "Hey, Theo, it's Stephanie." "Hey, Stephanie," I said. "I did not recognize your voice immediately because I was knocked out!"

I looked around the room and saw that Dennis was snoring on the couch, arms flailed across his chest. "Damn, it looks like Dennis and I crashed out. We went to the baseball game and got back here around 7:30p.m. or so. The last thing I remember, we were listening to music and asking each other what we wanted to do tonight. What time is it?"

Stephanie said it was just after 9:30p.m. She apologized for waking me and asked what time I was leaving for Los Angeles. I told her my flight departed from O'Hare at 11:00a.m. and she asked if I needed a ride to the airport. "Actually, Dennis and I did not even talk about that yet. I know he has to work, so I'm unsure if he is dropping me off or if I need to catch a cab." She barked, "I am *not* letting you catch a cab to O'Hare!"

Dennis moved about on the couch and started to wake up. He, too, was groggy. "Man, I was out of it!" he said. "What time is it? Are you serious, it's really 9:30? You mean I've been asleep almost two hours?" I asked Stephanie to hold so I could respond to Dennis, so I told him "We both fell asleep. The last thing I remember was talking about Weather Report and Joe Zawinul! I just woke up because my phone rang. We've been moving non-stop for the last couple of days and today we sat in the blazing sun and drank a lot of beer. Hell, we are lucky to have pulses! By the way, Stephanie says hi."

Dennis sat up on the couch and rubbed his eyes so vigorously it looked like he was summoning a genie from a bottle! "Tell her I said hi," and continued, "I leave for work at 7:30a.m. I can take you to the airport, but we need to leave here around 6:45a.m." I looked at him, stymied, and said, "I hate sitting in airports just waiting, so I thought about catching a cab. I think Stephanie is going to take me, though."

I returned to the conversation with Stephanie. "Dennis said we would have to leave here at 6:45a.m. if he takes me to the airport. I will take you up on your offer because I do *not* want to wait in O'Hare for over three hours. Stephanie confirmed she would take me to the airport, and that we should leave *The Ridgecrest* no later than 9:30a.m.

Dennis stood up from the couch and yawned like a bear unleashed from hibernation. He said, "I'm going to take a shower and hit the sack. Since Stephanie is taking you to the airport, you may as well ask her to spend the night here since I live closer to O'Hare than she does. She will run into some traffic coming from her place to mine in the morning. I guess the practical accountant in me is surfacing, huh?"

"Actually" I said, "that is a good idea." I returned to my conversation with Stephanie and asked her if she would spend the night with me at Dennis's. The pitch of her response indicated that she, too, thought it was a good idea. "I think that's a fantastic idea! My schedule is wide open tomorrow. The only thing on my calendar is showing a duplex in Hyde Park at 5:30p.m." "Perfect!" I said. She told me she would be at Dennis's in "about an hour."

I heard the bathroom door open and saw the steam curl from within. Dennis asked me if Stephanie would be spending the night. "She thought it was a good idea," I said. "She'll be here in about an hour." "See, I told you," he said. "I'm going to check to see if I have any messages on *Global Connections* or *Lifestyle Rendezvous* and then I am going to bed. I will pop in to say bye in the morning before I go to work. I suspect you and Stephanie will be fucking tonight, so all I ask is that you keep the noise to a minimum, Mr. Max Julian." I laughed and said, "I am so tired, I doubt there will be any major fireworks. When I wake up in the morning, though, ***that*** will be another story. You know that morning 'wood' is like a Ginsu knife!"

Dennis retreated to the bedroom to check his email. I went back to the couch and turned on the television to watch CNN. After hearing a continuous loop of recycled stories, I grew annoyed and decided to take a shower. I wanted to be fresh and clean for Stephanie, especially since I had been sweating profusely at the baseball game. When I finished showering, I went to the bedroom and lightly doused my body with CK Cologne. Dennis was just shutting down his computer and told me he was going to bed.

"Goodnight, Dennis, and thanks again for a hell of a weekend." "No problem, Theo" he said. "I thoroughly enjoyed your company, and it's good we got a chance to vibe. The next time we connect, I will visit you in Los Angeles." "Perfect!" I said. "There is one catch, though." "And what is the catch?" he asked. "You recall I said I am thinking about moving back to Philadelphia to be closer to my mom, right?" "Oh," he said, "yeah, I remember that. It sounds like you are serious about that happening sooner than later."

"Very much so," I said. "Stephanie told me her realtor connection in Philadelphia is going to start looking for me, so I definitely will do it. It is just a matter of when I find the right property. Premier Cosmetics' global headquarters is in New York City, and we have local offices in Philadelphia. So, transferring offices will not be a problem at all." I continued, "I very well may be living in Philadelphia by this time next year, if not sooner." "Well," he said, "wherever you are, I will visit. Is that a deal?" "Deal!" I said. We hugged and then he trudged to his bedroom and closed the door.

Chapter 27

At 11:00p.m. my cell phone rang. I suspected it was Stephanie letting me know of her whereabouts. In fact, I thought she was going to tell me she was en route to Dennis's. I asked her what time she thought she would arrive and she responded, "Psst! Go to the door and look out the peephole." I exclaimed, "You're here?" and she said, "Hurry! It's freezing out here!" I ran over to the door, looked through the peephole and saw her standing. I whisked the door open. "Come on in Stephanie. Why didn't you ring the doorbell?" She said, "It is late and I did not want to make too much noise in case Dennis was in bed. You told me he has to wake-up early, so I figured he would be in bed."

She walked through the doorway and stood alongside me in the foyer. I closed the door and we started kissing. When I looked at her, my brain registered, "Why is she dressed so formally in a London Fog trench coat and wearing 6-inch black pumps?" So, I asked her, "How in the world can you be cold in that big ass trench coat?" My eyes dilated like a mutated cartoon character when I saw what lie beneath the trench coat! She unbuttoned it and my loins recognized why she was cold. The only thing she wore underneath was a black satin lingerie ensemble. She smiled and asked, "Can you warm me up?" I hung her coat in the closet while admiring her body, mentally undressing her. Finally, I rhetorically asked, "Can I warm you up?

Are you kidding? They don't call me 'Microwave' for nothing, my sexy friend!"

I turned off all the electronic equipment, closed the balcony sliding doors, and led her by the hand to the guest bedroom. The comforter had already been pulled, so after I turned the lights off, I lay her on the bed. I massaged her feet as I removed her pumps and proceeded to suck her toes one-by-one. She took the liberty of peeling off her lingerie while I sucked her toes.

I laid on top of her while her open legs welcomed my hardness. Her back arched as I slide into her gently, yet deeply. My body demanded that I continue while my mind echoed, "Theo, you did not put a condom on!" I pulled out and said, "Sorry, about that. I got caught-up in the moment." "I understand," she said. "I did, too. I have to admit I would like to feel you without one." "*That* is an understatement," I said. "You felt so damn good, and you're already soaking wet! I think we better do the right thing for now, though. To be honest, I have been working so many hours that I have not had sex in damn near five months! I better think with the right head."

I grabbed a condom from my luggage. Stephanie lay on the bed masturbating while I placed the condom on. She motioned for me to get back on top of her. Just as we did the first time we fucked, we tried a variety of positions. For the next hour, we pleased each other in myriad ways until I could no longer hold back. "Stephanie, I'm ready to cum, I can't hold it anymore." She replied, "Wait! Let me get on top." She mounted me and rode hard while I pinched her nipples. She, too, was ready to have an orgasm, actually, her third! The pace of my upward thrusts increased until she sensed my impending ejaculation. "Give it to me," she said. I had the most intense orgasm of the entire weekend, and I was satiated.

Our bodies continued to pulsate, and I could feel her rapid heartbeat against my chest. "Damn!" she said, "that was amazing!" "I have absolutely no energy left," I said. Finally, she got up and retreated to the bathroom. I followed her and we decided to take a shower. Afterward, we went back to bed. I stroked her face with my hand while she looked into my eyes intently. "I can get used to this," she said. I followed with, "I can, too. The next time, it will be at my place in Los Angeles. But, who knows. If things work out in Philadelphia, it may be there. So, would you mind visiting me in Philadelphia?" "Wherever it is, Theo, I am there." She kissed me on the lips and pulled me close to her warm body. Within a couple of minutes, she was snoring lightly.

I was tired, but my mind raced and I could not immediately fall asleep. I continued to think about the efficacy of two issues that seared into my brain: One was the prospect of having a serious relationship with a *swinger* and the second was the impractical nature of a long-distance relationship. I asked myself, "How would I introduce Stephanie to my mother?" *Hey mom, this is Stephanie. She and I fuck other people and we have each other's permission.* I also thought, "How would I respond if one of my male friends said to me, 'I recognize you, Stephanie, don't you have a profile on *Lifestyle*

Rendezvous?'" I was besieged by ambivalent feelings about a woman whom I cared about, but was afraid of the stigma associated with being a *swinger*. What kind of man would I be perceived if other people knew my girlfriend had sex with others and I was aware of her trysts?

My mind drifted back to the contradiction of men being rewarded for having multiple partners while women who took multiple partners were labeled as "loose" or, worse, whores. I tried, desperately, to put all those thoughts out of my mind, but they resurrected until I assuaged myself, "If she is a good person and you *really* like her, don't concern yourself with others' perceptions." My thoughts settled and I was finally able clear my mind, but before going to sleep, I decided that I *had* to make a telephone call.

Chapter 28

When I awoke in the morning, I reached over to hold Stephanie, but she was not there. I wiped my eyes and headed to the living room. She was not there either, but I heard noise coming from the kitchen. I walked into the kitchen and saw her leaning over taking slices of bread from a toaster. She was dressed in one of my button-down shirts, and I could tell from the outline of her body she had nothing underneath.

She turned around and said "Good morning, honey!" "Hey!" I said. "You slept like a baby last night. Damn! It's 6:00a.m. What time did you wake up?" "I think it was around 5:45a.m. I thought I would cook you and Dennis some breakfast. I had to improvise because Dennis's refrigerator was, to put it lightly, empty. He did have some bacon, eggs, and coffee, so that will have to do if that's okay with you. There were no biscuits so I had to make toast." "Stephanie, you did not have to do that. You are so thoughtful." She walked over to me and put her hands around my waist. "I take care of my man morning, noon, *and* night!"

Just as we were kissing, Dennis walked into the kitchen, clad in a thick cotton robe. "I see you horn dogs are up early. Or, should I ask, are you up late?" I said, "No. We did get some sleep although not a hell of a lot!" Stephanie swatted me on the butt because of my comment. "The food is ready," she said. The three of us sat at the table eating and then Dennis said, "I cook the same thing every morning, but the way I cook it does not look like *this*!" "That is because you cannot cook worth a damn," I said. Stephanie had a way of transforming the mundane into the exciting, and the meal she cooked was no different. He countered, "Oh, and I guess you are *Wolfgang-fucking-Puck* in the kitchen, huh?"

We all laughed and then I went to the living room. I treaded through CDs and found a tune by Leon Thomas, *Precious Energy.* When I returned to the kitchen, I told them, "This is the ideal cut for now. I'm feeling the precious energy of two *really* good people. Thanks to you both for showing me one hell of a weekend! "Aww, that is so sweet, Theo." Stephanie said. Dennis sat up briskly and asked, "Have you ever thought about being a DJ? You have a keen sense of choosing the perfect tunes at the right time." "Me? Are you kidding? I'm not sure if I am DJ material." "Sure you are!" he said. "You have a good ear for music and I know you have a 'killer' collection at home." "Well," I said, "my Pop left me a ton of vinyl and I have been a novice collector since college. Come to think of it, remember how I used to DJ the parties in grad school?" "Hell, yeah, I remember," Dennis said. "That is yet another reason you might consider it. Besides, I'm sure you can pick-up a few extra dollars in a place like Los Angeles." I said, "Maybe you have a point, Grasshopper. I just may look into that!"

Dennis was the first to finish his meal. "That was abso-damn-lutely delicious! Thank you very much, Stephanie. I better get ready for work." "You're very welcome, Dennis. It was my pleasure to cook for you and Theo. I just hope my cooking will not scare him away." I laughed, "You need to stop, Stephanie. You've piqued my interest in every facet that I can imagine. It's too bad you don't live in Los Angeles." She replied, "Maybe you need to move to Chicago, hint, hint!" "Theo," Dennis said, "you can always stay with me as long as you wish although I suspect someone else at the table would *prefer* you stay with them, hint, hint" With that, he walked out of the kitchen.

"So," Stephanie said, "what do you think about what Dennis said?" "You mean moving to Chicago?" I asked. "Yep, that's what I mean," she said. "Right now, my focus is on moving back to Philadelphia to be closer to my mom since she is there by herself. As tempting as Chicago is, in every way, it's going to be either Philadelphia or, at the very least, moving her to Los Angeles. I know she doesn't want to leave Philadelphia, so it looks like I'll be moving eastward." "I understand," she said. "For quite some time, I have thought about moving east, too. I've lived in Chicago for a long, long time, but I want to go somewhere that is vibrant culturally and socially. New York City is out of the question. I prefer somewhere where the pace is not as frenetic, but still has a lot of history and culture." "Maybe you should consider Philadelphia, too. I think you would enjoy the area, and it is close enough that you can get to New York City in a couple of hours. That is what I miss about the East Coast. In Los Angeles, things are so spread out, but in Philadelphia and New York, you really don't need a car and there is so much to do."

Leon Thomas was just concluding *Precious Energy* with *"Power from the sun... the one and only one... Precious... ennnergy... won't you flow right into me..."* when I leaned over and kissed Stephanie. "You exude nothing but precious energy, Stephanie, and I really dig that!" She transformed into Scarlett mode again, saying, "There you go again, tryin' to seduce this innocent lil' damsel. Well, Mr., I do deeeclare! What's an innocent girl to do?" She recognized the naughty look in my eyes when I responded, "Oh, I can think of *several* things you can do..."

I quickly washed the dishes and turned the stereo off. "Let's go back to bed and take a catnap until we leave for lunch. Surprised, she asked, "Lunch?" "Yeah, lunch. We can lie around until noon or so and then go to lunch. What is your favorite restaurant for lunch?" "I thought your flight was at 11:00a.m.? We won't have time for lunch, duh!" "Who said I was leaving at 11:00a.m.? My flight leaves at 4p.m., my dear. When you went to sleep last night, I called the airlines and rescheduled my flight, a direct flight to Los Angeles. I'm a *Platinum Member* so they did not even charge me to change the flight. So, where do you want to go for lunch?" She said, "You are just a bundle of surprises! I guess that means you want to spend a little more time with me, huh?" She jokingly added, "I can't say I blame you. After all, I *am* a good catch. Seriously, Theo, I'm glad you will stay a little longer. If you decide you want to take the rest of the week off, rest assured you have a place to stay." "That is very appealing, Stephanie, trust me on that. I damn-sure would like to, but I better get back today, though. We will have a few extra hours to hang out, so let's make the best of it!" "Indeed we will, Theo." She put her hand on my cheek. "I like it when a man surprises me with good news." I kissed her hand and responded, "And I like to surprise a woman with good news, so we will get along perfectly."

We went back to bed and cuddled before drifting off. We awoke to a knock on the bedroom door. "Theo," Dennis said, "I'm about to take off for work." He cracked the door and asked, "Can I come in?" I got up from the bed and put on my shirt Stephanie wore when she was cooking breakfast. I walked over to Dennis and gave him a big hug. When he drew back, he said, "My brother from another mother, it's been a blast, and I hope I you enjoyed your stay. Theo, you *know* you can visit anytime you wish, brother." I said, "I know, man, and the sentiments are mutual. Anytime you want to come out to Los Angeles, my place is yours. I can only hope by then that I can show you an equally good time." I added, "I surprised Stephanie and moved my flight back a few hours. I'm leaving at four o'clock. It's not much, but I wanted to spend a little more time with her." "Yeah," he said, "I had a feeling you were going to do that. See, I know you better than *you* know yourself."

"Alright, I have to get moving so I won't be late for work. Lock-up when you leave." I responded, "Thanks, Dennis. I will call when I get to Los Angeles." Stephanie stayed in bed, but before Dennis walked away, she told him, "Thanks, Dennis, for introducing me to a wonderful man!" "It was my honor, Stephanie. I told you Theo was 'da bomb' did I not? I don't mess around with scrubs." We all laughed and then Dennis left. I hopped back in bed with Stephanie, but made sure to discard my button-down shirt.

We were lying on our sides with her back resting against my chest. I nibbled on the back of her neck while my right hand reached around to caress her erect nipples. I then treaded my tongue around her earlobe and darted it inside her ear. She moaned while her hips slowly gyrated against my loins, her right hand reaching backward to explore and stroke my growing erection. I felt her feet pulling at the sheets, pushing them off our bodies until they reached the foot of the bed. She stroked me vigorously until I was fully erect and then she turned around to face me. Our lips locked together as she moved her body on top of mine. Her hips bucked forward, backward, and I could feel my hardness rubbing against her moist cavity.

The sensation was driving us rabid with carnal anticipation, and just as my mind said, "Get up and get a condom," I felt her delicate hand guiding me inside her. I was just beginning to mouth, "Stephanie, I am not wearing a con..." when she placed a finger against her lips and said, "Shh! I want you like this." She leaned over and kissed me on the mouth, her tongue jockeying against mine as she slowly bounced up and down, allowing me to penetrate her deeply.

We both recognized I was not wearing a condom, but our bodies were in a rhythm whereby her downward pelvic motions met my upward thrusts. Our eyes seared into each other's while no further words were exchanged... only grunts of primal reciprocity! She removed her mouth from mine and uttered, "Give it to me, Theo! You feel *so* damn good inside me." I mouthed back, "That's it, Stephanie, ride it, baby… ride it." We continued to thrash one another until I finally came inside her. She emitted a long "Ohhhh God, I'm cumming!" and then crashed her breasts against my chest while wrapping her arms around my upper torso. Exhausted, we embraced and stared into the other's eyes. I asked, "How did that feel?" and she replied, "That was so intense! You have a way of making me have multiple orgasms, and I love it!" "I guess we got caught-up in the moment," I said. She apologetically agreed, "Yes we did, and I am sorry I did not let you put on a condom. The fact is, Theo, I wanted to feel you inside me like that. I know I let my emotions get the best of me, and I should not have done that. There's something about you that I trust, something in me that wants you all to myself."

While my body and mind were erotically full, I, too, felt a sense of guilt about having unprotected sex, so I said to her, "I understand what you mean. The fact is, if I wanted to stop, I would have, but there is something about you I trust as well. I paid attention to you at Barbara and Rick's party, and while you were taking some serious dick, I noticed how you made sure the men were 'wrapped up' before and during sex. There are no guarantees, but that told me something about you." "Trust me," she said, "I have not had unprotected sex in over ten years. The *only* other man I allowed to do that was my former boyfriend." We let the matter rest and then curled-up against each other and drifted off to sleep.

Chapter 29

The alarm on my cell phone chirped promptly at noon, just when I had rolled over and started nibbling on Stephanie's ear. She was in a deep sleep, but slowly began to awaken. "Hey handsome," she said. "You and I just can't seem to get enough of each other, huh?" I gave her a peck on the lips and said. "That seems to be the case. Hell, if I'm not careful, I may mess around and reschedule my flight yet again." "Well," she said, "that's perfectly okay with me. In fact, I think you should do it anyway. You certainly don't need to be catching a plane in the late afternoon. Everybody knows it's bad luck to fly after 3:00p.m." I gave her a half-cocked look as we both laughed at the absurdity of her comment. Yet, we both searched for reasons to delay my departure. "Well," I said, "if that were the case, there would be a hell of a lot of unlucky people all over the globe. Where did you hear *that* bullshit?" She responded, feigning a scientific tone, "Well… uhhh… studies show that… sixty percent of airplane accidents occur between the hours of… Hell, I don't know, it was the first thing to come to my mind. I just want you to stay longer." "I think you better stick to real estate, that is *the* biggest crock of shit I have ever heard," I said. This time there was no laughter. We just sat quietly and stared into each other's eyes. I pulled her close, this time tighter than previously.

I whispered in her ear, "Stephanie, I had a hell of a weekend, and I'm so damn glad I met you. You were and are *the* highlight of my trip. I'm going to miss you, and I know I'll be thinking about you during my entire flight home." "I'm going to miss you, too," she said. Laughing, she continued, "Hell, I may even do an updated version of Henry "Box" Brown. You remember the story of Henry "Box" Brown don't you?" "Oh, hell yeah," I said. "He was the Black man during Reconstruction that hid in a box and had his associates ship him north to freedom."

I suspected she was simply enthralled with me and enjoyed my company, as I did hers. Because Stephanie was a *swinger*, I surmised she was not accustomed to men really paying attention to her for reasons unrelated to sex. That was unfortunate because well beyond her physical beauty, she was indeed the "total package" of intelligence, humor, drive, and compassion. She sensed I was in deep thought and instinctively asked, "What's wrong?" I was caught off guard by her question, and responded, "Huh? What? Oh, I was just thinking." "I see," she said, "and you were 'just thinking' about what?"

Ironically, I felt very comfortable telling her the truth. In years past, I would have given a woman a line of bullshit or would have quickly changed the topic when queried about my emotions. However, I was candid and told her the truth. "I was thinking about you. I won't lie, Stephanie, I like you and everything about you. Yes, the sex is phenomenal, but you've got *that* extra something that appeals to me. I don't know what it is, but you have that effect on me. That's the good news." A slight frown came to her face after the latter comment, and she swiftly retorted, "The good news? I suppose you're about to let me down easy and give me the bad news?" I protested, "No, it's not that. It's just that... uh... I don't know what to do with you, Stephanie. On one hand I *really* like you. On the other, I'm nervous as hell because you're a... uh..." My tongue and mind were not in concert, and I had a tremendous amount of difficulty articulating my sentiments. Before I knew it, I blurted out, "You're a *swinger!*"

"Oh," she said, mildly irritated, "and now you're judging me? What's next, *Reverend* Theo, are you going to submit a special Papal request for my exorcism?" The acrid sarcasm in her voice numbed my senses, and I knew I screwed up royally! "Who the hell are you to judge me? I *thought* you were different, but I guess I was wrong. You sit here and chastise me because I enjoy having sex. What's up with you men? All of you will fuck anything that moves, and you are encouraged by society to do so. But, when we women like to fuck, we are labeled sluts. Is that not hypocritical, **Reverend** Theo? How ironic is it that you've been fucking the hell outta' me the entire weekend and *now* you're judge me?"

As I peered into her eyes, I saw disappointment and anger, not to mention tears welling up. She cornered me and called me to task for my hypocrisy, and, admittedly, she was correct. I was guilty of believing it was okay for men to have multiple partners, but sexually gauche when the inverse occurred. I also recognized I guarded the full extent of my apprehension. Frankly, it wasn't so much I was jealous of her having had multiple partners. The more salient issue was about *my* fragile ego.

Essentially, I dreaded the idea of others discovering I was in a relationship with a *swinger*. I envisioned male friends of mine exacerbating the situation by saying, "Man, you mean your lady is fucking other men *and* you know about it? What the hell is on *your* mind? What kind of freak are you?" The male ego can often be as fragile as *Tiffany China*. Metaphorically, mine was now on the verge of being trampled by a herd of livid bovines during Pamplona's annual *Running of the Bulls Festival*! Desperately, I tried to assuage her by saying, "Stephanie, please listen. Don't misunderstand what I'm saying. The bottom line is that I *really* dig you. It's just that I don't think I could handle sharing you with other men. I want you all to myself, and the idea of seeing you with other men has me confused as hell."

She was not impressed, cocking her head sideways. "Oh, so you're okay with fucking me and Lupe, but not okay with two men fucking me? That sounds even more hypocritical... *Reverend*." She sensed calling me Reverend was woefully irritating, and her acerbic tone added to the verbal incision cut into my heart. Still floundering, I tried the tactic reserved for uncomfortable moments when someone pulled my trump card – humor. I knew it could backfire, but at the rate I was going, hell, I had nothing to lose. "You keep screaming at me and I'm going to spank that ass of yours." She was not amused.

"I think I better leave," she said, pulling away from me as she started to get out of bed.

It was now time to summon every instance of Teddy Pendergrass I could, begging her, "Wait! Look, Stephanie, the fact is, I like you a *lot*, and, admittedly, I'm just insecure about the whole idea of *swinging*. Do I want you? Hell yes! Can I handle knowing you being sexually involved with another man? I doubt it, but, the fact is, I want to at least see how things develop between us. Let's just take things slowly. *One*, I don't even know if you feel the same way about me! *Two*, the reality is we don't even live in the same city, so, at least for starters, it would definitely be a long-distance relationship. *Three*, we would have to make decisions about all this *swinging* stuff."

By now, Stephanie was seething, and I could feel the venom she was about to spew all over my poorly-articulated words. Emphatically, she interjected, "What do you mean *we* would have to make decisions about all this *swinging* stuff? Theo, I enjoy being in the *Lifestyle*, and I have *no* plans of changing that. Do you think you can just waltz into my life and make decisions about *my* life? Who the hell do you think you are? What is it with all this bullshit you men try to pull, trying to make decisions *for* women? Who and what gives men the right to play God with *our* bodies?" My ego was already beaten to a pulp, but she did not relent, and the skewering continued, and rightfully so! "You know what, Theo? You act like you're pussy-whooped! If you want your docile, homemaker version of June Cleaver, I am *not* the one! You can have that frigid bitch and play Ward Cleaver if you wish, but *not* with me!"

She kicked the sheets completely off the bed and was about to get up when I grabbed her by the wrist. Instinctively, she pulled away from my grip. "Stephanie, please listen to me. I'm not trying to tell you what to do in *any* way. I would never do that because I care about you, and I respect you too much for that. You have to remember this *Lifestyle* stuff is brand-spanking-new to me, and I have yet to fully understand what it's all about. So, please work with me on that." She was standing alongside the bed, peering at me. "Look, Theo, I like you, too, but this is probably not going to work out. I think I better leave." She turned and proceeded to walk towards the bedroom door. I jumped out of bed, completely naked, and followed her. By the time I caught up to her, she was in the living room.

"Stephanie," I said, "please, let's talk about this." She turned around and saw that I was completely naked, my manhood swinging from left-to-right as a result of running after her. I underestimated her sense of humor as she thumped the head of my penis and said, "It's a shame you have two heads and *neither* one has a brain that actually works!" I wanted to laugh, loudly, but I couldn't gauge how pissed off she was. So, I treaded lightly and coyly smiled before attempting to appeal to her emotions. "Stephanie, I *know* what I want in life and I am not afraid to do anything to get it. And, right now, I am telling you that I want *you*!" My strategy worked. We stood there, silently.

I took the lead and inched my lips towards hers. She did not recoil, so I continued, eventually meeting her lips. The clothes in her hand dropped to the floor.

I pulled her closer to me and started leading her back towards the bed, confidently telling myself, "If I can just get her back in bed I'll be okay." She followed. "We should start getting ready to leave shortly. But, before we shower and get dressed, let's make-up the right way." She laid on the bed and spread her legs. "Well," I said, "you have no complaints from me." I knelt on the side of the bed and then wrapped her outstretched legs around my shoulders. "I want to kiss you in *all* the right places." I kissed her toes, ran my tongue against her legs and nibbled on her inner thighs. I was back in her good graces because her legs tightened around my neck, and her back arched.

It was not long before I lay on top of her as we proceeded to indulge in yet another round of bliss. She moaned, "We need to make this a quickie unless you're going to change your flight again. Hint, hint!" My mind raced, and I briefly considered her proposition as I looked at the clock. It was now 12:45p.m. As much as I considered altering my departure again, my head, the one with the brain, prevailed. I said to her, "As much as I want to stay longer, I really should be on that 4:00p.m. flight."

We finally crawled out of bed at 1:30p.m., showered, and got dressed. I packed my bags and then we left Dennis's. Stephanie said, "This time of day, we're about 25 minutes from the airport. Do you want to grab a quick bite for lunch before we go to the airport?

There's a restaurant, *The Backbeat*, a few blocks from the airport. The service is fast and the food is good. I'm sure you'll like it because they have jazz playing. The owner used to be a recording engineer, and word is that he recorded a "Who's Who" among jazz musicians during the '50's. "Sure," I said. "It sounds like a cool place, and as long as we can get to the airport as close to 3:00p.m. as possible, I'm game. Since I'm a *Platinum Member* with United Airlines, I won't have to wait in line. Once I get through security, I can pretty much walk right through."

The Backbeat was an intimate, cozy restaurant, and as soon as we walked inside, I heard Art Blakey's tune *Indestructible* playing. Posters of jazz musicians adorned the walls and there were several autographed pictures of the owner, whose name was Fred Weinstock, with artists like John and Alice Coltrane, Dexter Gordon, Ron Carter, Tony Williams, Herbie Hancock, and, my favorite, Lee Morgan. I recognized Fred's name because I was a voracious reader of album liner notes. I suspected most people read album covers only to see who the featured musicians were, but I enjoyed reading every inch of them. I wanted to know the entire personnel, including the producer, engineer, photographer, and everything associated with the album. I took to heart jazz drummer Max Roach's maxim, "Jazz recordings are the textbooks of history," which addressed the premise that during any given historical period, society could be analyzed simply by examining the music during that era.

A waiter seated us, handed us menus and took our drink orders. Stephanie ordered a glass of Zinfandel while I opted for a Heineken. The menu was a creatively designed replica of a music chart. And, all the items on the menu incorporated titles of jazz tunes or actual names of jazz musicians. I ordered a submarine sandwich, *The Sidewinder Grinder*, which was a play on words for Lee Morgan's popular tune, *The Sidewinder*. Stephanie ordered a *Blue Note Burger* and side order of *Footprints* (French fries), the latter being the title of Wayne Shorter's classic arrangement.

"This is a cool spot," I said. "I thought you would like it, especially the jazz motif," said Stephanie. It took less than ten minutes for our food and drinks to arrive, and the *Sidewinder Grinder* was much bigger than I anticipated. There was no way in hell I was going to be able to eat the entire sandwich. Stephanie's burger was huge as well, and the *Footprints* were the thickest fries I had ever seen. The food was fresh and absolutely delicious, so I made a mental note to assure *The Backbeat* would be included on my itinerary whenever I returned to Chicago.

We finished eating a couple of minutes before 3:00p.m. and then headed to the airport. Along the way, there was abject silence, but not for want of talking. Our lack of discussion, I was certain, was the result of us begrudgingly accepting the fact I was really leaving, this time with no itinerary alterations. While she drove, I caressed the back of her neck and, periodically, she turned to gaze into my eyes. At one point, she even took her right hand off the stick shift and stroked my face with the back of her hand. I turned my head to meet her hand and, in the process, kissed it.

As we pulled into the parking lot of O'Hare Airport, Stephanie said, "It looks like the trip is finally over, huh?" "Yeah," I said, "it's been a hell of a weekend, and I really wish I could stay longer, but I really need to get back. I'm not the type to check my email and answer my phone when I'm on vacation, so I'm sure I'll have a ton of messages waiting for me. Besides, I want to leave room for the imagination the next time I see you." She responded, "Oh, so you want to see me again?" "Stephanie," I said, "I wouldn't have it *any* other way. I really, really enjoyed meeting you and, frankly, I can't wait to see you again."

She parked the car and then we walked towards the Departure Terminal, all the while holding hands. I put my arm around her shoulder and pulled her close to me. "Stephanie, I want you to come visit me in Los Angeles when you get a chance. I'll be sure to show you a great time and you won't have to move a muscle. You'll be pampered in every conceivable way, and I do mean *every*!" She smiled. "Well, I believe you, but I seriously doubt I'll not have to move any muscles. I think you just want to get me into your home and keep me locked-in for a weekend of sex. You are so, so naughty... but that is *not* a complaint. I just may take you up on your idea. Seriously, though, I want to see you again, too."

Finally, we reached my gate and had several minutes to spare. For a minute, we just stood looking at each other. I broke the silence first and said, "I want to apologize again for explaining myself so poorly before we left Dennis's place. I certainly didn't mean to offend you, and I want you to understand I was just confused. I like you, a *lot*, and I want to be with you. Let's go with the flow and see how it works out. I'm willing to at least give the *Lifestyle* a chance, and I'll delve further into it when I get home." "Well," she said, "I recommend you just take your time. The *Lifestyle* is truly a global network of *swingers*, so I'll contact some of my friends to see if I can get you connected in Los Angeles. As far as you and I go, I also would like to see how things develop. I assure you, Theo, it's all about trust and open communication. I can tell you are a good person, and I trust you. Just open your heart with me and I'll do the same. Is that a deal?"

I considered her words and responded, "You got it, that's a deal. Oh, before I forget, please keep me posted on your real estate friend in Philadelphia. If the right property comes along, I'll definitely move there, so tell him I'm *very* serious." "He actually called and left a message yesterday, but I haven't gotten a chance to return his call," she said. "I'll keep you informed, especially since Philadelphia is closer to Chicago than Los Angeles. I have a vested interest in this, too, ya' know."

Over the airport loudspeaker, I heard, "United Airlines Flight 263 to Los Angeles will begin boarding in five minutes." The announcement reverberated in my ears, and I saw a look of sadness in Stephanie's eyes as she, too, heard the announcement. "Well, Theo, looks like this is it. Thank you for a wonderful time, and call me as soon as you land!" "I will," I said. "I'll give you a buzz the moment we land." We hugged and kissed deeply, oblivious to onlookers. As I was about to start walking away, she called out, "Theo!" I turned around and saw her blowing me a kiss. I did my rendition of the Dentyne commercial and acted as if I caught the kiss on my cheek, smiling. She mouthed "You are a goofball!"

Alas, I walked through the *Platinum Members* line, and before I walked inside the hallway, instinctively, turned around. Stephanie waving fanatically. There was something about the chemistry between us that appealed to my every sense, and I liked that feeling. Frankly, I had never had feelings so strong, and what struck me most was that I had known her only a short time. Who knows, perhaps she might be ***the one***. My emotions were going in every direction, and my mind raced – Stephanie, Dennis, my weekend trip, and getting back to work. I was wired-up, and looked forward to sitting back in my First Class seat, having a drink, and letting my mind wander wherever it wanted. Even more, though, I was anxious to get home to surf the internet and delve, headfirst, into *Global Connections* and *Lifestyle Rendezvous*!

Chapter 30

During the entire flight back to Los Angeles, my mind focused on *Global Connections* and *Lifestyle Rendezvous*. My thoughts were going in every direction and, admittedly, I started to get horny as hell. I began to mentally assess every woman I looked at on the plane, and secretly queried, "I wonder if *she's* in the *Lifestyle*" by picking and choosing which ones I surmised indulged. I thought, "No, not her, but I can tell **that** lady is, and that one, too! Yep, that one is, but not that one over there." I even had wild visions of the Captain saying on the loudspeaker, "This is your Captain. Welcome to *Flight Lifestyle*. Ordinarily, this flight is about three and a half hours, but since we'll be having an on-flight orgy, we're going to alter our flight plan a bit."

I was awakened from this semi-fugue state at the sound of a flight attendant's voice. "Sir, may I get you something to drink?" Shaken, I responded, "Huh? Oh, yes, may I have a Bloody Mary, please?" She replied, "Coming right up, sir." As she walked away, my mind sped again, thinking, "I just **know** she's in the *Lifestyle*, I can tell!" even though I had no clue. I quickly recognized my sophomoric enthusiasm and intrigue about the *Lifestyle* was jading my sense of reality, and that it was very unlikely I would be fucking *any* woman on this flight. My mind, though, kept rehearsing Skip's words at *The Spot*: "Man, I am meeting women everywhere I go, from all walks of life!"

I finally was able to drift asleep, but, as expected, dosed-off with erotic, carnal visions etched in my brain and stirring my loins.

190

I was awakened by the Captain saying, "Ladies and gentlemen, we know you have a choice when you fly, so we appreciate you flying "the friendly skies of United Airlines. We're beginning to make our descent into LAX, so please fasten your seatbelts and put all try tables to their upright positions. Flight attendants, please prepare for landing."

I pulled my seat forward and no sooner had I done so, the flight attendant swooped-up my empty cocktail glass. She inquired, "Did you find everything okay on your flight, sir?" to which I replied, groggily, "Yes, very much so. I always fly United, and I've no intention of stopping." She smiled brightly. "Thank you very much, and we hope to see you again, soon." My *Lifestyle* fantasies resurfaced as I said to myself, "Yep, I *know* she's a freak, I can tell a mile away!" Of course, I had no idea of the flight attendant's sexual interests, let alone anything else about her. Likely, she was just courteous and doing her job, but my weekend, albeit brief, excursion into the *Lifestyle* had me on full-throttle, and horny as a toad!

When we landed at LAX, I all but sprinted to my car, anticipating getting home, having a beer, and firing-up my computer. I dashed to the luggage carousel and, as usual, there was a delay with bags arriving. Others on the flight, like me, waited patiently and then we heard a bellowing voice on a speaker: "Baggage for Flight 263 from O'Hare to Los Angeles can be picked-up at Carousel 5. We apologize for the inconvenience." We were told on the plane our bags would be at Carousel 2, so we trudged three carousels over and waited. Finally,

I saw my black weekend bag tumble down the ramp so I jerked it up and slid it over my shoulder. After showing my claim ticket to the attendant, I walked briskly to my car.

After I tossed my bag in my car, I pulled my cell phone out and called Dennis. "Dennis! Hey man, thanks for a great time. I had a ball and I look forward to doing it again. Next time, you come out here. Is that a deal?" Dennis said, "Hey Theo! Man, it was great to see you, too. I'm glad you had a good time because I sure did. And, you made a favorable impression on Stephanie. She called me a half hour ago to see if you landed yet. You might want to give her a call. "Absolutely," I said. "I'm going to call her on my way home, and thanks for looking out for me. Thanks again, brother!" I smiled to myself as I hung up the phone because immediately after the conversation, I thought about all the good, fun people I met, not to mention Stephanie.

After I paid for parking, I zoomed out of LAX and headed north on Lincoln Boulevard. I decided to take Lincoln through Venice and hop on the Pacific Coast Highway at Lincoln and the I-10 Freeway. The weather was beautiful, par for the course in Los Angeles, so I soaked up the scenery and, once on the PCH, popped in a CD. Considering the week-end I experienced, the drive was perfect for jazz guitarist Wes Montgomery's *Bumpin' On Sunset*. Wes had always been one of my favorite musicians, and *Bumpin'* resonated, albeit on a different thoroughfare. I thought, "This tune **should** be called *Bumpin' Anywhere*" because I've yet to play it anywhere where it sounded out of context.

Cruising up the PCH, I took time to enjoy the wonderful ocean view. The reason I moved to Malibu was to enjoy the ocean. I loved the smell of it, envied its power, and warmed to its beauty. There was something about the ocean that always made me reflect on larger philosophical issues. I thought about how we humans are so insignificant in contrast to the expansiveness of the ocean and how we, as much as we try to fool ourselves, are no match for the voracity of the ocean's thrust – beautiful, but dangerous if not respected.

I knew I did not have much food at home, so I stopped at a deli near Sunset and the PCH. As I ate my sandwich, my thoughts began to drift back to *Global Connections*. The primary reason for my digression was the abundance of beautiful, scantily-clothed women at the deli. I secretly played the "I can tell she's in the *Lifestyle*" game as women walked in and about the establishment.

I called Stephanie and she picked-up on the first ring. "Theo! I've been waiting to hear that you made it to Los Angeles safely. You know those afternoon flights are cursed." She laughed and interceded, "How was your flight?" I told her I spent most of the flight fantasizing about her, *Global Connections*, and *Lifestyle Rendezvous*. I also confessed to having dreamt the flight turned into a 30,000 feet, in-flight orgy. She burst out laughing. "You are too much! I hope Dennis and I have not created a monster."

"I'm actually in a deli now, looking out at the Pacific Ocean, so I thought I'd give you a buzz to let you know I had a great time with you. I wish you were here now enjoying the Pacific Ocean view with me." She countered, "That sounds so, so good. Wouldn't it be nice to be on the beach together watching the sun go down on the horizon?" "Oh yes," I said, "That definitely would be nice." Instinctively, I broke into Stevie Wonder's classic song and began singing, *"You are the sunshine of my life... that's why I'll always be around. You are the apple of my eye..."* She warmly responded, "That's sweet of you, Theo. You know how to make me feel special, and I appreciate that." "Okay, my dear," I said, "I'm going to get a bite to eat and then head home. I'll give you a call tomorrow, okay?" "That's a deal, and I look forward to it," she said. "Get some rest, babe, and I'll talk with you tomorrow." I finished my sandwich, peered out into the ocean, and headed home.

Chapter 31

When I got home, I fished through mail and was happy to see I received two CDs and one album I ordered from what I called my drug of choice: *Vintage Vinyl*. *Vintage Vinyl* is a record store in St. Louis, Missouri where I purchase an insane amount of music online, most of it from labels such as *Blue Note,* Impulse!, Savoy, and ECM. In fact, I buy so much music online that I forgot what I ordered. My plan was to unpack my clothes, have a beer, put my new music on, and fire-up the computer to find out what all the fuss was about *Global Connections* and *Lifestyle Rendezvous*.

After I unpacked, I showered and put on my silk pajamas. Then, I unwrapped my packages and smiled to myself when I saw the gems I ordered – Duke Ellington's CD, *The Afro-Asiatic Experience*, Art Tatum's *Greatest Hits* CD, and a High-Fidelity album, Oliver Nelson's classic, *Blues and the Abstract Truth*. With Heineken in hand, I sauntered into my home office and flicked on my computer. I knew there would be tons of email messages awaiting my response, but I did not want to be distracted by them. I truly was on an internet mission of the carnal type, so I had no interest in sifting through, and wasting time on, a barrage of so-called inspirational emails, jokes, and the commensurate amount of messages with subject lines such as *I usually don't forward these types of messages, but...* Hell no!

I called Dennis when I found *Global Connections* online. "Hey man," I said, "I'm on the site. I do not believe this shit! I thought you were bullshittin' me, man. There are people naked as hell on this site, with their faces shown! They even have their email addresses included. Is this the internet equivalent of that 1-900-number shit that was huge years ago? What the fuck is this all about?"

Dennis was laughing at the top of his lungs, and finally settled down to say, "I told your ass it was real. Why did you think I was messing around? I'm telling you, Theo, the *Lifestyle* is a motherfucker. It's very much real, and *Global Connections* doesn't have shit on *Lifestyle Rendezvous*. There are some real swingers on *Global Connections*, but too many people are just bullshitting around, either perverts collecting pictures or wannabes *acting* like they're serious *swingers*."

"I have to be honest, Dennis, I believed you, but just thought you were exaggerating just to fuck with my head. I bow down to your ass now, man. Enough chit-chat! So, should I go straight to *Lifestyle Rendezvous*?" "Not really," he said. "I wanted you to go to *Global Connections* first to get your feet wet. You gotta crawl before you can walk, Grasshopper." He burst into laughter again, poking fun at my naïveté about *swingers*. "Fuck you, man" I blurted. "Before you know it, I'll be a legend on this site! Motherfuckers will be calling me Platinum Dick!"

"Seriously," he said, "take your time and just check out both sites. However, I do recommend that you join *Lifestyle Rendezvous*. You can sign-up for various packages – monthly, six months, or twelve months. The longer your membership, the cheaper it is. And, as well as you write, I *guarantee* you will get laid within two weeks *at the most*!" I interjected, "You're kidding me, man!" "No," he said. "In fact, if you post your profile tonight, you'll probably have messages in your box when you get up tomorrow morning. It's all about having a well-written profile that attracts chicks. Trust me, the shit works!"

I asked Dennis what he meant by writing a profile and he told me it was only a description of my personality, physique, and the type of woman or couple I was interested in meeting. "Wait one minute!" I said. "Did you say 'the type of woman or *couple*'? I recall you telling me that husbands are pretty open about helping their wives find some extra dick, but how in hell do you actually *say* that in a profile?" I continued, mocking a profile – *Hi, I'm Theo and I'm hung, so let me fuck your wife later this evening.* "No, jackass, what you do is… Fuck it! I won't waste time telling you. When you go to *Lifestyle Rendezvous*, look-up my profile and you'll get an idea of why I always get a ton of messages from folks on the site. Do you have a pen and paper handy? My profile name is *HungWithClass*."

I was thoroughly intrigued, yet also embarrassed about the prospect of being involved in *swinging*. So, I took the easy route of masking my feelings, attempting to say something humorous as I feigned writing his profile name down. "*HungWithClass*…. I spell that with a small *H*, right?" Dennis jabbed me back to reality – "Oh, you got jokes, huh? Seriously, write the damn name down and read my profile. Even though the site is about fucking, women *still* like to be romanced and mentally enticed. Distinguish yourself from men who don't know shit about appealing to a woman's *mind*! If you intrigue their minds, you'll get more pussy in a month than most dudes get in a year!"

For a moment, I went silent because everything Dennis was telling me just didn't make sense. I was struggling, big-time, with the premise of the *Lifestyle, swinging, playing,* and all the other amorphous, seemingly harmless descriptors that translated to fucking another man's wife – *with* his permission, mind you! This was *not* how my parents raised me! This was against *all* the lessons I learned in Bible Study on Sundays when I was growing up. *"Thou shall not covet thy neighbor's wife"* reverberated in my head like an ear-piercing Hendrix riff! How could people so callously and flippantly disregard religious tenets that denounced infidelity and adulterrr... Ohhh shit! For some reason, my mouth would not even allow me to enunciate the word... adultery. I always considered adultery to mean that a married person was creeping around on their spouse. However, my moral compass went berserk when I remembered spouses had no sexual secrets in the *Lifestyle*! I wondered aloud, "How in the world do married people fuck others' spouses? Whatever happened to the Ten Commandments?" I was thoroughly confused.

Dennis stirred me back into focus. "Theo. Theo! Are you there, man? What the hell is wrong with you? Are you falling asleep on the phone?" "My fault," I said. "I dosed off for a second because I'm tired from the flight." Of course, I was lying through my teeth because I was the antithesis of exhausted. In fact, I was wound-up from the time my flight landed. I simply could not wait to rush home and learn more about *Global Connections* and *Lifestyle Rendezvous*.

"Well," he said, "one of the reasons you'll find a higher caliber of serious *swingers* on *Lifestyle Rendezvous* is because it's a pay-site. That tends to weed-out the flakes. *Global Connections* primarily is a free site, so some of the people are not as serious. You're more likely to run across jackasses who're there just to trade X-rated pictures or some bullshit like that. With *Lifestyle Rendezvous*, you have to pay for a subscription, so that usually attracts serious *players*."

I said, "Okay, man, let me get off this phone and see what's going on with both sites. I'll give you a call tomorrow and let you know if anything happens." "Have fun, Theo, and remember everything I told you about how to approach things. Write the profile, and you might even post a nude body-sized picture, but do ***not*** show your face! I'll talk with you tomorrow. Thanks again for coming to Chicago, it was good seeing you, brother." "You too," I said. "I'll talk with you soon."

Chapter 32

I hung-up with Dennis and started reading profiles on *Global Connections* and *Lifestyle Rendezvous*. Just seeing all the naked, attractive women convinced me… Actually, they convinced my loins to at least consider moving forward with investigating the *Lifestyle*. One advantage of *Lifestyle Rendezvous* was that it allowed me to conduct a geographical search. Aloud, I said, "Damn, this is very convenient!" Then, I had a revelation: *If this regional search function is legitimate, I can meet a lot of women since I travel all over the globe!* I read the *Search* preferences and started getting aroused even more. I was so horny that were there a category, *"Any woman with a pulse and heartbeat who is available NOW!"* I probably would have chosen it. The *Search* option allowed me to select preferences based upon how I prioritized them.

Welcome to Lifestyle Rendezvous! Complete Your Search Preferences Below

Fill-in Your Search Preferences:

- *Gender:*   x Women   _ Men   x Couples   _ TS/TV   _ No Preference
- *Activities:* x Anal penetration   _ BDSM/Fetish   _ Gang bangs/Groups   x Oral sex

     _ Phone sex   x Vaginal penetration   _ No Preference
- *Ethnicity:* No preference   *Age*: 25 – 55   *Weight*: 110lbs.– 160lbs.
- *Eye color:* No preference   *Hair color*: No preference   *Distance*: 0 – 50 Miles

Click! *Oh, shit!* I pushed the *Enter* button to begin the search and 275 profiles arose, sorted by distance from closest to furthest. My mouth dropped open when I saw there were at least 23 women and 15 couples in *my* zip code area alone! A litany of questions raced through my mind, firing like neurons. *"Who are these folks?"* *"Could people on my block be swingers?"* *"What would I do if I were at a swinger party and saw people I knew professionally, or even socially?"* *"What should I do next?"* *"What the fuck am I getting myself into?"* Sweat began to percolate on my forehead, and I felt like I was hyperventilating. I needed another cold beer, fast, so I zipped to the kitchen to grab another Heineken and opened it. Instead of sipping, I rubbed the bottle's frosty exterior on my face for temporary relief.

When I sat back down to my computer, I thought I would take Dennis's advice and write a profile because I was starting to get tired, even though my hardon suggested otherwise. "What the hell, I'm diving in," I said, as I began my profile:

> Hello ladies and couples. I'm a single African American man in my 30's, tall, fit, and serious. Personality-wise, I am easy-going, good sense of humor, sane, and fun to be around. Sexually, I have a lot of energy and have been described as a "giver" in that I get a lot of pleasure seeing how a woman responds to things I'm doing to/with her.

I enjoy giving a woman a massage, taking my time to caress every part of her body... and mind. If you are looking for a guy who'll pounce on you, pump for five minutes and then roll over to watch ESPN, I am NOT the guy for you. Physically, I'm very well-groomed, attractive, and absolutely drug and disease-free. Finally, I am *not* interested in phone sex, trading naked pictures, or any other types of games unless, of course, the games are of the carnal persuasion. Women and couples only, please. And, serious replies only. Thank you.

"That should do it," I said. Now came the embarrassing part of taking a nude picture of myself. I went to my closet to retrieve my digital camera. Months had passed since using my camera, and it certainly was not to take nude pictures of myself. In fact, the last time was during an outdoor jazz performance at Los Angeles County Museum of Art. During the summer, LACMA hosted free outdoor jazz concerts and I always bumped into friends and musicians I had not seen in months.

I peeled off my silk pajamas and stood in front of the full-length mirror attached to my bedroom door. "How the hell will I do this?" I asked myself. Maybe I could put the camera's timer on and pose with my erection standing at attention like the Statue of Liberty. Dennis's admonition came to mind: "Do *not* show your face!" Perhaps it would be better to place the camera on my desk, making sure it was positioned such that nothing in the background or in my home could be recognized. I put a small dab of *Wet* lubrication on my manhood and gently stroked until I was fully engorged. I felt like a horny teenager doing all this, and chuckled to myself, "A man with a hard dick will go to great lengths to get laid!" Ten seconds... Flash! I looked at the picture and saw it was a bit fuzzy because I moved abruptly at the last second. Ten seconds... Flash! Better, but not an optimal picture. I accidently showed my face. Ten seconds... Flash! Perfect! The picture was clear, my body cooperated, and my head was turned so as not to show my face.

It took less than five minutes to upload my photograph and profile on *Lifestyle Rendezvous*. Satisfied, I pushed my chair back from the desk, thinking, "Okay, here goes, *Lifestyle Rendezvous*, show me what you got." Click!

Chapter 33

My alarm clock buzzed promptly at 6:30a.m. on Tuesday. I was still lethargic from the weekend, and my body was not quite ready to leave my warm bed. It was tempting to work from home, but I thought better of it and decided to go to my office. Begrudgingly, I got up and trudged into my walk-in shower. The shower revitalized me, so I got dressed, engulfed a hearty breakfast of turkey bacon, an English muffin, and carrot juice while I read the front page of the Wall Street Journal. I shuddered at the thought of Dennis finding out I drank carrot juice! Forever, I would be regarded by him as "one of those Los Angeles tree-hugging, meditating, and yoga-practicing health nuts."

I was ready to leave home at 7:30a.m. in hopes of beating the Pacific Coast Highway's insane morning traffic. If I left any later than that, it would take me at least forty-five minutes to get to my office in Santa Monica. Los Angeles traffic was always torturous. Without traffic, the drive to my office was less than fifteen minutes! Just as I was about to leave, I stopped at the door with a strange feeling I was forgetting something. Did I misplace my keys? No, they were in their usual spot. Habitually, whenever I walked inside my home I placed my keys inside a crystal bowl in my foyer. Did I leave the stove on? I rushed to the kitchen and found the stove was not on, nor were any other appliances. Ten minutes elapsed as I ran around my home trying to ascertain what it was I was forgetting.

Finally, a flash shone in my brain – *Lifestyle Rendezvous*! That's it. I forgot to see if anyone responded to my newly-created profile. "Shit! It's 7:45a.m. and I need to get my ass outta here." That's what the sensible, intellectual, and practical Theo said. However, the spontaneous, adventurous Theo chimed, "It'll only take a minute to check. You might as well do it! If traffic is too bad, take the side streets." I dropped my briefcase at the door and sprinted to my computer and flicked it on.

Within seconds, I was logged-on to *Lifestyle Rendezvous*. My eyes sprang wide open and my heart raced when I saw the prompt – *You have 4 new messages!* "No way!" I clicked on the *New Messages* tab and read the first passage.

> Hello there. We read your profile and were intrigued. We are a straight, married White couple in our mid-40's. We have been in the *Lifestyle* for about 10 years, and we are very much secure in our marriage. You sound like the type of gentleman we enjoy getting acquainted with, and would like to hear from you. If, after reading our profile, there is a mutual interest, let us know. I am 5'4", 120lbs, 40-28-34, witty, Ivy League educated, **very** sensuous, and attractive. I should warn you in advance that I've an affinity for handsome, well-groomed, well-hung, and professional Black men. We live in Pacific Palisades and would like to meet you

for drinks if you're amenable to that. Should things develop, we can travel or host. I have attached a recent picture. *Ciao.* Susan and Craig

I clicked the picture to enlarge it and immediately shouted, "Holy shit! She is abso-damn-lutely gorgeous! This **cannot** be real." My thoughts meandered like a raging river, and I was torn between responding immediately and waiting until I settled down, literally, from reading her message and seeing her picture. I clicked on the second message.

Single Black woman, 37, from Chatsworth here. I really liked your profile and, of course, the picture. I am looking for a single Black man who enjoys dancing, movies, concerts, and just hanging out. I am not in a rush to hop in the sack, but once I decide I want to do that, watch out! I'm a professional, drama-free woman, and very much a tigress in the bedroom – if it gets to that. To me, honesty is paramount, so I am not interested in game-players or insincere men. I am highly sexual, but my mind must be stimulated first. Feel free to respond when you get a chance. Damn, your profile picture looks delicious! Kisses 'n hugs. Gladys

I read both messages again and kept shaking my head. Internally, I was besieged with questions and my moral compass went into flux again. *What should I do? Is it too late to turn back? What would they think if I do not respond to their messages? What the fuck is going on in the world?* I looked at the clock – 8:15a.m. "Damn!" I said. "I guess I'll have to take the side streets. Maybe I should call into the office and inform my executive assistant I would work from home." The rational Theo surfaced and reminded me, *Take your ass to work! These messages will be here when you get home.*

Reluctantly, I pushed back from my desk and, despite my erection, decided to go to my office. Predictably, Pacific Coast Highway traffic was complete mayhem, so as soon as I could, I merged onto Ocean Avenue. The blaring horn of a blue Audi TT jolted me, interrupting my daydream at a stoplight at the intersection of Ocean and Pico. I looked in my rearview mirror and mouthed "Impatient jackass!" when I saw a twenty-something *Yuppie* banging on his steering wheel while flipping me the bird. Los Angeles' patented road rage overcame me as I thought to myself, *I bet if I jumped out of this car and snatched your little pussy ass by the collar that you wouldn't be so impatient. Yuppie motherfucker!*

I pulled out my cell phone and punched #5, which was the speed-dial number to my office. It was now 8:45a.m. My goal of getting to work by 8:00a.m. was reduced to a sordid, unfulfilled wish. "Hi Andrea, how are you? I'm on my way there. Of course, traffic is a nightmare, so I should be there a few minutes after 9a.m." "Hello Mr. Williams," she said. "You do not have any appointments this morning. If anyone calls before you arrive, do you want me to forward them to your cell?" "No, Andrea, just take a message," I said. "Sure thing, Mr. Williams, I will see you soon."

Andrea was my Executive Assistant, and an excellent one at that. She was hired two weeks after I began my tenure at Premier Cosmetics, so we had developed a comfortable, trusting working relationship. Andrea had been widowed for five years, and whenever she met women I was involved with, assumed the role of surrogate mother. She was an attractive woman in her late 50's who reminded me of Nancy Wilson – slim, distinguished, elegant, classy, and attractive. I tacitly solicited her advice about some of the women I brought to the office, and she always proved to be correct in her assessment of them. Her husband, Carl, died of lung cancer after twenty-five years as an engineer at Boeing.

I arrived at my office at 9:10a.m. "Good morning Mr. Williams!" bellowed Andrea. "How was your trip to Chicago?" "It was great, Andrea," I said. "It went by fast, but it was a blast, and I enjoyed the time away." She reminded me that my vacation, albeit short, was long overdue. "Mr. Williams, you need to get away from the office more often. I can't remember the last time you took a *real* vacation. Remember, life is short and there will always be work, so you should treat yourself without feeling guilty." Her sentiments, I sensed, were out of concern for my well-being because it had been at least two years since I took any substantive time off work.

Equally, she saw traits of me her late husband possessed. His passing was unexpected, and over the course of twenty-five years, he and Andrea had taken only three vacations together. She was reminding me, not so subtly, that Carl always had excuses to work even though he accumulated months upon months of vacation time. "Andrea," I said, "I promise you I'm going to start using more of my vacation time. And, you're right. Life is short, so thank you for your concern." "You're very welcome, Mr. Williams. I hope I was not being too forward, but I think you understand the context of which I say that." "I sure do," I said, "and I know you mean well. Thanks, Andrea."

I strolled through our expansive office and said hello to employees. Everyone knew I took a mini-vacation to Chicago, and my greetings to staff were met with a variety of responses. The first person I ran into was Benito Tucci, a District Manager. Benito possessed classic Italian features. His olive complexion accented a thick mane of jet-black curly hair, which was always well-coiffed. An attractive man, he was thirty-eight, 6'2", about 180 pounds, well-groomed, and had a healthy self-concept that bordered on arrogance.

Benito and I occasionally confided in each other about our personal lives, he more often than I, so he was quick to inquire, "Okay, Sport! Give me the rundown. Did you get laid or not? You've got that 'glow' about yourself, so it's obvious you did. I want details, too! Are you free for lunch?" I laughed and responded, "First of all, *stop* calling me Sport. That's not my name, and I damn-sure don't like it as a nickname. Second, what's up with all the questions? Are you preparing for a career at *The National Enquirer* or some shit?

Third, to answer your primary question, yes, I did get laid and you will never, ever believe how it all went down. It was absolutely insane!" I continued, "I can't do lunch, though. Let's hit Happy Hour at The Warehouse after work. "I can do that," he said. "How about six-thirty?" "Okay," I said, "six-thirty it is."

One of the temporary secretaries overheard us, and as she walked by, looked at me demurely and said "Hello Mr. Williams. Welcome back. I hope you had a good time." "Thanks, Toni, it's good to be back." Physically, Toni was the quintessential temp. She was an attractive African American in her mid-twenties, killer body, long legs, and always keen on revealing a commensurate amount of cleavage. When she was out of range, Benito whispered, "I think Toni has the 'hots' for you. I know you recognize that, so you may as well 'hit' it." "Well," I said, "I can sense something, but she is *definitely* off-limits. Yeah, she's fine as hell, but I'm not going to let my dick get me into trouble. That's a lawsuit just waiting to happen. However, if we don't hire her full-time and I see her little hot ass out and about, then it's on. I advise you to keep it strictly professional, too." "Hell yeah," said Benito. "She's fun to look at, but I'm not going to screw-up my career either just for a hot lay." "Oh?" I chided. "Suddenly Mr. Torpedo Dick has a conscious? What happened while I was away, you met a nun?" "Nope," he said, "I'm just trying to slow down a bit, that's all. I'm *still* the man in this office."

Benito and I were the only two men who were senior-level managers, so we frequently endured the wrath of women attempting to peer into our personal lives. I did a better job than Benito of keeping my antics separate from work. On more than one occasion, his past lovers made spectacles of themselves, and him, too. His most embarrassing experience was when a former lover, Carmella Rossi, used a key to scratch his brand new black Mercedes S-Class, which was parked in a *Reserved for District Manager* space. As if that were not dehumanizing enough, she used fluorescent orange lipstick to write, "Cheater!" on the hood of his car. One of the Sales Associates, Donna, noticed the occurrence and screamed, "Benito, somebody's keying your car!" as staff rushed to the window to get a clear view. By the time Benito sprinted to the elevator and got to the parking lot, Security had detained Carmella, but the damage was already done. Staff watched intently as Benito and Carmella screamed at each other, in Italian, while Security kept the other at bay. I tried, unsuccessfully, to save Benito some honor by screaming out to staff, "Okay, everybody, let's get back to work." That was just one of several missteps on Benito's part related to bringing personal drama on the job. He almost lost his job because of that fiasco, too.

At six o'clock, Benito buzzed me on the intercom and asked, "How're you coming along? Are we still on for six-thirty?" "Yes," I said. "I'm wrapping things up now, and just turned off my computer. I'll meet you at The Warehouse soon." "Good deal," he said. "I'm wrapping things up, too. See you soon." I grabbed my briefcase, turned off my office lights, and said goodbye to staff as I walked towards the elevator. When I reached the parking lot, I felt a renewed sense of energy because the day felt long, and I was mentally exhausted. Further, I still had not physically recovered from my trip. I hopped into my car and, within minutes, was zipping through traffic and cruising down Lincoln Boulevard towards Marina Del Rey.

Benito and I were regulars at The Warehouse. When I walked in, I was immediately greeted by the hostess, Tessa, who gave me a hug and kissed me on the cheek. "Hey Theo, how're you doing? Welcome back to The Warehouse! Where's your partner-in-crime, Benito?" "Hey Tessa! He'll be here any minute, and it'll only be the two of us. Can you please set us up at a private table near the back? We need to catch-up on some work, but we might sit at the bar after we eat." "You got it!" she said. She led me to a secluded table near the rear, which was perfect because I knew my conversation with Benito would get animated once he heard about my trip.

I did not have to ask Tessa to bring me a drink because I virtually lived at The Warehouse, and even had personal and corporate accounts there. She knew my tastes for drinks, appetizers, main courses, and desserts. A minute later, she approached my table, smiling and holding an Apple Martini. "Here you go, Theo. Do you want a dinner menu now or are you going to wait for Benito?" "I'm kind of hungry," I said, "so I'll start off with an appetizer." "Calamari it is," she said. "You know, Tessa, you should consider being a mind-reader. You never cease to amaze me in terms of knowing what I like." She responded, "Well, you've been coming here regularly for three years." She winked and added, "Besides, I pay attention to my special customers." I barely had time to thank her before she rocketed towards the kitchen. I settled into my seat and reflected on my trip.

Benito walked in right as my calamari arrived, and before he could sit down, Tessa returned to the table and placed a glass of red wine on it. "Hey Benito!" she said. "Would you like an appetizer or would you prefer a dinner menu?" He responded, "You're right on time, Tessa. I'll pass on both. I'm in the mood for a good steak, so I trust your judgment." "Good choice," she said. "I have the perfect meal for you, then. A salad, medium-rare filet mignon, and baked potato with sour cream and chives." Benito sat down. "Perfect! You're awesome, Tessa." "That's why they pay me the big bucks, sweetie," she said, smiling. "What about you, Theo?" "Well," I said, "that does sound good. I think I'll have the same thing."

Tessa had barely left the table before Benito leaned over and asked, "So, what happened in Chicago, Sport?" He pissed me off with that silly name, so I barked, "If you call me Sport one more fucking time, I'm not telling you shit!" "Okay, okay!" he said. "How did it go, Mr. Exalted Fucking Thelonious Ellington Williams? You were walking around on a cloud all day at work, so you obviously had a great time. What happened?" "Well," I said, "I went to see my old roomie from graduate school, Dennis. He lives in Chicago..." Benito interrupted me and said, "I know all that shit. Get to the *real* details. You said earlier that I would not believe what happened." "Be patient, man," I said. "I'm trying to put things in context for your horny ass, so relax." I continued, "Anyway, I went to see Dennis and he took me to a *Lifestyle* party." Exasperated, Benito barked, "A what party? What the hell is a *Lifestyle* party?" "Benito," I said, "what I'm about to tell you shall remain **strictly** confidential. If you ever, ever repeat this to anybody, I will deny it and swear down that you are a borderline psychopath! In other words, I trust that you will not run your mouth and will shut the fuck up about this. Are we clear on that?"

"First," he said, putting both hands in the air, "is this something illegal? If it is, I do **not** want to hear it! You can just stop now and we'll eat our dinner, have some drinks, and act as if nothing happened." I laughed hysterically until he asked, "What the hell is so funny?" "Hey man," I said, "it's **not** anything illegal. Dennis took me to a fuck party." Benito choked on his wine, and some of it dribbled down his chin onto his tie and the tablecloth. After regaining composure, he screamed, "You went to a fuck party?" "Hey man," I said, "you want a damn microphone so everyone in the restaurant can hear you? Shut the fuck up and relax!" I went on to say, "It was unbelievable, Benito. The women were drop-dead gorgeous, and I fucked about four or five of them at the party. And, to top it off, I met this bad-ass 'sister' who fucked my brains out the entire weekend!" Still amazed, Benito reeled off a barrage of queries. "What was it like? Was it at a club or something? Were the women hookers? You mean to tell me they were beautiful, too? How did Dennis find out about it?" "Actually," I said, "there is a **whole** community of folks out there, from all walks of life, involved in what's called the *Lifestyle*. I met all types of people, professional folks, who just like to fuck. And, get this… many of them are married!"

Benito plopped back in his seat, dumbfounded, mouth gaping. He finally gasped and said, "That is *truly* un-fucking-believable… Wait! You said you met people from all walks of life, right? If there are *swingers* in Chicago, then surely there must be some out here, right?" "Oh, I almost forgot," I said, "Dennis turned me on to a couple of *Lifestyle* websites. Man, it's a global phenomenon! Dennis told me there are people all over the world who indulge. I checked the sites out last night and, get this, I had two messages this morning!" "You must be shittin' me, Theo!" Benito barked. "Not one bit," I said. "One message was from a white couple in Pacific Palisades and the other was from a Black woman in Chatsworth. The Black chick is fine as hell and the wife of the couple is nice, too." Benito queried, "What do you mean the wife? She's cheating on her husband? You better be careful sneaking around with married women because…" I cut him off in mid-sentence by saying, "You don't understand, Benito. Her husband *does* know! They've been *swinging* for several years and are secure in their relationship. So, I guess her husband is okay with her having sex with other men."

Tessa brought our meals to the table and immediately asked, "What in the world are you guys talking about? You're sitting in this secluded corner and Benito has wine all over himself and *my* tablecloth!" I laughed and responded, "We're just catching up on things because I haven't seen him in a few days. I went to Chicago over the weekend and the wannabe private investigator here, Benito, aka, *Columbo*, is asking me a million questions. Please give him his steak so he can shut the hell up." "I'll second that," said Tessa, as she placed sumptuous dishes before us. She continued, "I'll leave you guys alone, so just holler if you need anything." "Thanks, Tessa," I said. She was no more than five feet away before Benito blurted, "Wow, Theo! I never would've imagined people do shit like that." I responded, "Yeah, that's what I thought. I tell you, Benito, in some ways it's strange, and I **still** don't get it even though I saw it with my own eyes. It was like a modern-day scene from the movie *Caligula*. I mean, people were fucking all over the place: the backyard, in the Jacuzzi, alongside the pool, all the bedrooms in the house, the living room. Actually, I stand corrected. The wife, Barbara, took me to the master bedroom because that was the only place that was off-limits to others to fuck. Man, she just about wore my ass out! She has a thing for Black men, and she wasn't shy at all about letting me know that. Now for the crazy part! While I was fucking the daylights out of her, her husband, Rick, comes into the bedroom and watches me plow her!"

Benito dropped his fork into his plate, shocked. "No fucking way! That is bizzzzarre! You're bullshitting me, right? What did you do? Did you keep fucking her? Did he join in and bone her, too?" I said, "There you go again with all those questions, *Columbo*. One at a time, okay?" "Look, just tell me what the hell happened," he screamed. "Well," I said, "he just watched for a while. At first, I felt

216

uncomfortable and I started to lose my hardon. I mean, come 'on, man. I was laying there banging his wife and he's there watching! What the hell was I to do?" "Well?" Benito asked.

I peered into his eyes, deadpan expression, and said, "What do you think I did? I tore that pussy up!" We laughed and then I told the truth. "Seriously, I fucked her thoroughly, but for a few minutes, my mind was racing like crazy. It obviously felt good. But, it was weird because I felt like I was doing something immoral by having sex with a married woman. So, when Rick walked in, I was confused as hell. I was thinking, 'Why am I feeling guilty when he's right there watching?'"

"Further," I said, "at least initially, it was just antithetical to my moral compass. My parents did not raise me to do any shit like that, man! Strangely enough, my mother's voice echoed in my head." *Boy! What in the world are you doing? You better stop that nonsense! Don't you know adultery is against **God's** word?* Benito's only wide-eyed response was, "Moral compass? What the fuck! Don't give me that Dali Lama bullshit. Was she pretty or not?" Ignoring his tirade, I continued, "At first I just thought it was some WPS…" Again, he interjected. "WPS? What the hell is that?" Laughing, he continued, "Let me guess, you started performing an exorcism on the pussy?" "No, jackass," I said. "That means White People Shit. You know, the idea that white people do some crazy ass things. You gotta admit, man, ya'll do some crazy stuff. Look at the Roman Empire. Hell, you don't have to look back that far! What's that stupid motherfucker who

217

goes around fucking with alligators, lions, and shit like that? I can't remember his name, but you get my point."

We laughed, but I continued, "Seriously, though. Initially, that's what I was thinking until I saw *all* types of people there, literally, from all over the world! There were some Russians, Hispanics, African Americans, and just about everybody else in-between. And, these were not broke-ass people, Benito! I'm talking doctors, realtors, professors, and the whole shebang." Benito caught Tessa's attention and held up one finger, meaning he wanted another glass of red wine. I was still working on my Martini, so I declined his offer of another drink. Tessa brought his wine and asked how our meals tasted. We affirmed both meals were delicious, and that we probably would not have room for dessert. "I don't know, guys," she said, "a great way to finish up your meals would be our delicious cherry sorbet with a dash of Brandy." "We'll see," I said, before she whisked away.

I picked up where I left off with Benito. "Anyway, that part was fun, but there's something I haven't mentioned. I met a woman who's a *swinger* and there was a connection that was more than physical. I really dug her and she dug me, too. I'm not as confused about everything as I was before, but it's still a bit surreal." He burst into laughter and sneered, "Wait! You mean to tell me you're in a houseful of gorgeous women, and can have any one of them, and you fuck around and fall in love? Damn, Theo, you hopeless romantic bastard! You're confusing sex and lust with love, my man. I'll tell you what. The next time you're bonin' some fine woman and start feeling like the Pope, call me and let *me* worry about the moral dilemmas." "See," I said, "that's why your ass is always meeting psycho chicks and stalkers. That's your problem, man. You think with your dick! I, however, think with the right head." "Okay, cool down Sporrr…" He stopped in mid-sentence because my immediate stare told him *You call me Sport one more time and I'm going to knock your fucking teeth out!* He relented.

The banter finally subsided, so we finished our meals in silence. Periodically, Benito looked up from his plate to say, "You lucky bastard! Why can't that kind of shit happen to me? Why am I always meeting these psycho women?" "Well, for starters…" Before I said another word, he snapped, "Shut the fuck up. Those were rhetorical questions. I'm not ready for one of your relationship therapy sessions, but thanks anyway." This time, I relented.

We passed on dessert, in part, because I was too damn anxious to get the hell out of there and get home to my computer. I mentally drifted at the table, saying to myself, *I wonder if I have any more "hits" from my ad.* Unconvincingly, I told Benito, "It's getting late. I better get home and get some rest." Benito wasn't the brightest bulb in the box, but he was keen enough to call my bluff. "Yeah, I'm sure you're tired, Theo. You better get home to check your email… oops, I meant get home and get some rest." "Okay, you called me on the carpet, and you're right. I won't lie, Benito, I can't wait to get home to check my email." "I don't blame you," he said, "and I feel you on that.

Let's get outta here, but make sure you let me know what happened tomorrow at work." "You know I will," I said.

Benito waved Tessa over. She was prepared to give us dessert menus, but I stopped her by saying, "We're going to call it a night, Tessa. I'm still a little tired from the trip, so I'm going to get home." "Benito," she asked, "are you leaving, too, or can I get you some tasty dessert?" "I'm done for the night, too, Tessa. I'll take a rain check on that dessert, though, it sounds damn good. I don't know about Theo, but I'll be back over the weekend. Premier Cosmetics wants to land Paula Abdul as a spokeswoman. I've been tapped to schmooze her agent, so I'll be back on Saturday night." Tessa countered, "Thanks, gentlemen. You are two of my best customers, so you better not stay away too long. As for Saturday, leave it all to me, Benito. Come Monday morning, Paula will be ready to sign on the dotted line!" I arose from the table and gave Tessa a hug and kiss. "Put both dinners on my personal account and add $50 for your tip," I said. Tessa hugged and kissed Benito as well before sending us off with "Thanks, Theo! Have a terrific evening, gentleman, and I'll see you Saturday night, Benito."

Chapter 34

Benito's Mercedes S-Class was adjacent to my Carrera on The Warehouse's parking lot. When we reached our cars, I said to him, "Okay, B.T., I'll see you tomorrow. Drive safely, and don't get your horny ass into any trouble tonight." "Trouble?" he asked. "Hell, I should be warning *you* about trouble. *You* are the one who's about to go home to an email box full of messages from horny, hot housewives. Me? I'll probably be the first person in California to get prosecuted under the *Three Strikes and You're Out* law for committing felonious assaults on my dick!" We burst out laughing before giving each other a hug and telling the other, "See you tomorrow at work."

Surprisingly, I was the first to peel-off from the parking lot. My mind feebly attempted to tell itself, *I need to get home immediately because I have a lot of work to do.* However, that was eons away from the ***real*** truth. In fact, I knew it was total bullshit! *You need to hurry home to see how many women left you messages on Lifestyle Rendezvous. There may even be some on your block who want some hot sex tonight. Hurry!*

I found myself impatiently driving down Lincoln Boulevard, summoning traffic to disappear as if I were Copperfield himself. The conjurer's voice echoed in my ears, *Damn! Whose bright idea was it to place all these stop lights on this street? Why is everybody driving so damn slow? Poof! Make all these damn cars disappear or, at least, get the hell out of my way!* Impatience, especially when

221

accompanied by vacuous, wishful thoughts, can be torturous because you focus on immediate gratification and not rational, well-thought out consequences and solutions. We often get into the "I want it now" mindset in contrast to "Relax and think about consequences" frame of mind. The former was where my mind ventured until I approached Lincoln and the I-10 Freeway.

I was jolted to my senses when a high school-aged kid almost ran me off the road at the on-ramp. Of all contraptions, this snotty-nosed, pimpled-faced brat was piloting an emaciated buggy, a ratty-ass mobile inferno better known as a Pinto! *Didn't they outlaw those four-wheeled fire bombs? Isn't it illegal to even **think** about driving a piece of shit like that?* When I jarred my brakes, I noticed the little imp was pecking buttons on a cell phone, oblivious to an abundance of tired, restless drivers around him. *I wish I could call your parents and tell them what just happened, you little bastard!* I hammered on my horn and he looked upward, embarrassed. He screamed out the window, "Dude man, I am so sorry!" as he held up a hand to wave. I flipped him off and sped away. Another thought came to mind: *Why do reckless Los Angeles drivers courteously wave at those whom they almost cause fatal accidents?*

The Pacific Coast Highway was not too crowded, so I reached Malibu in about fifteen minutes. Shunning Porsche manufacturer safety warnings, I started closing the convertible top while my car zipped towards my garage. Premier Cosmetics work was the last thing on my mind, so I tossed my briefcase in the back compartment.

I envisioned myself as Olympic medalist Bob Beamon, long-jumping several steps at a time before reaching my front door. As soon as I opened the door, I felt a sigh of relief, and started singing the patented introduction to Etta James' signature tune… *Aaaat laaast!* Home.

Surprisingly, the desire to whisk directly to my computer was secondary to wanting to methodically take my time. *Why rush, Theo? Relax, take your time and have a drink. Put some jazz on. The women on Lifestyle Rendezvous are not going to disappear.* Shower taken, drink in hand, and wrapped in a blue, Egyptian cotton robe, I approached my stereo rack. What artist's music would be apropos? Hmm. I stood before my stereo, but soon recognized the necessity of going to my "chill room," the space I converted to house over 3,000 albums, most of which, if not all, were in pristine condition. *This is a moment for high fidelity vinyl, the real deal, not those CDs, which were often sterile reproductions of reproductions!* I knew I wanted to hear a saxophone, but who would it be? I flipped through the albums, which were alphabetized. It was less cumbersome, and more convenient, to alphabetize since the sheer magnitude of vinyl was staggering. Bingo! There it was, its dark greenish cover still crisp and shiny as it was decades ago when I secured it for my collection: *Ballads* by John Coltrane. Satisfied, I floated from the "chill room" back to the living room and delicately placed the iconic recording on my Clear Audio turntable. Satisfied, I picked-up my drink and floated to the computer in my office.

"Okay," I said to myself, "show me what you got, *Lifestyle Rendezvous!*" After I typed in my password, and saw the site's main page, I froze, completely stupefied: *You have 7 new messages!* "No fucking way!" I whispered. Then, I thought about what transpired that morning. When I abruptly left for work, I had four messages, and viewed two. So, from the time I left for work and returned home later, I accumulated five more hits to my profile posting!

I decided to retrieve the two previous messages since they arrived before the latter five. The first message said:

> Nice cock! Oh, sorry about being so direct, but your profile picture ***immediately*** caught my attention. I am a widow, 58, who is looking for a relationship of substance. I recognize this is a 'sex site,' but I want quality over quantity. My children are grown, out of the house, so it's time for me to pursue *my* interests. I am a free-spirited woman who is 58, educated, financially independent, and worldly. I am not looking for sex only, but a meaningful, stable relationship with a man who should treat me like the queen I am. Respond *only* if you, too, enjoy the finer things in life, and want a serious relationship. Looking forward to hearing from you.
>
> XOXO
>
> Allison

My first reaction was, "What? Is this bitch crazy?" Admittedly, I was taken aback by her admission she liked my dick, yet essentially lectured me about how she was a woman of substance and all that bullshit. It was humorous, but also insulting to a degree. Further, she was a bit out of my age preference, and definitely sounded like a drama queen. I deleted the message and went to the next one. It read:

Hello there. We are a professional, attractive African American couple in Torrance. She is 37 and I am 40. We have been on this site for two months and have yet to meet a man she feels comfortable with. We are looking for a man who definitely is DDF, discreet, professional, and has a good sense of humor. She liked the content of your profile, and sees you as someone she would like to meet socially to see how things develop. We are interested in someone who is not pushy and understands/respects the fact that our marriage comes first. I have attached her picture for your review. Discretion is important to us, so her face is *not* included in the picture. You can see, however, that she is well-built. If you are interested, please contact us and include your phone number. Also, please tell us a little about your experience in these matters. Thank you.

Keith and Delores

I clicked on the picture and, immediately, my dick protruded through my robe, like a genie released from its bottle. Delores had a fantastic almond-colored body, firm breasts and long legs. I reminded myself not to fuck-up by accidently deleting their message, so I immediately clicked on a prompt labeled **Saved Message Bin**. Then, I responded to their message.

> Hi, Keith and Delores. Thanks for your message. I appreciate it and your candor. I have no "drama" in my life, so I am interested in meeting people just as you describe yourselves. To me, this is about having fun with like-minded folks, creating memories to last a lifetime. I am very clean, respectful, honest, sane, and easy to get along with. I live in Malibu, but know the Torrance area. I am certainly amenable to meeting for drinks/conversation. The way I see it, Keith, this is *all* about Delores. I am not the pushy/ arrogant type, so I think you both would find me to be trustworthy, witty as hell, intelligent (book sense and the all-elusive common sense), and just plain ol' fun. I have included my number, and I look forward to hearing from you both.
>
> Sincerely,
>
> Brian

I remembered Dennis' admonition that went along the lines of: *Don't use your real name until you meet someone and develop trust. There are too many flakes out there, so be cautious.* His words echoed in my brain because I was just about to write my real name at the conclusion of my message. I also thought, "What the hell does DDF mean?" So, I fished through other profiles on the site and was able to surmise it meant Drug and Disease-Free. In fact, it seemed as if I would need a damn *swingers* glossary to interpret the barrage of acronyms: DDF (disease and drug-free), BBW (big, beautiful woman), DP (double penetration), DVP (double vaginal penetration), MWF (married white female), MBC (married black couple), SWF (single white female), SBF (single black female), WM (white male), BM (black male), TV/TS (transvestite/transsexual), CP (cream pie), NSA (no-strings attached), NS (non-smoking), GB (gang bangs), and many more! Admittedly, some of the acronyms were confusing, such as *cream pie*. I dug further to find out what it meant and discovered it referred to women who liked to get "filled-up" with cum! Venturing into the *Lifestyle* would be interesting indeed!

I was about to read the next message when I heard a ding sound, a bell. A prompt popped-up in the middle of my screen that said, **Instant Message**. I clicked on the prompt, and was immediately greeted with, "Nice profile!" I responded by saying "Thank you" and then read the sender's profile: Straight MWC (41m/38f) visiting Los Angeles looking for NSA sex with clean, distinguished BM. You must be DDF and NS. I uttered to myself, "There go those fucking acronyms again." The prompt illuminated again. "What are you up to?" and I responded, "Just relaxing right now, and you?" "My name is Brad and my wife's name is Julia. We are at the Beverly Hills Hotel and Julia is horny as hell. We are from Tampa and she loves BBC! She read your profile, saw your picture, and wanted to know if you're able to play now." I thought to myself, "What the fuck is BBC?" so I scurried around the site: Big Black Cock! I laughed aloud and then reality set-in: *Did he just ask me to come over to their hotel and fuck his wife now?* I looked at the clock: 9:30p.m. "I read your profile, too, and saw Julia's picture," I said, continuing, "I'm **very** much interested." Brad replied, "Here is our cell number. Call us now so you can talk to her. And, yes, we're very serious." "Okay," I typed, "let me sign-off and I'll call in about 10 minutes." "Okay, we'll talk soon, but hurry, Julia's pretty damn horny and wants some BBC, now! ☺"

I signed off, but did not call immediately. My first reaction was to call Dennis. "Hey Dennis! It's Theo. How're you doing, man?" He sounded groggy, and his response was, "Well, I **was** doing okay sleeping my ass off until some dickhead decided to wake me up. Have you forgotten the time-zone difference, Mr. Cosmetics?" "Oh shit!" I said, "I forgot about that, my fault. I **had** to call you because I was on *Lifestyle Rendezvous* and a couple sent me an instant message. The wife, a white chick, claims she wants to get fucked now. What should I do?" Dennis' voice was now more energetic. "Have you seen a picture of her? If she's fine, then you need to get off the damn phone, stop fucking up my sleep, and go get some pussy!" I responded, "The hubby sent me the instant message, and said they're visiting from Tampa. I thought I'd call you since you know about all this shit. Remember, this is *all* new to me! They asked me to call them in a few minutes, and I said I would. Do you think I should call them or do you think it's just somebody joking around?"

"In my experience," he said, "it's those instant messages in the wee-hours that are actually *most* reliable and serious. I think you should call them. Send me a text of the particulars, so I'll know where you are. Text me the number they gave you to call as well if it's their cell phone." He continued, "Do you know anybody locally that you can tell where you're going? You can *never* be too cautious, so *always* let somebody know where you're going. In other words, Theo, don't let your dick get you into trouble! Now, son, let a player get some sleep. Call me in the morning!" "Yeah," I said, "I'll call my buddy Benito. I was with him earlier this evening, so I'm sure he's still up. Thanks, Dennis! I'll give you a buzz in the morning to let you know how everything went."

I hung-up with Dennis and recognized my breathing was heavy. And, my forehead and palms were sweating profusely. My nerves were shot, and my mind jolted, thinking about all the possibilities: *Is this real? Are they flakes? Will I be too nervous to get it up?* Finally, I summoned the courage to call. "Hello, may I speak to Brad?" He responded, "Yes, this is Brad." "Hi Brad," I said, "This is Brian from *Lifestyle Rendezvous.* We just sent each other an instant message on the site." "It's nice to meet you, Brian, and thanks for calling. Like I said, we're originally from Tampa, but we're visiting Los Angeles. Julia's horny as fuck, and she liked your profile and picture. You can tell from our profile that she's a knock-out." I interjected, "Brad, that's a dire understatement! Julia looks gorgeous, and I'm flattered she liked my profile."

I was attempting to be calm, making sure not to appear too anxious or, worse, desperate. However, Brad shocked me with is candor, and asked, "So, do you want to come over now and *play*?" Before I could thoroughly digest the reality of the situation, I blurted, "Hell yes! My profile is very accurate. I'm disease and drug-free, non-smoker and have absolutely no drama in my life. To me, this is **all** about meeting like-minded people who've common, carnal interests. I have no trite fantasies of trying to 'steal' your wife or any nonsense like that. So, Brad, count me the fuck in!" He laughed, and responded, "Brian, we've been swingers for about eight years, and we're pretty good at spotting bullshit profiles. Yours definitely stood out, and we appreciate guys like you who, like us, understand what this is all about." "Agreed!" I said. "I'm in Malibu, and, at this hour, probably about thirty minutes or so from the Beverly Hills Hotel. I'll have to shower first. It's just after 9:30, so I should be there around 10:15."

"That's perfect, Brian," he said. "Let me put Julia on the phone so you two can get acquainted. I look forward to meeting you." I could hear the phone change hands, and then a sensuous voice purred, "Well, helllllllo Brian! I'm glad you called. I *really* like your profile and, I confess, have a weakness for attractive, endowed Black men. You seem like the type of gentleman I enjoy being with." "I'm flattered, Julia," I said, "Thank you very much!" She continued, "We've been married just over eleven years, and very secure in our marriage." I responded, "I'm very happy to hear it's a secure marriage, Julia. I'm *not* into home-wrecking or doing anything dishonest. To me, this is *all* about having fun and creating memories with others who're like-minded." "Well, Brian," she said, "based upon that, your profile, picture, and that lovely cock, I think I need to give you our room number! We're in room 402, and I'll see you around 10:15. Hold a second, here's Brad. Byyyyyyye, Brian," she cooed. I peaked at their profile again, and my dick got harder than a petrified tree! "I'll see you soon, Julia," I said.

Brad picked up the phone and asked, "So, what do you think? Do you still want to come over?" "Are you kidding?" I asked. "Hell, if I had a helicopter I'd be there in five minutes." We laughed and I said, "Absolutely, Brad. I'm interested, and look forward to meeting you both. I'll see you soon." I was about to hang up, but Brad caught me, "Hey, Brian? Before you come over, I just want to give you the heads-up about Julia. Don't worry, nothing's wrong. Just a reminder: we're very clean, no diseases, no drugs, and serious. We liked your profile, and expect the same for you. Condoms are mandatory, so if you're not okay with that, we'll have to pass on the idea. Also, you need to know she has a *lot* of energy! She's not shy one bit, so do not

231

be surprised if she's already naked when you arrive." Again, my mind raced: *Dayyyum! I do not believe this shit is happening to me, now!* Brad continued, "She'll likely answer the door in sexy lingerie and drop to her knees and start sucking your cock as soon as you walk in. She likes assertive men, so don't be bashful. As for me, I'll just kick back and enjoy watching. We fucked right after dinner and I haven't recovered. Julia, though, wants more, which is why we love *Lifestyle Rendezvous* so much. Give me a call if anything comes up. I'll see you soon." "Okay, Brad," I said. "I'll see you soon. Do you want me to bring anything to eat or drink?" "No," he said, "we already had dinner and there's a bottle of wine here. Otherwise, buddy, depending on how much time you have, just bring enough energy and condoms to last a good three hours, if not more!" "You go it, Brad. Bye, bye."

I hung-up the phone, thrust my robe off, and sped to the shower. Even though I had taken a shower a short time ago, I savored another, just to make sure I was ultra-fresh. Within fifteen minutes, I was showered, shaved, and dressed – dashingly, I might add. I firmly believed in making lasting first impressions, so I donned a navy blue Calvin Klein two-piece blazer and slacks, white silk pocket square, white button-down shirt, Movado watch, black Bruno Magli loafers, black silk boxer shorts, and black sox. I completed the ensemble by strategically spraying my favorite Armani cologne on my neck, inner thighs, and behind both ears. I looked at myself in the full-length mirror: task completed. I looked casually elegant. And, I remembered that Dennis had given me five Viagra tablets, so I made sure to put one in my pocket.

I knew where the Beverly Hills Hotel was located, but did not remember the cross-streets. It was best, I thought, to take the route I was familiar with instead of risking getting lost. I was sure there was a more direct route, but "Fuck it," I said. "It's better to be safe than sorry." I decided to cruise south on the Pacific Coast Highway until I reached the I-10 Freeway heading east, and then exit LaCienega Boulevard heading north, then west on Wilshire. Just as I was turning west on Wilshire, my phone rang. "Hello?" "Brian? This is Julia. I'm just checking-in to see how far away you are." "Hi Julia," I said. "I'm turning left on Wilshire now, so I'm probably less than ten minutes away." "Mmm," she purred, "that's not far at all. Just come on up to room 402. Call me when you're about to get on the elevator so I can greet you at our door. See ya' soon, sexy." I responded, "Julia, you're going to mess around and make me get a speeding ticket talking like that. I'll be there shortly, and I can't wait to have you wear me out." Before she hung up, she said, "We'll see about that, sexy, bye, bye for now."

Shit! I almost forgot to call Benito! I pulled over just past Rodeo Drive and called Benito. "Hey, Theo! What are you up to?" he asked. "Hey, Benito!" I said. "Do you have a pen and piece of paper? I want you to write down some information." "Sure," he said, "hold on a sec. Okay, shoot!" "Take down this phone number. It's a cell phone with a Tampa, Florida area code. And, write down Beverly Hills Hotel,

Room 402, Brad and Julie from *Lifestyle Rendezvous*." He barked, "What the fuck is this about, Theo?" and I replied, "I met a couple on *Lifestyle Rendezvous* about an hour ago and they invited me to their room at the Beverly Hills Hotel. I just want someone to know where I'm going, and with whom." "No shit!" he screamed. "I'm serious, Benito. I spoke with them on the phone and they seem like cool people. But, you never know, so I'm just trying to be a lil' cautious, especially since this hook-up is different from the Chicago party. This is **completely** different, and I'm on my own here. Call me in about thirty minutes just to check-up on me, okay? I'll catch-up with you tomorrow and let you know how things went. Don't forget to call me in about thirty minutes!" I had to remind Benito because his memory was not the most efficient, and it was especially hampered when he was aroused. "Got it! I'll call in thirty, and let me know if you need any help. You know I'm less than ten minutes from the hotel, right?" "Yes, Benito, I remember" I said. "I'll be **sure** to call you if I need any help. I'll talk to you soon." Before I whisked from the curb, I remembered to take the Viagra pill, and crossed my fingers it would have an immediate effect.

I pulled into the valet parking area of the hotel and a cheerful young lady zipped up to me. "Good evening, sir, and welcome to the Beverly Hills Hotel. Do you have any bags, sir?" Peering at her nametag, I said, "Good evening, Drea, and thanks for the warm welcome. I don't have any bags, but thank you for asking." "Enjoy your stay," she said, as she hopped inside my car and drove off.

When I reached the lobby, I took out my phone and called Julia, who answered in the middle of the first ring! "Hello, Brian. I take it you're about to get on the elevator?" "Yes, coming right up." "Oh," she said, "you'll be coming alright, and I suspect I will, too."

I looked myself over in the lobby mirror one last time before stepping onto the elevator. When I reached the fourth floor, I felt semi-nauseous again, confronted and annoyed by petulant queries that pecked, like dirty Philadelphia pigeons, at my confidence: *What the fuck am I getting myself into? This is real, Theo, so **now** what are you going to do? What type of married people go around fucking others? What if they're actually thieves and want to rob you? What happens if Brad tries to touch me when I'm fucking Julia?* Finally, *Theo, shut the fuck up and knock on the damn door!*

I was about to knock on the door and then, open sesame, it seemed to open on its own. Of course, that was not the case. It was Julia, who poked her head from behind the door, which opened just enough to allow me to squeeze through. I immediately saw why she did not open the door completely: she wore a red silk negligée top, matching panties, and black high-heeled pumps. As soon as the door was closed, she descended to her knees and began unbuckling my pants. *Damn! This chick is no joke!* "Uhh, hello, Julia," I muttered. She looked upward, while rubbing my crotch, "Hello, Brian," she said. "It's a pleasure to meet you. Now, let me see what this bulge is all about." I stood motionless and let her work her magic. Seconds later, my pants hugged my ankles, and she unabashedly started sucking me.

"Hello Brian. I'm Brad. I see Julia is up to her antics again. She simply can't get enough cock, so I'm glad you were able to help her out tonight." Brad, who was fully clothed, walked over to me and we shook hands. I was embarrassed to be shaking hands with a guy while his wife was on her knees slurping my dick like it was a Popsicle. *Nobody is going to believe this. This is straight out of those old Penthouse Forum letters, all of which began, 'You won't believe this, but...'* As much as I found those letters to be comical and total bullshit, *now*, I know what the hell they were talking about!

"Honey," Brad said, "will you at least let our guest take his clothes off? Geez!" Julia continued fellating me while skillfully removing my loafers. She slid my pants from beneath my feet, which allowed me to step out of them. Then, she handed them to Brad, who placed them on the sofa. "Wow," she said, "that is such a lovely cock. I hope you don't mind, but I *had* to sample the appetizer." She stood up and, to my surprise, shook my hand, almost a formal introduction, and said, "Nice to meet you, Brian. I hope I wasn't too forward." *You just finished sucking my dick and now you want to introduce yourself with a formal greeting? You didn't even say hello first, you just started munching on the dick. Nobody's going to believe this shit!* "Uh... Julie... err... not at all... I love it when a woman's assertive, especially sexually. "That's good to know, Brian," she said, "because I make *no* apologies for loving cock, and I'm especially unapologetic for admiring a nice, black cock like yours. Now, let's get you out of all those clothes."

She slowly undressed me, and when I was completely naked, rubbed her body against mine. "Mmm, you smell absolutely delicious. I love that cologne." She asked me to take a seat on the couch, which I did, and then Brad brought over the bottle of wine and uncorked it. Julie proposed a toast: "Here's to hoping this may turn into a long-lasting friendship." "I second that," I said. We clicked our champagne flutes. Julia and I sat on the couch, naked, while Brad stood across the room.

"So," Julia asked, "how long have you been on *Lifestyle Rendezvous*?" "Actually, Julia, I ***just*** joined the site and posted my profile last night. A friend of mine in Chicago told me about it. I visited him this past weekend and he took me to my first *Lifestyle* party. This is all brand new to me." "Oh really?" she asked, surprised. "From reading your profile, we figured you have been in the *Lifestyle* a number of years. Usually, the 'newbies' write those silly, 'I have a huge dick, let's fuck' type of profiles. Yours, however, gave no indication you're new." She continued, "That's not a bad thing with us at all, though. We just like being around clean, discreet, professional people, and your profile caught our attention." "And I'm damn glad it did," I said. "I actually put a lot of thought into it, hoping people would understand the type of person I am, my interests, and my perspective about it all."

"Well," Brad said, "it's a great profile, and we're glad to have met you. We only play with people who are disease-free, clean, and respect discretion. I am a banker and Julie works for an auction firm. We're in Los Angeles, in part, because our oldest son is a junior in high school and he's doing a campus visit to USC. He wants to study film production, and USC has a good program. Julia came out to do some work with Sotheby's and I, my friend, decided to take a few days of vacation time. We try to play when we travel, which is why we joined *Lifestyle Rendezvous* a few years back."

I was struck by their sense of openness, freedom, if you will. They seemed to be so relaxed, honest, and drama-free. There was no pressure, but I felt compelled to share a bit about myself. "For starters, my real name is Theo. My friend in Chicago suggested that I be cautious and discreet with others, not divulge too much information until I felt safe and comfortable. "A point well taken, and good advice," Brad chimed in. I went on, "I work in senior management for a Cosmetics company and Los Angeles is my home, for now. I've been here a few years, and considering moving back east, but that's not concrete at the moment. I love my work, and, of course, am spoiled by the weather here." "Well," Brad chimed in, "if you decide to move, keep me in mind if you're going to buy property. My bank is one of the most successful with getting people home loans." I responded, "I certainly will, Brad. I have a realtor looking for property, so I may take you up on that offer."

Brad and I, briefly, got so involved in the prospect of doing business together that we ignored Julia, at least until she warned, "You boys can talk business if you want, but I am **not** going to be a 'happy camper' if I don't get me some cock… now!" I quickly shot back, "Uh, Brad, we'll have to continue this conversation at a more, dare I say, appropriate moment. This beautiful lady needs some attention, and I need to oblige." Julia arose from the couch and stood before me. She had long brunette hair, piercing gray eyes, about 5'4" tall, 120 pounds, firm, supple 40D breasts, shapely legs, and a perky butt. I massaged her legs and nipples as I sat, and she moaned immediately when I darted my tongue around her navel. "I think that's my cue to get out of the way," said Brad. "Don't mind me, Bri…, I mean, Theo. Do you mind if I take a couple of pictures? I **assure** you, your face will **not** be included. Julia likes to have a couple of pictures taken when she *plays*. She turns into a little slut with a camera in her face and a cock in her mouth. Don't you, honey?" I was now standing and Julia was on her knees again with a mouthful of dick. She whimpered, "Oh, yes!" Then, she took it out of her mouth, looked at it admiringly, and said, "Mmm! I *love* cock and just can't seem to keep my panties on! I'm a slut for a nice cock!" I told Brad I didn't mind him taking a couple of pictures, but reminded him none of my face.

Brad took a camera from his luggage and walked over to me and Julia. My mind raced again. *Did he just call his wife a slut? Ain't thattabitch! Apparently she likes it because she's moaning like a*

239

motherfucker, and she's got a Kung-fu grip on my dick! To hell with it, go with the flow. "Okay, honey," he said. On cue, Julia stuck her tongue out, and placed it on the tip of my dick. She looked straight into the camera lens, aimed inches from her face. "Next!" For the second picture, she put the head in her mouth, and for the third, half of it down her throat. She wanted a fourth, demonstrating her deep-throating skills, but my girth and length were unmanageable. *This is some strrrrange shit!* "A couple more, honey, and then I'll be out of the way. Theo, did you bring condoms? If not, we have some." "I'm prepared," I said. "I don't think Julia wants me to move." She was slurping up and down in a frenzy, using her hands to stroke me simultaneously.

Brad handed me a *Magnum*, which had a Pavlovian effect on Julia. She smiled, stood up, and said, "I was wondering what took you so long to pull that out." She moaned as I put it on and then led me to the edge of the bed. "Okay, Brad, let's not get carried away with that damn camera! Take two pictures, max, and then Theo and I need to fuck!" She laid me back on the bed with my legs hanging over its edge, then straddled me. She arched her back and bent forward so our chests met. Brad was able to get a picture of her sliding down on my full erection. "Okay, now my favorite position," she requested. "I'll lay on my back, spread my legs as wide as possible and you go balls-deep in my pussy. Is that okay?" "Is that okay?" I asked, "You *must* be kidding me!" She laughed and said, "I thought so." "In fact," I said, "let's do one of me teasing you with just the head in, and the second with me buried in you deep. Deal?" "Oh, you're a naughty man," she said, "but I like how you think." Snap! Snap!

"Brad," I said, "please email copies of those to me. I can't wait to see how they look." "No problem," he said. "I'll block out Julia's face, but not so much that you can't see her sucking cock." "Thanks," I said, and continued "Now that pictures are out of the way, let me *show* you what my profile is all about." Brad dimmed the lights and sat on the sofa while I lay Julia on the bed. I massaged her feet, kissed her toes, and began running my tongue, upwards, on her legs. Instinctively, she spread her legs and allowed me greater access to lick and nibble. I kept my hands busy, rubbing her nipples, until my lips reached her semi-shaved mound. Parting her labia, I flicked my tongue to-and-fro, and then, gently, put her clit between my lips. I pressed my lips together, putting a little pressure on her clit. She responded by thrusting her hips upward, screaming, "Wow!"

We both were in the moment, and just as I was about to slide my tongue inside her, my phone started ringing. *Who the fuck is calling me? Talk about bad-timing! Oh, shit! It's probably Benito.* I was in the midst of a sexual quandary: Do I sabotage the mood by answering the phone or do I ignore it? Initially, I chose the latter, but thought better of it. I did not want Benito to panic in case I did not answer, but did not want Julia to feel shunned. I compromised and chose the honest route by telling her "I hate to spoil the moment, my dear, but I told my friend Benito to call me to make sure I was safe. As I said, I'm new at this, so I just want to let him know I'm okay." Julia was amenable, and understood. In fact, Brad did, too, and was helpful. "Do you want me to answer it, Theo? I can put the phone up to your mouth and you can let him know you're okay. That way, you can get back to business." "Good idea" I said. Brad brought the phone over to me and held it to my ear. I answered, "Benito!"

Are you safe? Yes.

So, you're really meeting them at the Beverly Hills Hotel? Yes.

Is she pretty? Oh, she's absolutely beautiful!

What are you doing now? I'm eating her pussy.

Stop lying, you bastard! Julia, please tell my buddy Benito what I'm doing. *"He's eating my pussy Benito, and doing a wonderful job!"*

Where is her husband? He's holding the phone up to my face. I'm safe, now can I get back to eating this delicious pussy? *"Hi Benito, this is Brad, I'm Julia's husband."*

You lucky motherfucker! Do you need help? No! Bye, Benito, I'll see you tomorrow.

Theo, I'm not too far. Tell them... Click!

"Now," I said, "where did I leave off?" Julia used her hands to guide my face back between her legs, "Right there!" she said. I sucked and licked her for several minutes, and then slid my finger inside. Her pussy was soaking wet, and not only from my saliva. She was thoroughly turned-on, so I told her, "Let's get in a 69 position. I know you want to suck me some more, but I'm not through eating this delicious pussy." Without hesitation, she positioned herself atop me and pulled the *Magnum* off before devouring me. I have never been particularly enthused about receiving blowjobs, but Julia's technique was atypical. First, and most important, she never used her teeth. Second, she went slowly, skillfully taking her time from tip-to-base. Third, she used her hands to stroke the shaft as her mouth moved up and down on it, and, fourth, she *loved* doing it! Julia was groaning, literally, while sucking me. I had never met a woman who possessed so much enthusiasm for sucking dick, but she was that person. Sensing how wired-up she was, I started talking to her between flicks of my tongue on her clit, "I think you're ready for this dick inside your tight pussy." "Mmph, yes, mmph!" she stammered.

I moved her from atop my body, but remained on my back. Brad brought over another *Magnum*, but this time, Julia put it in her mouth. *What the fuck is she doing with the condom in her mouth?* Without using either hand, she rolled the condom down my dick using just her tongue! *Damn!* "Have you ever seen that?" she asked. "Hell no," I said, "but you damn sure have my attention. You need to join a damn circus! You'd be a millionaire within two goddamn weeks!"

Brad chimed in, "You're damn right, Theo! Imagine how our income would soar if she made some instructional videos."

I lay on my back and she stood up in the bed, admiring my dick as it, too, stood upward. "I like the seduction," she added "of standing and, slowly, oh-so-slowly, lowering my pussy on that thick cock of yours. I'm so fucking wet just thinking about it being inside me." She tossed her lingerie off, but kept her high-heel pumps on. *What is it about women being butt-ass naked, but keeping their high-heels on when they fuck?* Teasingly, she placed her index finger in her mouth and sucked on it, as if she were savoring dessert, and proceeded to lower herself, as promised, very slowly. "Mmm, Theo, I'm going to put the head in." "Fuck yeah," I whispered, "give me that pussy, Julia." She put my engorged head in and wiggled her hips in a circular motion. "Ohhhh God! That cock feels so damn good." Lower... Her head thrust back, she took me inside, and was now bouncing up and down as her heels clawed into the mattress. Brad encouraged her, "That's it, honey, take that cock! You like Theo's cock, don't you?" "Yes!" "Is he stretching you out, honey?" "Yesssss!"

I had only been fucking Julia a few minutes before she *gushed*! "I hope you don't mind," she said, "but I'm a squirter. I should have told you that earlier, but I got so damn excited, I forgot to tell you." "No, no, Julia. I don't mind at all," I assured her. "In fact, that's a *major* turn-on to me! It tells I'm doing something that pleases you mentally and physically." Moaning loudly, she said, "Oh, Theo, you got *that* right! Fuck me with that big cock! Make me squirt again!" I increased

244

the frequency and intensity of my upward thrusts, hammering her womb with abandon, relishing her passionate whimpers. *Gush!* "You made me cum again," she wailed, "You're making me cum so hard..."

For the next two hours, we sucked and fucked... and fucked again, virtually non-stop. Brad was correct in saying Julia had an abundance of energy, but it was the final position, me on top with her ankles resting on my shoulders, that proved the final blow. I emptied three *Magnums* before we lay exhausted, complimenting each other for being attentive and helping the other cum; in her case, she squirted a total of six times throughout the night, and the mattress was soaked! We peeked over at Brad, whose pants were around his ankles. He was jerking his dick while screaming that he was cumming. "Whew!" he said, "That was some show!" Julia responded, "I hope you liked watching it as much as I enjoyed *getting* it!"

We indulged in small talk, laughed a lot, and had one last glass of wine. Ironically, even after I had cum several times, the Viagra was still working on me, and Julia marveled, "You are something else, Theo. I've not been fucked like *that* in ages! I hope we can do it again, and soon." I got dressed and told them I'd like to connect again, too. We agreed we would meet again before they returned to Tampa, and I invited them to my place in Malibu.

Finally, I left and headed to the lobby as I adjusted my clothes in the elevator. My legs felt like rubber, but I was able to walk straight. *That was unbelievable. Incredible! There's no way in hell anybody is going to believe that. I'm glad Brad took pictures.* I gave my parking ticket to the valet, Drea, and, within seconds, she sped my Porsche up to the hotel's main entrance. I gave her a $50 bill and she thanked me for telling her to keep the change.

My body felt like it was 4a.m., but it was just 2:00a.m. when I looked at my watched. I pulled away from the Beverly Hills Hotel with a smile on my face, and in disbelief. I whispered to myself, "*Lifestyle Rendezvous* is the shit!" as I drove east on Wilshire. I was tempted to call Dennis, to give him a full account, but I remembered I woke him previously, so I would wait until later in the day. I was also tempted to call Benito, but quickly discarded that idea because I knew he would have a barrage of questions, and I was just too tired to entertain them.

When I reached home, I showered and checked to see if I had any messages on the site. *You have 8 new messages!* Before I left to visit Brad and Julia, I had 7 messages and read 2. So, from the time I left until now, I received 3 more messages! "Wow!" I said, "This is amazing. Hell, the membership fee has paid for itself already in terms of my experience with Brad and Julia." It was tempting to read all the messages, but I did not have the energy. I did notice, however, there was a message from Brad and Julia, which I did read.

> Theo,
> Thanks for coming over at such short notice. We thoroughly enjoyed your company, and you gave Julia what she craves – a thorough fucking. Most important,

your personality and approach to the *Lifestyle* are congruent with ours. We hope the feelings are mutual, and certainly hope to see you again before we return to Tampa. And, should your travels take you to Tampa, be sure to let us know!

Brad and Julia

p.s.

Here're the pictures I promised you. Mind you, when Julia saw Them, she got horny again and, well, you know what happened next. ☺

I looked at the pictures and, sure enough, got horny again, too! Brad dutifully blocked out a portion of Julia's face in the pictures, but her delicious body was readily evident. I said to myself, "When Benito sees *these* pictures, he'll talk my ear off for weeks at a time!" I decided I'd respond to Brad and Julia when I woke up. For now, my bed called me, and, shortly, I would be sound asleep.

Chapter 35

I woke up at 5:30a.m., refreshed, but still be bit sluggish from the previous night's activities. I lay in bed a few minutes, letting the *Lifestyle* sink-in. In less than one week, I attended a sex party with people from all over the world, met a couple at the Beverly Hills Hotel, had several messages and, I'm sure, invitations for more sexual forays. When Dennis first told me about the *Lifestyle*, I was dumbfounded, awestruck, angry, and jealous. Suffice it to say, I was an emotional rollercoaster because all the tenets conflicted with my upbringing, my ethical and moral foundation. Now, I felt more amenable to the *Lifestyle*. I met some fantastic people from all walks of life. There were no hidden agendas, false pretenses, or, misrepresentations from anyone I met. Perhaps this was my opportunity to explore further. After all, as long as everything involved consenting adults, what could be wrong with that?

As soon as I walked into the office, Benito waltzed up to me, virtually accosted me, actually, and asked, "What happened last night? I heard their voices, so it's obvious you weren't bullshitting me on the phone. How long did you stay? Was she **really** pretty or were you exaggerating?" I smiled, but was somewhat annoyed by his interrogation. He hadn't even allowed me to get to my office to put my briefcase down. The tone of my voice reflected my exasperation: "Will you back the fuck up, Benito, and let me get to my office? I'll be sure to tell your horny ass what happened over lunch. By the way, this time, your ass is paying for lunch." "Come 'on, Theo," he pleaded, "give me the goods, brother." I stopped, turned directly towards him and said, "Benito, I'll talk with you at lunch, later!" He knew my threshold for him being a pain in the ass, and always seemed to push until he recognized I had enough.

When I reached my office, I closed the door, set my briefcase down, and hung my sport coat on its rack. My first order of business: Call Dennis! "Hey Dennis," I said, "Did I catch you at a bad time?" "Not at all" he said. "How're you doing, Theo? How did it go last night?"

"Man," I said, "you would not believe it! I took your advice, went over to the hotel, and everything went down. A couple from Tampa is visiting Los Angeles. They're professional folks. He's a banker and she does something with auctions, Sotheby's, or something like that." "Enough of the pleasantries," he said, "Did you fuck her?" "Dennis, I was there about three hours! She was fine as hell, great body, and could take some dick! Her husband took a couple of pictures, but stayed out of the way, otherwise." I sensed caution in Dennis's voice. "You didn't let them take pictures with your face in them, did you?" "Oh, hell no!" I barked. "I took your advice, and speaking of that, my name is Brian, not Theo." Dennis burst into laughter and said, "I taught you well, I see." "Eventually," I said, "I told them my real name and a lil' about me after they gave me their personal information. I felt comfortable, and apparently they did, too. Dennis, I had a blast, and it wouldn't have happened without you. Thanks, man."

We talked a bit more about how things were going at his job, his *Lifestyle* experiences, and then our parents. As we wound down, I sensed Dennis going into sage-mode. "Alright, Theo, I have to get going, but let's talk this weekend. I'm glad you've had some good experiences, especially in such a short time From the party you went to here, to Stephanie, and the couple you met last night, it'll only get better." He continued, "Don't get too eager, and just take your time. Everything will work out because you're a good dude. Remember, think with the *right* head! Have fun, Theo, and get off your moral high-horse. Quite trying to over-analyze the *Lifestyle* and just accept it as it is. People like to fuck, period. The sooner you understand that, the better off you'll be and more fun you'll have." "Thanks, brother, I appreciate that," I said. "We'll talk this weekend." "Catch you later," he said, and then we hung up.

At 9:30a.m., my office intercom buzzed. It was my executive assistant, Andrea. "Hello, Mr. Williams. I wanted to give you the appointments on your calendar today. You have a phone conference with Regional Managers at 10:30a.m. that goes until 11:30a.m. Mr. Tucci asked me to put him on your calendar for a lunch appointment, but I told him I would confirm that with you. At 2p.m. you have a phone conference with Ms. Berry's representative to talk about our new line of products coming out in late July. That should last thirty minutes, at the most. Finally, at 4p.m. you have a 1-hour presentation to attend on Premier's internet growth strategy. That's it for today in terms of meetings. I will bring in the files for the conference calls. Is there anything else you need?" "Thanks, Andrea, I appreciate your help. I'm good to go for the day's tasks. Regarding lunch, please move Benito's meeting to 7:30p.m. for dinner at the Warehouse." "Will do, Mr. Williams, anything else?"

I decided to go, alone, to Santa Monica's Third Street Promenade for lunch. I was not in the mood for Benito, and, frankly, I knew that when he asked me earlier. I was having a burger when my phone rang. "Hello, may I speak to Brian, please?" Initially, I was taken aback, and almost told the caller they had the wrong number. Then, I realized *I* was Brian! "Yes, this is Brian. To whom am I speaking with?" "Hi Brian, this is Delores as in Delores and Keith from *the* site?" "Oh! Yes, I remember," I said. "How're you, Delores?" "Doing well, thanks. I wanted to touch base to see if you would be available for cocktails on Friday, early evening." Intrigued, I responded, "Yes, that can work." She continued, "Keith and I would like to spend some time with you to get acquainted. We don't *play* on the first date, so it's an opportunity for us to find out if there's some chemistry, without any pressure." "I appreciate that," I said. "I can do Friday, any time after 6p.m. I work in Santa Monica. What area will you and Keith be coming from?" "We'll be in the Beverly Hills area," she said. "I know a nice place in that area, The Stinking Rose. How 'bout we meet there at 7p.m.?" "That'll be perfect," she said. "We've been there before. I'll call you on Friday afternoon, just to check-in. How does that sound?" "Perfect!" I said. "I'll see you and Keith on Friday at The Stinking Rose, 7p.m

The last week had been a whirlwind for my social life. I hadn't had this much erotic fun in ages, and the future was uncannily bright! Perhaps I was too critical of the *Lifestyle*, and allowed my preconceived notions to jade my perspective. Now, however, I was beginning to feel more open. Free. "Life is too short," I said to myself, as I munched on fries, "seize life with the utmost zeal, and everything will fall into place."

My meet-and-greet with Delores and Keith went very well on Friday. Delores had a killer body, chocolate-colored, smooth complexion and exuded class and sex appeal. Keith was a handsome gentleman as well. Neither he nor I felt threatened by the other, and he was uncommonly relaxed about the idea of sharing his wife with another man. Fortunately, that other man was me! Delores worked in the Wilshire District as Editor of a Fashion Magazine and Keith was Finance Manager of an Audi dealership in Beverly Hills. We had a ton of laughs, and agreed to set-up a *play date*, as they called it, for the following weekend at my place.

Chapter 36

It was a lazy Saturday afternoon and the sun was reflecting off the Pacific Ocean with full vigor. The ocean was littered with surfers and the beach was peppered with sun worshippers. Five days had passed since my return from the *Windy City*. I went to work on Tuesday, so it seemed the week glided by, and a couple of eleven-hour days were actually bearable. Now, it was my time to relax and reflect upon the trip, and my life.

I grabbed a Heineken from the refrigerator and sprawled on the couch. Feeling refreshed yet pensive, I decided to listen to music. The sun shone through the open sliding doors, and I could hear waves crushing against rocks, drowning out customary Pacific Coast Highway traffic. This was a perfect environment for thought and reflection.

Usually, I am strategic about choosing which CDs or albums I play. This time, however, I pushed the *Random Play* button on the CD player so I could ingest any tunes that cued up. Like life itself, I would adjust to the variety of tunes the player churned out. Ironically, the first tune to play was one of Pat Metheny's signature tunes, *Are You Going With Me?* I wondered what the world would be like if others went with me, ventured into the *Lifestyle*.

Mentally, my journey began, as I thought about it in greater depth, many years ago when I sat in an undergraduate Human Sexual Behavior psychology class. I was inquisitive about sex even then, when my chain-smoking, Vodka-induced professor would saunter into class and promptly show erotic videos, then engage the class in discussions about sexual mores.

Beyond students' nervous laughter and trite giggles, I often left the class with more questions than answers. Sometimes, a classmate would nudge me out of my question-laden stupor. And, since it was a Catholic university, I was particularly curious, asking myself rhetorical questions like, "What might the world be like if we were less Puritanical about sexuality?" "Why is it some people are so hypocritical and intent on stating what others *should* do *behind closed doors* when these very same saviors' private behavior betrays their public, sentiments?"

Then, I thought about my Biology class when the lecture focused on the animal kingdom and how some animal species did not engage in monogamy. I wondered, "Why were humans so intent on extolling the virtues of monogamy? Why can't people just enjoy life and not feel guilty about having sex, even if it's not for procreation or on a wedding night?" I thought about my experiences working for various companies, and about women and men whom co-workers secretly chided; the workaholics who were so high-strung and married to their jobs, the ones whom co-workers quietly muttered, "She *really* needs a man or, at the *very* least, some dick!" or "He *really* needs to get laid, he's too high-strung!" I wondered why they, too, denied themselves opportunities to enjoy life to its fullest, but took out their sexual frustrations on others. I suspected, though, that the women had large, over-utilized dildos hidden in their clothes drawers and the men possessed various devices with which to masturbate. Poor bastards!

I thought about all these questions, life questions, intimacy questions, and it seemed as if I had more questions now as I had in prior years. I was certain, however, I would seize life and enjoy the journey, for that was how I now saw life – *a wonderful journey.* Ironically, the journey had little to do with sex, although that was a part of it. The journey was about exploration and overcoming fears, mental obstacles, and, most important, making decisions with *my* interests at the fore.

I heard the click of the CD player changing to a new disc, and as it did, I pondered all these questions, slowly drifting off as Coltrane's *After The Rain* massaged my soul… I thought long and hard about moving back to Philadelphia to be closer to my aging mother. My tenure in Los Angeles had been filled with challenges at work, lessons learned, erotic adventures beyond belief, and various queries that made me ponder the difference between love, sex, and intimacy. Metaphorically, I thought about my years in Los Angeles as a door. That door represented a part of my life; a door, initially closed, peered into, and then fully opened.

Sexually, I thought, how different was I from others? Based upon the sheer magnitude of *Lifestylers*, I knew with certainty I was not alone for my knowledge was garnered from first-hand experiences. The voice of my undergraduate Experimental Psychology professor echoed in my head: "No study is valid and reliable without solid data and empirical evidence! Everything else is just a belief." Surely, one could not ignore the fact that millions, globally, chose the *Lifestyle* over "traditional relationships."

My cell phone rang and interrupted my thoughts. Initially, I was going to let it go to voice mail, but my intuition suggested otherwise. I picked-up the phone and examined the caller's number to decide if I wanted to be disturbed. However, when I saw Stephanie's number on the Caller I.D., I quickly pushed the "Accept" button. "Well, hello, Stephanie, how are you? This is a pleasant surprise, and you have perfect timing. I'm just lying back enjoying the beautiful ocean view, listening to music."

Stephanie beamed, "Hey there, Theo! I'm fine, and it's so good to hear your voice. I wish I were there with you." She continued, "Well, I have some good news and some potentially greater news. Which do you prefer to hear first?" I responded, "Uh, you have me stumped on that one. I think I'll go with the good news first." "Well, the good news is that I heard from my realtor friend, Scott, in Philadelphia. He told me he has some excellent property available in Bala Cynwood. It's a stone's throw from Philadelphia. The property is a two bedroom condominium in a private neighborhood, close to excellent shopping areas, and is selling for a good price."

"Stephanie, thank you so, so much! I appreciate your helping me move closer to home. I'll have to find a way to show you my appreciation for your hard work. So, what is the potentially greater news?" "Well," she said, "as I mentioned before, Scott has a very successful firm, and he specializes in residential and commercial properties. He's expanding his business and asked me to consider moving to Philadelphia to become a partner! I'm thinking about doing it because I always wanted to move to the East Coast, but never had a real reason. I've been in Chicago for a long time, so the idea of moving is intriguing. Both my parents passed away several years ago, and I do have aunts and uncles throughout the eastern corridor. The offer would be even *more* appealing if a certain someone I know in Los Angeles decided to move there as well."

I was ecstatic about the prospect of moving closer to home, but then I had butterflies in my stomach when I thought about Stephanie's job offer and, by extension, spending considerably more time with her. I also thought about what it would be like to have a serious relationship with her, and, frankly, my stomach initially felt queasy. After considering the possibilities, though, I responded, "You know what, Stephanie? Life is short, go for it! You never know what's *behind closed doors* until you open them up."

Stephanie and I exchanged a few more pleasantries, briefly talked about the *City of Brotherly Love* and then hung up. The ocean whispered my name again, so I walked out onto my balcony. The vastness of the Pacific Ocean helped me put my life into perspective, reminding me to treasure the seemingly smaller things in life. I thought about the possibilities that accompanied being with Stephanie, and my heart raced! A smile came to my face as I reflected, so I pulled out my phone and punched in a few numbers. First, I called my childhood friend, Glen, who had recently moved to Los Angeles, to let him know my move back to Philadelphia was taking form. I knew he would apologize, yet again, for his outburst and misunderstanding when I initially told him I was considering moving, as well as getting more deeply involved with Stephanie. Of course, I apologized, too, for berating him. He was actually ecstatic to hear that I was happy about it, and sure it was what I wanted to do.

Most of all, though, I wanted to share my enthusiasm with someone else, the person who was integral to helping me peer **behind closed doors** of my life, so I called my other brotherly friend, Dennis. "Hey, Dennis, how are you doing? Hey man, I just finished speaking with Stephanie. Guess what I'm going to do…"

Post Script

Behind Closed Doors is largely, but not exclusively, a work of fiction so there are very accurate sentiments and activities therein. It attempts to bring to the forefront a *Lifestyle* that has largely been ignored despite millions of global adherents. In part, the *Lifestyle's* status as an appendage of dialogue is that some of its tenets are antithetical to our static, Puritanical perspectives about interpersonal and sexual relationships. *Behind Closed Doors* is not a polemic challenging "traditional" relationship mores. Nor is its purpose to encourage people to venture into the *Lifestyle*. From what I am told, these types of relationships are not easy to develop, let alone sustain. Sharing one's partner sexually with others, I suspect, encompasses a range of philosophical, moral, emotional, health, and intellectual decisions people must tease out. As someone told me, "The *Lifestyle* **is not** for everybody."

Frankly, my life-long curiosity about sexual mores stimulated me to pen *Behind Closed Doors,* in part, because I find the idea of *swinging* an intriguing one. Considering the massive numbers of marriages and/or relationships that end because one partner "cheated" on the other begs the question: Is there a better way? *Lifestylers* I have spoken with, and there were many, told me in varying degrees that their relationships were actually **more** secure. Why? One primary tenet is honesty, so partners make sure there are no sexual secrets, and that lines of communication are always open. If the mantra,

"Relax, it's just sex" is true, then perhaps it is worth investigating in greater detail the reasons for explosive rates of divorces and the levels of satisfaction among people in the *Lifestyle* versus those of "traditional" marriages.

Writing *Behind Closed Doors* helped me address many queries I have always had about sexual mores related to interpersonal and/or romantic relationships. Some questions have been sufficiently answered while others remain adrift. While I still have many more questions than answers, this novel was cathartic in that it allowed me to interview *Lifestylers* to gain *their* perspectives. What I found fascinating about speaking with *Lifestylers* is they represent **all** walks of life, hail from almost every continent, earn incomes from low to astronomically high, and have education levels from high school diplomas to medical degrees. So, when one asks "What do *Lifestylers* look like?" or "What do they do?" the answer is as simple as you looking in a mirror. They are just like you!

To all those who shared their insights and lessons with me, I am humbly indebted. Most important, and I emphasize this point strongly, *Lifestylers* who shared their insights with me may rest **assured** their identities *will go with me to my grave!* I recognize that, generally *(at least in public!)*, our society frowns upon the *Lifestyle*, and lambasts it with fatuous, negative descriptors. You entrusted me with information, and I would never besmirch your names and/

or personal information. If I may coin the mantra of Agents Mulder and Scully from the rabidly popular television show (and movie), *The X-Files*, we know there is a worldwide community of *swingers*. Yes, "they're out there," and in vast numbers!

Yours in spirit,
E. Lee Ritter

Author's Note

The author wishes to acknowledge the artistic production of each musician referred to therein. It should be blatantly obvious that jazz music permeates virtually every facet of my life. Without music, the trajectory of my existence assuredly would have meandered in alternate directions. Therefore, I am not only ecstatic, but my heart smiles, to have been able to pen work that incorporates my love for this wonderful art that many people call jazz.

I invite readers to cull through recordings mentioned in *Behind Closed Doors* and, further, add them to your collection. You will discover that the tunes I chose, as well as the environment/aura in which they were "played" by the book's characters, were not only suitable, but absolutely stellar! Finally, when you, too, are *behind closed doors* (and any other place/space you find yourself), summon the recordings and spirits of these musical icons for it is they who helped make African American Classical Music what it was, is, and will be… *forever and a day.*

I had the fortune of interviewing and/or meeting several of the musicians noted in this book. Therefore, it was my attempt to elevate the music so that readers will presumably embark upon their own journey to learn more about the musicians and their recordings. ***Musicians and actresses whom I have referred to, living or***

deceased, are in no way implied to have been, ever, involved in the Lifestyle. Again, musical selections were my preferences. Any and all shortcomings of this book are solely my responsibility, and any resemblances to actual people are ***purely*** coincidental.

CPSIA information can be obtained
at www.ICGtesting.com
Printed in the USA
BVHW032213281118
534296BV00001B/28/P